DARK ANGEL'S SURRENDER

THE CHILDREN OF THE GODS BOOK 16

I. T. LUCAS

NOTE FROM THE AUTHOR:
Dark Angel's Surrender is a work of fiction!

Names, characters, places and incidents are products of the author's
imagination or are used fictitiously and are not to be construed as real. Any
similarity to actual persons, organizations and/or events is purely
coincidental.

ANANDUR

*S*ometimes, the best of things happened at the worst of times, Anandur mused as he hoisted the body up, looping the noose fashioned from the guy's leather belt around the corpse's neck.

Mortal danger had a way of bringing out the worst or the best in people.

Love could flourish even when surrounded by pain, blood, and death. But then this was no news to him. Anandur had always been a romantic, and today's events had just proven what he'd already known.

But it was no doubt shocking news to Brundar. Poor guy was completely out of his element. The love part, that was. Brundar was no stranger to blood, pain, or death.

Taking one last look at the body swinging from the noose, Anandur admired his handiwork. An excellent job if he said so himself. The angle was consistent with the way he'd snapped the ex-husband's neck.

I wonder how long it will take until he's found.

Did the psychopath have friends? A family that gave a shit?

Calypso should know.

To spare her the gory sight, Anandur had loaded the girl and his brother into Brundar's Escalade. Later, he would drop Callie at her home, deposit Brundar into the capable hands of Doctor Bridget, and then take an Uber back to the scene of the crime for his Thunderbird.

The neighborhood seemed safe enough to leave a car overnight. Besides, he had one hell of an alarm system, and a tracker he'd installed himself on top of the LoJack. Whoever dared to steal his baby wouldn't get far with her.

His next task was to clean the blood off the tiled floor. A roll of paper towels in hand, Anandur got down on his knees, not an easy feat given the protective suiting he was still wearing, and got to work. It was a good thing Brundar hadn't made it past the entry and onto the carpet before getting shot. Nothing save torching the place would've eliminated all traces of his blood if any of it had gotten on the carpet.

He finished the job with a thorough wipe down, using up an entire container of bleach. When the cleaning was done, including the ex's guns, Anandur put the empty bleach container into a large trash bag, then filled it with the wadded paper towels.

The guns went into a dresser drawer in the bedroom.

Trash bag in hand, he walked out the door. The fireplace in his and Brundar's apartment would finally be put to good use.

Dropping the bag in the trunk, Anandur glanced at the back seat, where Brundar was lying propped against the door with his legs resting in Calypso's lap. Apparently, the girl wasn't scared of a little blood. As badly bruised as she was, her main concern was to keep Brundar as comfortable as possible throughout the drive.

The thing was, after dropping her off at her apartment, Brundar would have to manage without her support for the rest of the ride.

"How are you holding up?" he asked his brother.

"I'll live," Brundar said. "The bleeding's stopped."

"That's good. I don't think you could've gotten any paler." Anandur turned to the girl. "I need your address, Callie."

"What for?" She lifted her chin and threw him a challenging look. "I'm not going home. Wherever Brundar goes, I go."

With a slight tilt of his head, Anandur signaled Brundar to take it from there and explain why it wasn't possible.

Instead of doing the smart thing, Brundar did the opposite. "Bridget should take a look at her bruises."

"I can take Calypso to a hum—" Anandur stopped himself in time "—hospital before I take you to Bridget."

Brundar shook his head. "They will ask questions."

"So what are you suggesting we do? If we bring an outsider in, Kian is going to tear us new asses."

"I have clean strips of fabric in the glove compartment that I can use to blindfold her."

Calypso snorted. "Aren't you guys going a little overboard with this? I'm sure your cousin is not going that mean."

"He is," Anandur and Brundar said simultaneously.

"Maybe we can sneak her in to see Bridget and then I'll take her home."

"I'm here, guys. Don't talk about me as if I'm not."

"Sorry," Anandur said.

Brundar shifted, a pained groan escaping his throat. "Call Bridget and tell her we're coming in."

To make that sound, Brundar must've been in unbearable pain. Anandur punched the glove compartment open and pulled out one of the soft white cloths. "I don't want to know why you keep this in your car." He tossed the fabric to Brundar.

"To clean my weapons. What do you think I use it for?"

"Never mind." Anandur turned the engine on and eased into the street, then called Bridget once he reached the freeway.

"What's the emergency?" She sounded tired.

"I'm bringing Brundar and his lady friend in. He was shot in both knees, and his friend is badly bruised. They are both in the car with me, and you're on speakerphone."

"ETA?"

Smart woman. Not that he'd left much room for misinterpretation. "Fifteen minutes or less."

"I'll bring a gurney."

"Much obliged." He ended the call.

In the back, Calypso took the cloth from Brundar's hands, folded it on the diagonal to fashion a blindfold, and then tied it loosely around her eyes.

"Everything hurts too much for me to tie it securely, but I promise not to peek."

"It's fine. I trust you." Brundar took her hand and brought it to his lips for a kiss.

Anandur barely managed to stifle a shocked gasp, forcing himself to look at the road instead of spying on his brother in the rearview mirror. But what he'd just witnessed had been a fucking miracle. Brundar acting affectionate?

Anandur had thought he would never live to see the day.

The woman deserved sainthood for pulling that off.

It was imperative that he keep her safe from Kian and anyone else who might think to separate her from Brundar. Given what she'd accomplished, her humanity was almost irrelevant.

Brundar needed her.

"Listen, Calypso. When we get there, don't wander away from us. You stay glued to either Brundar or me, and you do exactly what we tell you. Understood?"

"Yeah. I got that. I have to hide from the big bad wolf."

"You have no idea."

CALLIE

*T*he blindfold kept sliding down Callie's nose and, even though the fabric was incredibly soft, it hurt every time she had to move it back up. Pushing it into position one last time, she leaned against the headrest, hoping to anchor it in place.

The guys were most likely exaggerating their cousin's hostile disposition. Either that or he was indeed a terror of a man.

She couldn't imagine those two cowering before anyone.

On the other hand, it might have not been fear. The brothers held their boss in the highest esteem, and breaking his rules didn't sit well with them.

Whatever.

As long as she got to be with Brundar, she didn't care what she had to do.

Besides, a blindfold was nothing new. Except, she associated it with hot sex and not clandestine operations. Callie was almost grateful for the all-consuming pain she was in, which prevented the Pavlov-like sexual response to the blindfold. Under the circumstances, getting horny would've been grossly inappropriate.

She wondered how come she was so calm. Everything hurt, from her bruised face to her scraped wrists to her arms and legs and everything in between. But she was alive and free, which less than an hour ago seemed like an impossible dream.

Oh God, Shawn was dead.

Callie still couldn't wrap her head around it, nor could she summon even a smidgen of sorrow or regret. After all, she had some memories with him that weren't horrible. She should've felt something. But there was nothing, not even shock. Not even horror at what had transpired over the last couple of hours.

Maybe it was a typical response for survivors—feeling euphoric for the simple reason that they were alive. Especially when that survival was nothing short of miraculous.

Brundar's cold hand closed around hers, reminding her that they weren't out of the woods yet. Her injuries were superficial, and the most she had to worry about was some scarring. But, despite his and Anandur's reassurances, Brundar might never walk again.

If he ended up crippled because of her, she would never forgive herself for getting him involved in her crap.

"Are you okay, sweetling? Are you in pain?" Brundar asked.

Her injuries were nothing compared to his, and yet he was concerned about her. God, she loved this man. The thing was, if she told him that, he would run off, or crawl away as was the case.

Hey, maybe this was the perfect opportunity to spring it on him.

In his condition, he couldn't get far.

"If you're smiling, I assume it's not so bad. Want to tell me about it? I could use a distraction."

If he only knew.

"I'm worried about you. I would never forgive myself if

your injuries crippled you. But as shameful as it is to admit, I smiled thinking that there is one advantage to you being in this state. You can't run away from me. You can try crawling away, but I will have no problem catching you."

He squeezed her hand. "I'm not going anywhere. I'm done running."

Anandur sighed. "Oh, man. We are in a shitload of trouble."

It made her angry to think that what she and Brundar shared could be considered a problem. It was like they were stuck in a story from a different age or place, where social status and other crap like that stood in the way of love. "Why do you work for a tyrant like that? You can quit and find better employment, where you are free to be with whomever you choose."

"It's complicated," Anandur said.

Evidently.

Did their cousin hold something over their heads? Or did they owe him a debt of gratitude? It had to be something huge to justify such sacrifice on their part.

She wondered what on earth could merit such loyalty to a guy who didn't allow them to have a life. The thing that bothered her most, though, was that Kian was happily married, meaning the rules against relationships didn't apply to him. That wasn't fair. If he demanded it from those in his employ, he should at least abide by the same rules.

The car slowed and turned, then went through a series of downward spirals until it stopped. Callie heard what sounded like the pneumatic hiss of a mechanism, then the screech of a heavy door sliding on rails. When the noise stopped, Anandur pulled forward, driving for a few feet before coming to a full stop.

Brundar patted her thigh. "You can remove the blindfold."

"Thank God." She untied the loose knot at the back of her

head and let the cloth drop to her lap. A blindfold wasn't fun when it had nothing to do with sex.

As she'd guessed, they were in an underground parking lot. It was dimly lit, and even though her eyes had been closed throughout the drive and therefore accustomed to the dark, it took Callie a moment to notice the small form standing next to the entry to the building proper.

The shadowy figure detached from the wall she'd been leaning against and headed their way, pushing a wheeled gurney in front of her. As she got closer, Callie saw more details. The woman was young, mid to late twenties at the most, and was dressed in jeans and a T-shirt. And yet, Callie had no doubt that the woman was the doctor Anandur had spoken to before. She had that unmistakable air of confidence and competence about her.

Anandur got out, and, after exchanging a few words with the doctor, he opened the back door. "I'm going to lift you up and place you on the gurney," he told Brundar.

Brundar nodded.

"Wait, can't the doctor give him something for the pain before you move him?" Callie asked.

Anandur hesitated for a moment, looking from the petite doctor to Brundar and back.

"Just do it." Brundar leaned forward, then groaned and fell back against the door.

"Let me." The doctor put her hand on Anandur's bicep, motioning for him to move aside.

"Hello. I'm Doctor Bridget." She offered her hand to Callie as if there was no injured man in the vehicle, waiting for her to alleviate his pain.

"Callie," she said as she offered the doctor her hand, which the woman shook quickly.

"I'm going to squeeze by you, okay?"

"Sure." Callie cast the woman a puzzled look. Was she going to get inside and give Brundar a shot for the pain?

"Anandur, push the gurney up to the seat and adjust the height until it's level with it. We are going to slide Brundar over."

Callie lifted her hand. "Aren't you going to give him a shot first?"

"No." The doctor snaked her arm under Brundar's back. "When I say go, Callie, scoot as gently as you can toward the gurney, one inch at a time. I'm going to push Brundar at the same rate, so there is no pressure on his knees. When you reach the end, Anandur is going to lift you together with Brundar's legs. You'll provide the support while I lift his torso from behind."

Callie cast her an incredulous look. "How are you going to lift him?" The woman looked to be no more than an inch or two over five feet, if that, and delicately built. She could never lift a big guy like Brundar.

"Don't worry about that. I'm stronger than I look. Just do exactly as I say, and we will have him on that gurney with minimal pain. Understood?"

Neither guy argued with the doctor about her plan, so they must know something that Callie didn't. Like maybe Bridget was moonlighting as a bodybuilder.

"Yes, ma'am."

"Small movements, Callie. On three. One, two, three!"

BRUNDAR

*B*rundar gritted his teeth as Bridget moistened his pants and then cut them off him, all without giving him anything for the pain. Was she punishing him for involving her in harboring a human?

"Bridget."

"What?" She didn't look up from her task of examining his knees.

"Can I trust you to keep Calypso a secret?"

"Anandur said he is taking her home as soon as I'm done treating her."

"He is."

"Then it's all I'm going to say if asked. As a doctor, it is my obligation to treat her. But nothing more."

"Thank you."

"I need to knock you out to reset your knees, which I will have to do without the help of a nurse because there is a human here I can't allow her to see. The bones are already mending, but not in the right way."

"Can I have a local shot? I don't want to be out completely."

"Fine," she grumbled. "You're lucky that I just discharged

Roni and no new patients have come in. I don't know what possessed you to bring her in here. You're aware that you can't hide her for long. Even if she is hidden from sight, her scent and her heartbeat are going to give her away."

"I know. But I couldn't leave her alone after what she's been through."

"I'm still waiting to hear all about it, like how the hell the clan's best fighter got both of his knees shot by a human. It's not very confidence inspiring."

He had never heard Bridget talk so nastily to anyone, let alone a patient.

"Why are you angry?"

She waved a hand. "I don't have all night. Talk to me."

By the time Brundar had finished telling Bridget a very condensed version of the night's events and what had led up to them, the anger in the doctor's eyes had subsided.

"Callie must be traumatized. Even if she hated the guy, his violent death must have been difficult for her. After I'm done with you, I'll see if she needs anything for the shock."

"Thank you."

As always, Bridget worked quickly and efficiently. It took her about thirty minutes to administer the local epidural, reset his knees, and put them in braces to keep him from accidentally moving them.

When she was done, Bridget put her hands on her hips and glared at him. "Don't even think about putting pressure on your knees until I tell you it's okay. Your brother will have to carry you to the bathroom and back for a couple of days. After that, you can use a wheelchair, and crutches to the bathroom."

"How long?"

"As long as it takes."

Bridget was still in a nasty mood.

He rephrased his question. "When can I go back to work?"

"After your knees are fully mended, which should take about two weeks. I don't want to have to re-break and reset them again because you didn't listen to me." She looked evilly at him. "I will do it the old-fashioned way, with a belt between your teeth to bite on and no painkillers."

Fuck, he'd been there, done that. It was easy to forget how bad it used to be.

"I promise you that I'm going to follow your instructions to the letter. Contrary to popular belief, I'm not into pain."

That got a smile out of her. "Good boy." She patted his shoulder. "Rest here while I treat your girlfriend." Bridget stepped out of the room and closed the door.

A moment later it opened again, the irate redhead letting Calypso and Anandur in. "She wants to check on you first." Bridget grimaced.

Calypso's face looked bad. Splotches of purple and yellow and black covered most of it.

Had it gotten worse, or had he been in too much pain to notice it before?

"You need to let the doctor treat you, Calypso."

"I will in a minute." She walked up to his bed. "What's the prognosis?"

"He is going to be as good as new in a few weeks," Bridget said from behind her.

Callie lifted a brow. "I'm not a doctor, but even I know it's impossible to heal from such severe injuries so quickly."

Bridget put her hands on her hips and glared at the three of them. "I used a new experimental procedure that speeds up the healing process significantly. You have my word. In a few weeks, there will be no sign of the injury."

Calypso smiled for the first time that night. "Thank you, Doctor. That's the best news I've ever gotten." She leaned to kiss Brundar's cheek. "Now I'm ready to get treated."

Behind her back, Bridget rolled her eyes and mouthed, "You owe me big time."

He nodded. Bridget had lied for him. She sure as hell hadn't enjoyed it.

Calypso pushed up and turned to the doctor. "Any chance you can pull a miracle treatment like that for me? Something to get rid of those bruises overnight so I can go back to work?"

"Sorry. That procedure works only on bones and tendons and cuts, not bruises."

To Bridget's credit, she handled Calypso with way more care than she had him, touching as gently as she could and apologizing for hurting her every time Calypso winced.

"Nothing is broken. I'll give you something for the pain. How are you holding up emotionally?"

Calypso shrugged. "Surprisingly fine." She tugged her T-shirt down. "Is there something wrong with me? Shouldn't I feel something?"

"I'm not a psychologist. I guess that you didn't have time to internalize what happened yet and that it will hit you later. I'll give you a mild relaxant in case it does."

The doctor walked out, returning a few moments later with three containers of pills. "The instructions are right here." She showed them to Calypso, then waved her hand in Brundar's direction. "Okay, people. It's late, and I want to get some sleep tonight. You're free to go."

Anandur pointed at the gurney. "Am I taking him up with that?"

"Unless you want to carry him in your arms, then the answer is yes."

"I'll take the gurney."

"Smart move. Goodnight, guys. Call me if you need me."

"Thank you, doctor," Calypso said.

As soon as Bridget had left, Anandur closed the door behind her and walked over to the bed. "Am I taking Calypso home now, or is she staying the night?"

"Is that an option?" She looked hopefully at Brundar.

13

He didn't want her to go. Not now, not ever. But that wasn't on the table. The next twenty-four hours was the best bargain he was going to get. "She comes with us. You can sneak her out tomorrow night."

"That's what I thought." Anandur leaned over him, lifting him an inch off the bed and repositioning him as far as he could go to the right.

"Up you go." He motioned for Calypso to get on.

Brundar extended his arm, pulling her to him as soon as she climbed up. With Calypso pressed against him, he inhaled her scent, taking his first deep breath of the day.

Anandur grabbed a blanket, shook it out, and covered them both with it. "Not much of a plan, but that's all I got."

"There are no cameras in the clan's elevators," Brundar offered.

"True. This is just in case we bump into someone."

As if a blanket would help.

Even if they managed somehow to mask Calypso's scent, an immortal would immediately pick up on the additional heartbeat. But Anandur was right that there wasn't much to be done about it. They were taking a risk.

His brother opened the door and then took up position behind the gurney. "Let's roll, kids. May the odds be ever in our favor."

4

CALLIE

*T*he painkillers Bridget had given her hit Callie on the way up to Brundar's apartment. With the gurney sliding quietly on its wheels, and her tucked against his side, warm and safe, she closed her eyes and let herself drift off, waking up only when Anandur lifted the blanket.

She shivered at the loss of warmth and cuddled closer to Brundar.

"Up you go, Calypso." Anandur showed her no mercy.

Brundar was as reluctant to let her go as she was to get up. "Can we sleep here?" She grabbed for the blanket.

Anandur yanked it off. "You'll be more comfortable in the bed, and I bet you would like to shower first."

Right. She vaguely remembered being dragged over the pavement. Her clothes were covered with dirt, and her hair was all tangled up. Going to bed without a shower was not happening no matter how exhausted she was.

As Callie waited for Anandur to pull down the railing on her side of the gurney, she took a look around the apartment. It was a typical bachelor pad, complete with a big screen, correction, a huge screen, open boxes of pizza with leftovers sticking to the cardboard and empty beer and whiskey bottles galore.

In short, it was a pigsty.

"Don't look at the mess, Calypso. All of it is Anandur's doing. I refuse to clean up after him. I'm not his maid."

Anandur humphed. "Yeah, as if I was eating pizza and drinking beer by myself. Half of this mess is yours."

Brundar ignored his brother. "Come to my room, and you'll see. It's spotless."

Frankly, Callie couldn't care less about the state of cleanliness of their bedrooms, what she cared about was the bathroom. She was too tired to start cleaning it, but if the brothers were as disgusting as Shawn had been, and the toilet was covered in pee, she would have no choice but to clean it first.

"Can you guys point me in the direction of the bathroom?"

Heck, she needed a clean towel and a change of clothes as well.

Brundar must've noticed her despondent expression. "You can use my bathroom, and I have brand new T-shirts and underwear you're welcome to."

"Thank you. What about you? How are you going to shower?"

Brundar glanced at his brother.

Anandur patted his shoulder. "It won't be the first time I had to wash his ugly butt."

"And I washed yours, more than once. I think we're even."

"Yeah. When you're right, you're right. Come on, Calypso, let me show you where he keeps his underwear." He took her elbow and leaned to whisper in her ear. "I wonder if he keeps his lacy thongs in there too."

Callie laughed. Imagining Brundar wearing women's panties was hilarious, but Anandur deserved some of his own medicine back. "I bet his butt looks better in a thong than yours."

Anandur waggled his brows. "There is only one way to find out. Should I demonstrate?"

"Over my dead body!" Brundar called out from the living room.

The guy really had bat ears.

She took the pack of T-shirts and another one of boxer shorts Anandur had handed her. "I don't know how he does it. He hears everything."

"Maybe he is a mutant," Anandur deadpanned as he opened the bathroom door. "There are extra toothbrushes and soap in there." He pointed at a tall cabinet. "As well as clean towels."

"Thank you."

Thank God the bathroom was spotless, and she didn't need to clean a thing. Avoiding her own reflection in the mirror, Callie took off her clothes and folded them on top of the vanity. A glimpse of her face in the clinic's bathroom had been enough.

Awful didn't begin to describe it.

Stepping into the shower, she was relieved to find that Brundar had great hair products, including conditioner. Her scalp was tender from having been dragged by her ponytail. Even after the double dose of conditioner she'd applied, and the ten minutes she'd let it sit and work its magic, combing her hair out hurt like hell.

When she was done, she put on one of Brundar's plain white T-shirts and a pair of his boxer shorts. It was long enough to cover her butt, with only a fraction of the shorts showing, but regrettably too sheer to forego the bra.

"Here you are," Anandur greeted her as she walked into the living room. "Come grab something to eat."

The guy had been busy.

Gone were the empty pizza boxes and beer bottles. He'd

even wiped down the coffee table, which was topped with readymade sandwiches, an assortment of pastries, and a coffee carafe. She wondered where the food came from. Only gas station minimarts and Denny's were still open this late at night.

Brundar, who looked showered, was sitting in an armchair with his legs propped up on an ottoman and eating a sandwich.

"The coffee smells divine." She walked over and poured herself a cup, then debated where to sit. Next to Anandur on the couch, or try to squeeze next to Brundar in the armchair, which was what she wanted to do.

"Come sit with me," Brundar said.

"I don't want to make you uncomfortable."

"You're making me uncomfortable just standing there. Come." He lifted himself by bracing his arms on the chair's armrests, then moved over to make room for her.

Callie grabbed a muffin and her coffee mug and squeezed her butt into the tiny space, nestling against Brundar. As he wrapped his arm around her, they uttered a simultaneous sigh of relief.

Anandur put his hand over his heart and batted his eyelashes. "You guys are just too adorable."

He was so funny, mimicking the accent and hand gestures of a southern lady, that Callie couldn't help the laugh exploding from her mouth together with the sip of coffee she'd just taken.

She wiped her mouth. "God, Anandur, living with you is a health hazard. Don't joke while people are drinking or eating."

"I'm sorry. I'm so used to him reacting to nothing, I sometimes forget that other people find me funny." He threw Brundar a mockingly accusing glance.

"They don't. They are just polite," Brundar grumbled.

It dawned on her then why the two were such opposites.

Callie was willing to bet that what had triggered their polar opposite dispositions had something to do with what had happened to Brundar as a kid.

With the younger brother losing the ability to find joy in life, the older one had turned himself into a joker in a desperate attempt to bring it back.

Did Brundar know how lucky he was to have a brother who cared for him that much?

Did he know Anandur was clowning around for him?

Probably not.

5

CALLIE

"*L*et go!" Callie screamed, trying to pry off Shawn's vise-like grip on her arm.

"Never. You're mine, you little bitch." He lifted a fist, pulling his arm back to deliver a blow.

Callie cowered, covering her face with her hands, but the punch never came. Instead, he began shaking her.

"Wake up, Calypso!"

Calypso.

Shawn never called her that. And it wasn't his voice either. She was dreaming.

Callie forced herself to wake up, lifting off the bed and commanding her eyes to open. Her angel was there to keep her safe. Brundar was hovering over her, a worried expression on his handsome face. Even injured he would never let anything happen to her.

His name a whisper on her lips, she closed her eyes and dropped back on the bed. "Brundar."

"I'm here, sweetling. It was just a nightmare."

"Tell me about it. I dreamt Shawn had me."

His eyes blazing with a strange inner light, Brundar

kissed her forehead. "Never again. Anandur made sure of that."

"Thank God. Am I a horrible person for saying that?"

Tenderly, Brundar brushed a strand of sweaty hair from her cheek. "Shawn was evil. Anandur did you and the world a favor."

As a shiver ran through her, Callie covered her eyes with her hands. "I can't believe I lived with a man for two years and didn't see it. I mean I did, but I didn't internalize how bad it was. Or maybe I just didn't want to admit that I married a monster. I convinced myself that Shawn just had anger issues, and that he was controlling, but it was so much more than that. Why did he hate me? Do you know?" She removed her hands to look at her angel through a mist of tears.

"He didn't hate you. He hated everything and everyone. Don't ask me why. There was no reason. You said he came from a normal middle-class family, right?"

"He did. I don't think Shawn was ever abused. On the contrary. He told me he used to be a bully who terrorized others just because he could. But he wasn't stupid. He'd kept up his charming façade until after the wedding. Before that, I only had a gut feeling that something about him wasn't right. I should've trusted it instead of brushing it off. But I was young and pregnant, and I thought I was doing the right thing."

It felt cathartic to let it all spill out, to admit the guilt and self-loathing she'd carried with her for so long.

"You can put all of that behind you. I'm not telling you to forget it, that's never going to happen, but you can enjoy your freedom and safety without feeling guilty about it."

Freedom.

No more hiding. No more staying away from the people she loved. Callie could have her identity back. "I don't even need the fake name anymore. Do you think your hacker can change the name back in the university records so I can go as Calypso and not as Heather?"

"I'm sure he can."

Wow, she could have her life back. She could call her father and Dawn. Even go visit them. Having the freedom to just be herself and enjoy her family and friends was intoxicating. Heck, she could even go back to working at Aussie.

Except, too much had changed.

She could have her life back, but she wasn't the same woman she was a month ago. Her priorities had shifted, with the man leaning over her being number one. She owed him and his brother her life.

For some reason, the realization calmed her racing mind as if the cogs had finally realigned to work in perfect harmony. The problem was that once her mind had quieted, she started paying attention to her body's aches and pains.

"I think I'm going to take one of those pills Bridget gave me. How about you? Do you need yours?"

Brundar grimaced. "I do. But first I need to take care of another pressing need."

It took her a split second to realize what was bothering him. The poor guy needed to use the bathroom. "I'll get Anandur."

He looked so miserable. "Thank you."

Callie padded down the corridor to the other bedroom and knocked on the door.

A moment later the door flew open with Anandur in all his naked glory staring down at her. "Brundar okay?"

She averted her gaze. "He needs to use the facilities." As did Anandur, judging by the involuntary glimpse she'd gotten.

"I'll be right there." He closed the door in her face.

Apparently, the joker slept in the nude and was grumpy in the morning.

She rushed back to Brundar's bedroom, ducking straight

into the bathroom to empty her bladder before Anandur got there. She'd even managed to brush her teeth before hearing Brundar's groan of pain from the bedroom.

Quickly, she opened the door, holding it for Anandur who was carrying his brother in his arms, thankfully, wearing jeans but no shirt.

He must've worked out a lot. Callie felt horrible for noticing. The guy was her boyfriend's brother, and she liked him, but she wasn't attracted to him. Still, a woman had to be either blind or dead not to notice all those muscles.

"I'll wait outside." She closed the door behind her and went into the living room to search for the pills.

They were on the kitchen counter where she'd left them last night. Callie filled up a cup with tap water and took two.

While waiting for the guys to be done, she decided to start the coffeemaker and make breakfast. Those two needed a lot of food to maintain their bodies. She knew Brundar's appetite was healthy and was willing to bet that Anandur's was even healthier. He was a big guy.

The problem was, they had nothing to make breakfast from. The fridge was stuffed with beer bottles, but food-wise she found only a half-eaten pack of sliced bread and two jars of peanut butter, one of them empty.

It seemed the brothers either ate out or dined with their boss, enjoying his butler's vegan cooking. Or not. What was more likely, they didn't care what was served as long as someone else cooked it.

Brundar liked steaks, not veggies.

The coffeemaker was spewing the last of the brew when the brothers emerged, Anandur carrying Brundar and depositing him in the same armchair he'd sat in last night. It was touching to see how careful the big guy was with his younger brother. Anandur's heart was as big as his body.

She poured the coffee into three mugs, fixed hers with sugar and cream, and Anandur's with one cube of sugar like she'd seen him do last night, then brought them out to the living room. "I made breakfast if you can call peanut butter sandwiches that. You guys have nothing in the fridge aside from beer."

Anandur took his mug. "That's the important stuff. We stock up on Snake's Venom because it's not available in just any store. Food you can get anywhere."

Callie handed Brundar his coffee. "Then you won't mind doing a little shopping so I can make you guys a decent lunch?" She walked back to the kitchen to get the sandwiches and handed them out. "This is a travesty of a breakfast."

Anandur bit into his sandwich, taking half of it into his mouth and chewing with gusto. Apparently, he didn't share Brundar's refined table manners.

"I need to get Brundar a wheelchair from Bridget. If she doesn't have one, I need to find a place that sells them. But I can get more stuff from the café downstairs."

Callie shook her head. "No more sandwiches. To heal, Brundar needs proper food in his body. Wouldn't you prefer to eat Chicken Piccata with a side of spaghetti and a lettuce salad, to yet another sandwich?"

Anandur salivated.

"Calypso is an amazing cook," Brundar said.

"You win. It's good that today is Saturday and I have time. What I'm really glad about, though, is that I don't need to report to Kian yet, and inform him that both Brundar and I are out of commission. He will go ballistic when he hears that."

"I'm sure he is going to understand."

Anandur humphed. "Trust me, he will not. But never mind that. I know how to handle him." He waved a hand. "Make a list of what you need."

Callie smiled, the small victory feeling surprisingly good, giving her some sense of control in a situation where she had none. She was trespassing, hiding, and counting the minutes she had with the man she loved until forced to leave.

"I'm going to make you a list of items for meals to last you guys a week. Also, if you don't mind, could you stop by the club and bring me my purse?"

Crap, a split second later she realized that Anandur wasn't supposed to know where she worked. "I'll give you the address and the combination to my locker. I'll call to let them know you're coming."

Anandur rolled his eyes. "Anything else?"

There was, but she shook her head. "That's all."

The purse was a must. Callie's birth control pills were in there, and she didn't want to miss a day when she'd just started taking them. A change of clothes would've been nice, but it wasn't a necessity. Asking Anandur to pick up some stuff from her apartment on top of everything else was too much.

"I'll get you something to wear from Walmart. Don't put on your list things they don't carry. I'm not going on a shopping expedition. I'm getting everything on the list from there."

Stifling a grimace, Callie nodded. "I'll make sure of it." She didn't mind clothing from Walmart, but their fresh produce wasn't the best.

6

TESSA

*S*aturday mornings at Jackson's café, or as the sign over the door still proclaimed, Fernando's Café, were busy. That was why Tessa preferred to come over much later in the day. But she'd slept over at Jackson's, and he'd insisted she stay for breakfast even though he couldn't spare a minute to be with her.

Sitting at the back and watching the customers was kind of fun but felt awkward. People standing in line and waiting to be seated were giving her the hairy eyeball for taking up an entire booth to herself.

Maybe she could join Vlad in the kitchen.

Tessa pulled out her phone and texted Jackson even though she could see him standing behind the register. If she moved from her booth even for a moment, someone was going to claim it.

Can I sit with Vlad in the kitchen? I'm lonely.

She saw him typing away on his phone. *Of course. I'm sorry I can't be with you.*

Tessa grabbed her plate and her cup and headed for the kitchen, stopping by Jackson to give him a quick peck on the cheek. He was hers, and she wanted all those horny customers ogling him to know that.

"Hi, Vlad. I hope you don't mind some company. I don't like eating alone, and Jackson is busy." She sat on the only stool in the kitchen, using a corner of the worktable to put down her plate and cup.

"Saturday is busy all day long. But it's going to get a little easier in an hour or so."

Vlad worked like a machine, preparing plate after plate of sandwiches with sides of salads, then handing them over to Gordon who was running around taking orders and making deliveries.

"What happened to the girl who used to work for you guys?"

"She quit."

"Without notice?"

"Took her paycheck, said thank you it was nice, and walked out. No explanation, nothing." Vlad shook his head. "Humans." He blushed and cast her an apologetic glance. "Other than you, Tessa. You're awesome."

"Thank you."

Tessa watched for a few more minutes before deciding to help out. It wasn't as if she had anything better to do. The only thing on her agenda for today was Karen's class, which was much later in the day.

Walking up to the row of pegs, she lifted the last apron off and put it on. "What do you need help with the most? Making sandwiches, or delivering them?"

Vlad hesitated for all of thirty seconds. "Delivering. I need to stay here. Customers get weird when they see me out there."

She frowned. "Assholes, all of them. You're one of the nicest guys I know."

He blushed again. "Thank you."

A moment later he handed her a plate. "Table four. Table

one is the one next to the window and table two is the one across from it, and so it goes."

"Got it." She headed out with the plate.

Jackson stopped her. "What are you doing?"

"Helping out until it quiets down a bit."

He looked like he was about to argue, but the smile on Gordon's face when he saw her wearing the apron must've convinced him otherwise.

"It should get better after ten," he said.

The moment it did, Jackson walked over to her and untied her apron. "Thank you for your help, but now I want you to sit down. I'll join you for a cup of coffee for me and tea for you."

"Sounds awesome. I wouldn't mind a chocolate croissant with my tea."

Apparently, working on her feet had awakened Tessa's appetite. After years of sedentary office work, running around with plates and cups had been surprisingly invigorating. Especially since she was in pretty good shape thanks to her intensive Krav Maga training.

All in all, her life was getting good. She had a great guy for a fiancé, new friends, and thanks to Karen she was in great shape. The most significant change, though, was that she wasn't as anxious as she used to be.

Instead of a constant state of alert, her panic attacks were becoming less and less frequent. Occasionally, something would trigger her fight or flight response, and after that happened her adrenaline level would take forever to return to normal, but it was happening less and less. If she were to give herself a grade, Tessa would say that she was ninety-five percent okay. A vast improvement from the mere thirty she'd estimated not so long ago.

Jackson sauntered over with two cups and a plate, moving in that sensual and yet all male way of his.

Sigh.

She was one lucky girl.

"Hi, beautiful." He leaned to kiss her cheek the same way she'd done to him before, and only then put the cups and plate down. "I'm sorry I couldn't sit with you this morning. And for making you work for free."

"I'll collect my dues later." She winked.

Jackson lifted his coffee cup and leaned against the booth's upholstered back. "What do you have in mind?"

"I'll think of something. But whatever it is, I can't say it here."

His eyes started glowing, betraying his excitement. "Whisper it. I'll hear."

That's right. She kept forgetting her guy wasn't an ordinary human. Tessa leaned forward, making sure no one could read her lips other than Jackson. "I'm ready."

Jackson's expression turned serious. "I don't know about that."

"I am. This time I'm sure. I have never felt so good about myself as I do now. Not even before, you know." She didn't want to spoil the moment by bringing up the nasty part.

"You're right. This is not the time or place to talk about it."

"Then when?"

"Later. After closing."

"Here?"

He shook his head. "I'll think of somewhere with a better atmosphere."

"We need privacy. How about my place?"

He lifted a brow. "Your place and privacy is an oxymoron. Unless Eva and Bhathian are out."

"Right. What about your place?"

"The guys are not going out tonight."

Tessa slumped. "I wish we had our own place already."

"Yeah, me too."

29

JACKSON

"I feel like a teenager in one of those coming of age movies." Tessa chuckled. "Sneaking stolen moments in a car because we have no place of our own."

"I am a teenager, but I don't feel like one." Jackson was uneasy about Tessa's idea to stop at the deserted parking lot of the park. During the day it was okay, and he had even taken Nathalie's father on walks there, but at night the place turned into a different kind of playground. All sorts of dirty deeds were done in parks after dark. Gang meet-ups, hookers, drug dealers.

His eyes were busy scanning the area instead of focusing on the beautiful girl sitting next to him. Tessa had brought him here to talk him into having sex with her, and he still wasn't sure it was the right time to take the final step, cross the barrier, to boldly go where Jackson had never gone before with Tessa.

He had to admit that her confidence level was at a record high, as evidenced by her choice of location for their talk. The old Tessa would've been hyperventilating from a panic attack if he'd brought her to a dark, deserted place like this. The new Tessa seemed perfectly comfortable parking in the darkest spot of the small parking lot, while he was nervous as fuck. Maybe because it was up to him to defend her in case any one of those denizens of the night decided to bother them.

"What are you looking at?" Tessa followed his eyes as he snapped his head in the direction of a shadow darting behind the recreation building.

"I don't like it here. All kinds of shady characters come here at night. It's not safe."

She leaned her head against his bicep. "But you're Jackson--an immortal with superpowers. They need to fear you, not the other way around."

"I'm not afraid. I'm uneasy. You're still mortal, Tessa, and I'm just one guy."

Reaching out a hand, she caressed his cheek. "I don't want you to feel uncomfortable. We can go somewhere else to talk."

Hallelujah. "We can park across the street from the café and still have privacy. Gordon and Vlad's hearing is good, but not that good."

"Okay."

As Jackson let out a relieved breath and put the car in reverse, executing a K-turn, the shadow from before darted from behind the building, running toward the playground and then hiding behind the slide.

When he left the parking lot and turned into the street, Jackson took one last glance in his rearview mirror. The shadow hadn't moved.

Tessa turned to look back. "Did you see someone?"

"Yeah. Someone was definitely there, skulking, darting from one shadowy spot to another. I could tell he was up to no good." To put it mildly. It was all over the news that there was a serial killer on the loose. The rumor spreading throughout the keep was that he might be an immortal.

Tessa glanced at the new weird-looking ring she'd gotten

from Karen and fisted her hand, so the ring's triangular tip pointed out. "This can double as a weapon." She jabbed the air in front of her, then relaxed her fist and flexed her fingers.

"I bet it can. But it wouldn't do you much good against a guy with a gun or a knife, or against two guys coming at you at once."

Her heartbeat speeding up, Tessa sucked in a breath, then another.

Fuck, he shouldn't have said anything. Way to undermine her newfound confidence. "But what are the chances of that, right?" Jackson forced a smile.

"No, you're right. Bhathian told me that there is a serial killer on the loose and to be careful."

Damn. He'd thought Tessa didn't know.

Normally, Tessa avoided reading or watching the news because anything and everything triggered her anxiety, but she was getting stronger by the day, and he wouldn't be doing her any favors by shielding her from everything that might upset her.

"Did he tell you they think it's an immortal male?"

Tessa frowned. "Are you sure? He didn't mention it. I would think that as a Guardian he would know."

"That's what I've heard. The police are not releasing details, but apparently, the victims bleed to death from twin punctures to their necks."

Her hand going for her throat, Tessa smoothed it over his latest bite. "I thought a male couldn't harm a female that way. I never bleed after you bite me."

"Obviously, he is doing it on purpose, hitting the right artery and then not closing the wounds with his saliva." Jackson shook his head. "Unless it's a human who wants the murders to look like a vampire attack."

The more Jackson thought about it, the more he was

inclined to believe it was a human copycat. A nutcase with vampiric delusions.

Tessa sighed. "We are sitting in your car, and instead of talking about how I'm finally ready to have sex with you, we are talking about murders. I don't know about you, but I'd rather talk about sex."

Jackson chuckled and pushed his chair back. "Come here." Releasing her seatbelt, he lifted her into his lap. "I'd rather talk about sex too. But talking is overrated." He cupped the back of her neck and kissed her.

Her arms going around his neck, Tessa kissed him right back, their tongues not so much dueling as dancing. When her need for air forced her to release him, she took in a deep breath.

Looking at his mouth with hooded eyes, she rubbed her thumb over his lips. "I'm so ready, Jackson, it's not even funny."

A smile tugging at her lips, she leaned and whispered in his ear, tickling it with her warm breath. "Do you want to hear a secret?"

"Yeah."

"Do you want to know why I'm so sure I'm ready?"

"Please, don't torture me like that. Spit it out already."

She blew air into his ear, then nipped it playfully. "For the past week, every night when I went to sleep without you, I played with myself."

"Fates, Tessa, that's so hot."

She whispered, "Do you want to know what I fantasize about when I finger myself?"

"What?" Jackson hissed through elongated fangs. He was so turned on he was about to come in his pants like some runny-nosed preteen.

"I imagine you on top of me, inside me, making love to me."

"And?"

She blew another puff of air into his ear. "I climax every single time."

He was so ready to be inside her, right there and then, in the car, parked on the street where anyone could see them. All it would take was to push his pants down, and her skirt up.

Fuck no.

Their first time wasn't going to be in his car, or even his bedroom, or hers.

They had waited so long for this moment, and their joining was going to signify so much more than sex, the occasion called for an appropriately elaborate setup. He wanted it to be special for them. Like a honeymoon, special.

But that didn't mean they couldn't make love. He could still pleasure his girl with his fingers and his mouth and his tongue, bringing her to one climax after another.

Jackson pushed his hand under Tessa's skirt and slid his finger under her soaked panties.

She moaned even before he touched her folds. "Oh, yes!" She sounded triumphant.

"Baby, we are not going to do it here."

"Let's go up to your room." She made a move to slide back into the passenger seat.

Jackson held on. "We will go up, and we will make love to each other, but not all the way."

"Why not?"

"We've waited for so long, we can wait a little longer and make our first time super special. I want to find us a romantic inn and rent the honeymoon suite. I want to fill the room with flowers and candles and music. Can you let me do this for us? Can you wait until next Sunday?"

Tessa cupped both his cheeks. "I love you so much, Jackson. Of course, I can wait. I want the honeymoon suite and the flowers and the candles. I want our first time to be romantic and sweet and uniquely ours, a memory to cherish forever."

"I love you, kitten, and I want to give all of that to you, but I can't promise that all of it is going to be sweet." He waggled his brows.

"Neither can I. We will start with sweet, continue to hot and sweaty, and finish with fireworks."

"I like your plan."

8

ANANDUR

*B*ridget didn't have a wheelchair.

Apparently, since she'd opened her clinic in the keep, there had never been a case of an injury that required the use of one.

Luckily, his trusted old Walmart had one. Typically it was an order-only item, but someone had returned theirs to the store.

Anandur loved the place. One-stop shopping for all his needs. His snob of a brother would never set foot in the discount store, but the joke was on him. Brundar was going to use their wheelchair.

He'd even found another nifty item for the snob. A portable urinal. Brundar could pee in the plastic bottle instead of waiting for Anandur to carry him to the bathroom.

What other store could have had him in and out, his entire shopping list fulfilled, in less than thirty minutes? Altogether the round trip, including the stop at Brundar's club, had taken him a little over an hour.

In the keep's parking garage, Anandur unfolded the wheelchair, loaded it with all the shopping bags, then wheeled it into the elevator.

The lift stopped at the lobby level, and Andrew walked in, holding a paper bag with pastries. "What's that?" He pointed at the chair.

Fuck, Anandur had hoped to have a little more time before the keep's rumor machine started spinning and someone told Kian.

"Brundar got injured."

"How?" Andrew sounded incredulous, as would everyone else once they heard the news.

The invincible warrior having been incapacitated by a human was big news, and not good news, which meant that the rumor was going to spread even faster. For some reason, people hungered for drama much more than they hungered for good news and certainly more than comedy.

Fools.

There wasn't a shortage of drama in the world, while the other two were in short supply.

"It was a hostage situation. It was either him or the victim. Brundar chose the nobler path."

Andrew rubbed his jaw. "Damn. That's a nasty situation I'm well familiar with. How is he doing?"

"Cranky. You know how proud Brundar is. He doesn't want anyone to see him like that. So don't tell a soul. The last thing he wants is to entertain well-meaning visitors."

Andrew nodded. "I understand. No one will hear about it from me. But you can tell Brundar that I'm proud of him. That is if you think he is up to hearing that. Some men don't like praise for what they consider their duty."

"I'll tell him. The worst thing he can do is growl at me, which I'm used to."

Andrew slapped his shoulder. "You can take it, big guy."

"Say hi to your girls for me," Anandur said as the elevator stopped on Andrew's floor. "And kiss the little one's cheeks."

Andrew grinned. "Will do."

As soon as the doors closed, the smile slid off Anandur's face. Andrew was a good man, but he would no doubt tell Nathalie, swearing her to secrecy. But then she would do the same with Syssi, and *boom*—the news would get to Kian.

They needed to get Calypso out of the building as soon as possible.

The trouble was, to sneak her out they needed to wait until it was late at night, when there was less of a chance of bumping into someone.

Exiting on his floor, Anandur glanced at the third elevator door, the one dedicated to the penthouse level. As Kian's bodyguards, he and Brundar had access to it. If he made sure Kian was asleep, he could sneak Calypso into it.

The thing didn't stop at any of the other floors, not unless those inside it commanded it to do so.

The thing was, Kian was known to occasionally wander between his basement and home office, sometimes in the middle of the night. Doing business with companies across the Pond often required him to make phone calls when he was supposed to be asleep.

No wonder the dude was always so grumpy.

The guy needed a vacation, but Anandur wasn't the fool who was going to suggest it. Kian fumed whenever anyone even mentioned the word.

"I'm home!" Anandur called out as soon as he opened the door. Given Brundar's injuries, he doubted his brother was up to getting busy with Calypso, but it wasn't completely outside the realms of possibility. The girl was hot. This morning, she hadn't had a bra on, which meant that he'd gotten an eyeful of her impressive breasts, perfectly outlined under Brundar's white T-shirt.

Looking had been wrong on so many levels. First of all because Callie was Brundar's, and second of all because she'd been traumatized and beaten the night before and certainly wouldn't appreciate anyone ogling her breasts.

Especially not her boyfriend's brother.

Anandur had done his best to keep his eyes on her face, but that one glance had been enough to make him feel like a lecher. He would have to learn to do better, think of her as a sister, or a cousin.

Fates knew he'd had enough practice with that.

Callie pushed up from the armchair she had been sitting in snuggled up to Brundar. "Let me unpack the groceries, so I know what I have to work with."

He lifted the bags off the chair and put them on the counter. "Here is your purse." He handed it to her together with a bag of clothes. "I got you a pair of leggings, a couple of long T-shirts, a pack of panties, and a bra."

Brundar growled but said nothing.

Callie might have blushed, but with all the different colors on her face it was hard to tell. She reached into her purse and pulled out a wallet. "How much do I owe you?"

"Nothing. You can make us lunch, and I'll consider your debt paid in full." He winked, then leaned closer. "I'm getting one hell of a deal here. I'm sure your cooking is worth much more than the few bucks I spent on the clothes."

She smiled. "You need to taste it first."

"I can't wait. Chicken Piccata sounds so appetizing."

He left her to deal with the groceries and wheeled the chair to Brundar. "Want to test drive this beauty?"

"No, but I have to. I need to pee again. I think the painkillers Bridget gave me have a diuretic effect."

"Aha! I got something for you!" Anandur pulled out the portable urinal, presenting it to Brundar like a trophy.

Brundar grimaced but took the thing. "Thank you. It will make my life easier. Help me to the chair?"

Lifting his brother, Anandur gently lowered him to the wheelchair, then adjusted the leg supports. "Be careful navigating the corners, so you don't bang your legs into anything."

Brundar handed the bottle back to Anandur, grabbed the wheels and moved the chair forward, then backward and sideways. "I think I got it. Hand me back that bottle. I'm going to give it a try in the bathroom."

"I'll help you. It takes time to learn how to move in this thing." Anandur leaned closer and whispered, "We need to talk."

Brundar nodded. "But only this one time," he said for the benefit of Callie's ears.

"You got it."

Anandur pushed the chair down the corridor and into Brundar's bedroom, then waited until Brundar was done in the bathroom.

"I bumped into Andrew on the way up," he said as Brundar wheeled himself back. "He asked what's the chair for and I told him you got injured in a hostage situation. Which is the truth. I asked him to keep it to himself because you're grumpy and don't want anyone visiting, but I don't trust him not to tell Nathalie, who in turn might feel compelled to tell Syssi. Bottom line, we have to get Calypso out of here as soon as possible."

"Agreed. You need to sneak her out tonight."

"I have a feeling she is going to resist."

"Most likely."

"Are you man enough to stand up to her?"

Brundar cast him one of his more deadly glares. "Calypso is traumatized and bruised, and every instinct I have screams for me to keep her safe by my side. So if she resists, and I cave in, it is because I *am* a man."

Anandur was so proud of his little brother he wanted to pull him into a crushing bro embrace. He didn't, and not only because Brundar was injured.

Instead, he inclined his head. "I stand humbled and corrected."

9

BRUNDAR

"This is so good." Anandur paused for a moment to compliment Calypso, then shoved another piece of chicken into his mouth.

She smiled. "I'm glad you like it. What about you, Brundar?"

"Superb as always."

Calypso didn't look convinced. "Tell me the truth. I know you like beef."

He did, but whatever Calypso made tasted great. "I do. But I like sampling your creations even more."

Anandur reached for the platter and jabbed his fork into another piece of Chicken Piccata, put it on his plate and added a heap of spaghetti. "I wish we could keep you. I could get used to eating like this. But I'll have to double my workout time if I want to fit through the door."

Brundar felt his gut clench uncomfortably. He didn't like the reminder that Calypso was leaving tonight.

"If I stayed a little longer, you could get back to work while I kept an eye on Brundar. Wouldn't your cousin like that? Having both of his bodyguards out of commission must be worse than having harmless little me stay in his building."

Her logic was solid, and it would be hard to argue without giving away the real reason why she couldn't stay. Brundar exchanged glances with Anandur, hoping his brother would come up with something that sounded even remotely logical.

Anandur wiped his mustache with a napkin. "Unless Kian and his wife want to go out, he doesn't need us during the weekend. By Monday, Brundar is going to be okay to stay here by himself."

That had sounded very logical, but it had also given Calypso an opening for a new argument.

"In that case, I see no reason why I need to leave tonight. I can spend Sunday here, and you can take me home Sunday night."

Anandur scratched his beard. "It's risky, but maybe it's worth it. For me. If you stay with Brundar tonight, I can go out and have some fun. He can manage now that he has a wheelchair and a bottle to pee in."

Calypso ignored the comment about the urinal and smiled triumphantly. She lifted her hand, palm up. "There you go. I stay, and everyone is happy. As long as the big bad wolf doesn't sniff me out, that is."

A chuckle bubbled up from Anandur's chest. "An apt analogy."

"I can make dinner too, for today and tomorrow. And a Sunday brunch."

Poor girl, trying to justify her stay by cooking for them. Naturally, he wasn't going to phrase his objection like that because it would offend her. She would deny it and make up all kinds of reasons for why she just had to spend the rest of the weekend cooking. He would have to come up with an excuse, like her need to rest. In fact, it was the truth. Calypso was pushing herself too hard. He should not have agreed to her cooking lunch either. But then she would have felt bad.

Brundar shook his head. Calypso was changing him. A

few weeks ago he wouldn't have thought twice about saying what was on his mind regardless of how it would've been received.

Reaching over the dining table, he clasped her hand. "Slow down, Calypso. Anandur was just joking. You need your rest too. Takeout will do."

Anandur started to open his mouth, most likely to protest, but Brundar threw him a warning glance. His brother shut it without saying a thing, but his crestfallen expression and slumped posture spoke louder than words.

Something in Brundar's stern expression must have affected Calypso, either that or her fatigue had finally gotten the better of her, and she nodded. "I love having someone, two someones, to cook for who appreciate and enjoy it. But you're right. I need to take it easy."

He knew Calypso and waited for the catch. She never capitulated without a fight. Outside the bedroom, that was.

"When I make dinner tonight, I'll make double. It's not more work, and we will have dinner for tomorrow too." She eyed the empty platter with a satisfied smirk. "On second thoughts, I'll make it quadruple. I thought I made enough for lunch tomorrow as well."

He wasn't going to get a better deal than that.

"On one condition." Brundar cast his brother a warning glance. "You let Anandur help you. He can peel and cut and do other stuff like that."

Anandur shook his head. "I don't know about that. Having me around the kitchen is like the proverbial bull in a china shop."

"Can you wash dishes?" Calypso asked.

"I can do that."

"That's all the help I need. Cleaning up takes almost as much time as cooking, and it's my least favorite part of the process."

"Then I shall be your humble dishwasher, madam. I've already played a lowly deck boy, I can do this."

Calypso's eyes widened. "Are you an actor?"

"Not professionally. It was part of an undercover assignment."

Her eyes got even wider. "Can you tell me about it, or is it classified information?"

Anandur leaned back in his chair and rubbed his stomach. "I guess I can tell you the story without revealing any identifying details."

Brundar rolled his eyes. Anandur enjoyed drama. He could've told Calypso the name of each participant, and it still would have told her nothing. It wasn't as if the story had made the news.

"We suspected the owner of a luxury yacht of smuggling drugs, and since his crew was all female, I pretended to be a deck boy, offering my services to yacht owners in the marina." He winked suggestively.

It took a moment for his meaning to sink in, and when it did, Calypso gasped. "You didn't." She giggled.

Anandur inclined his head with pride. "Oh yes, I did."

10

CALLIE

$\mathcal{A}$fter Anandur had left, Callie leaned against Brundar and sighed. This was one of the best days of her life, and the good news was that the day wasn't over yet. She'd never felt such a sense of belonging, of family, even though she and Brundar were barely a couple, and she'd only met Anandur recently.

But then traumatic events had a way of creating a bond between people.

She'd read that people working in emergency rooms felt it, as well as soldiers in commando units. Superficial differences that meant something outside of those intense environments went up in smoke when people fought as a unit for survival, either their own in the case of commandos, or patients in the case of emergency room personnel.

But it was more than that.

Listening to Anandur tell his stories with Brundar's arm wrapped around her, holding her close, Callie had felt at peace. She had felt at home.

What a shame it was an illusion.

Tomorrow night, her carriage was going to turn back into

a pumpkin, but she wasn't going to leave a glass slipper behind.

"When is Anandur coming back?" she asked.

"Why? Do you miss him already?" There was an edge to Brundar's voice, his body tensing next to hers.

Did he think she was interested in his brother?

Silly man.

"He is fun, and I like him, but that's not why I'm asking. I'm trying to figure out how much alone time we have left."

Brundar relaxed back into the couch. "Plenty. He probably won't be back until the early hours of the morning. Do you have something in mind?"

"Maybe." If Brundar was up to it.

Though judging by how he'd gotten himself out of the wheelchair and onto the sofa, Brundar wasn't exactly helpless despite his injuries.

She still marveled at his incredible upper body strength.

Using the coffee table and the sofa's armrest for support, he'd lifted himself off the wheelchair and onto the couch with his feet never touching the floor.

Brundar hooked a finger under her chin and turned her head to look up at him. "Tell me what you want, sweetling."

She didn't want him to look at her battered face up close. It wasn't a pleasant sight, but he wouldn't let go. "Don't look at me like that."

"Like what?"

"Like you think I'm beautiful. I know what I look like and it ain't pretty."

He dipped his head and planted a chaste kiss on her lips. "You're always beautiful to me."

Who knew the guy was a closet romantic. "That's sweet of you to say, but I look like crap. If I didn't, you wouldn't be kissing me like I'm sick."

"I don't want to hurt you. Your face is so badly bruised

that I'm afraid that even the gentlest of touches will cause you pain."

He was right about that, and it wasn't only her face. Her whole body was one big ache, but for some reason, it didn't make her any less lustful. Was it a survivor's thing? Wanting to celebrate life because she'd almost lost it?

"I want you. Is it wrong to feel horny when both of us are such a mess? How can we even go about it without hurting each other?"

"You can sit on me," he suggested with a smirk.

The idea had crossed her mind, but there was a problem with that. "I can't do it with my hands tied up. I need them for balance."

"Can you do it with a blindfold?"

"I guess. Does it mean I can touch you?"

"Given the circumstances, I'll allow it this time."

"Maybe we could do without the blindfold as well?"

"No."

"Why not? I want to see the expression on your face when you climax."

By the sudden tenting of his loose pajama pants, the idea wasn't abhorrent to him, which made her hopeful.

"That's not negotiable, Calypso." Brundar's tone changed from playful to commanding, which had the desired effect on her.

So much for hope, but she had to give it one last try. "Please?"

"Go to my bedroom and get one of the ties from my closet."

"Yes, sir." She mock saluted him.

"And put a chair against the front door in case Anandur comes back early."

"As if a chair would stop him. I don't think a grand piano would."

"It will give us a second to cover up."

She could live with that. Besides, there was something exciting about doing it in the middle of the living room when there was a chance they could get caught. A small chance, but then if she thought it was likely for Anandur to show up in the next hour or so, she would've insisted on moving the fun to the bedroom.

"I'll bring a blanket."

After picking a dark silk tie from Brundar's small collection, she put it on top of the blanket she'd folded on the bed, and reached for her purse which Anandur had kindly delivered. The birth control pills hadn't been the only reason she'd needed her purse; the pack of condoms she had in there was the other.

After all, that antsy feeling had been dogging her since morning, and there had been little else she'd been thinking about while cooking lunch and then dinner. It was either a survivor's need to embrace life, or Brundar's pheromones.

It was a good thing her bra was the padded kind, not because she needed enhancement, but because it did a great job of concealing her stiff nipples. That was why she'd worn her own and not the one Anandur had gotten for her at Walmart.

It was the right size, which made her realize that he'd been sneaking peeks at her breasts, but it was one of those thin fabric ones that would have covered nothing.

With everything ready, there was one last thing she needed to do—get naked and try to renegotiate from a position of power. Brundar would have a much harder time sticking to his guns while staring at her bare breasts.

11

BRUNDAR

*B*rundar's breath caught when Calypso entered the living room without as much as a single strip of fabric on her.

The woman was perfection. From her high breasts and pink nipples, which were begging to be sucked, to her slim waist and narrow hips, to her long, toned legs. Except, it pained him to see the large bruises on her left hip and shoulder.

The memory of Calypso falling together with the chair she'd been strapped to would be forever etched in his brain, as would the backhand to her face that put that in motion.

If Shawn weren't already dead, Brundar would have taken great pleasure killing him, not with a quick and merciful snapping of the neck, but a slow and excruciating death. For every iota of pain the motherfucker had inflicted on Calypso, Brundar would have made him pay that times a thousand.

She stopped in front of him and put a hand on her hip. "Why are you glaring at me?"

He leaned forward and reached for her hips, pulling her to him.

"Careful," she said, resisting his pull when her thighs touched his.

"Straddle me," he commanded.

She put her bundle of a folded blanket, one of his silk ties, and two wrapped condoms on the couch next to him.

Brundar smiled at that. Apparently, Calypso had faith in his ability to satisfy her despite his injuries.

Climbing with her knees on the sofa, she lifted one knee over and lowered herself, so her naked core was on top of his aching, pajama-pants covered cock.

"At least someone is happy to see me," she said.

Brundar caressed her back. "The bruises on your arm and your hip reminded me of how you got them. I wish I could kill him again. But I wouldn't have granted him a merciful death like my brother did. I would've made him suffer."

Calypso frowned. "Your eyes, they look as if they are glowing."

Damnation. He should not have allowed himself to get carried away like that. The glowing eyes could be explained away, but he could feel his fangs elongating as well.

"It's an illusion created by the angle of the light fixture." He cupped her breast to distract her and reached with his other for the tie.

Calypso moaned and closed her eyes, giving him the perfect opportunity to slip the tie over her eyes.

"Sneaky," she said. "You know, I put down some hard limits, like paddles and other instruments of torture, but then moved some of them into the soft limits category. I don't see how the blindfold is any different."

"If you call paddles and floggers instruments of torture, you obviously don't know what those are." He thumbed both nipples.

Calypso arched her back. "Tell me," she breathed.

Naughty girl. Just from reading over the questionnaire in

the club she should have a good idea, but, apparently, talking about it aroused her.

"Nipple clamps, for one." To demonstrate, he pinched her nipples hard.

"Ouch!" She pushed his hands aside and cupped her breasts protectively.

"Never. There is nothing sexy about those nasty things."

Her scent agreed with her proclamation. No nipple clamps. Good. He didn't like them either.

"Okay. Those are crossed out."

"What else?"

"There are small vibrators to stimulate a woman for hours. In my opinion, when used like that those are worse than the nipple clamps. But in small doses they can be pleasurable."

"I agree. What about plugs?"

"Those are supposed to be more pleasurable than not, but I don't play with them."

"Good. They don't sound like fun to me either."

This time her scent didn't agree with her statement. Calypso was curious about that form of play. Regrettably, he wouldn't be satisfying that curiosity. He could never associate pleasure with that.

Deflecting again, he continued, "And then there are the real instruments of torture that deliver only pain, such as whips and the like."

"Masochists find pleasure in pain."

"True." He ran a finger through her wet folds. "But you're not one of them."

She shook her head. "No. I just like it when you boss me around. In bed, I mean."

He delivered a soft smack to her behind. "And you like being spanked."

"Yes. But not today."

"I know, sweetling. I was just teasing."

She leaned forward and kissed him, her tongue seeking entry he couldn't grant. He couldn't pull her hair either; her scalp was too tender from the assault. Instead, to stop her, Brundar wedged a finger between their lips.

"Turn around, Calypso," he commanded.

She hesitated for a moment, but then did as he asked, straddling him with her back to his front.

Brundar lifted up and pulled his pants down, freeing his cock, then lowered her to rub her moist center against it.

"I like it. Feeling you like that against my skin is so much better than through the rubber."

"How much longer before we can toss those out?" He cupped her breasts, holding her to him and letting her have all the control over their lower halves.

"Four days. And I don't even care that you didn't bring me a letter from your doctor yet."

"I'll get her to write it when she comes to check up on me."

"As much as I'm enjoying this, I have to ask you to please put the condom on and get inside me before I spontaneously combust."

"Your wish is my command."

She snorted. "Aren't those supposed to be my words?"

"Normally, yes." Brundar tore the wrapper and sheathed himself. He lifted her by her hips and pushed in an inch. "I'm making an exception today."

"Oh, yeah?" Calypso lowered herself another inch. "Doesn't feel like it to me. You're still calling the shots."

"Just the way you like it, sweetling." He surged all the way in.

"Oh, yes!" She threw her head back, her lush hair covering his chest.

He lifted her up, then lowered her, then did it again a couple of times. "You want to give taking over a try? I'll just provide the prop." He pushed up to demonstrate.

"Okay."

Brundar let go of her hips and put his hands behind his head, lacing the fingers. "I'm ready to be ridden by my lady jockey."

Calypso gave it all she had. For about a minute and a half before tiring. "I like it better when you do it."

"Of course."

12

ANANDUR

*A*nandur leaned back in his chair and popped open the top button of his pants. "I'm so full, I can't move."

Calypso was one hell of a cook. As she'd promised Brundar, dinner today was made from yesterday's leftovers, but she'd fixed it up, so it tasted like something new.

Dabbing his mouth with a napkin, Brundar cast him a hard look. "Too bad, because you're doing the dishes."

"I know. Just give me a moment to catch my breath."

Calypso started pushing to her feet. "There is no rush. Let's have coffee first."

Brundar reached for her hand and pulled her back down. "Anandur can make coffee."

She patted his shoulder. "It's okay. Let your brother rest. I don't mind."

Glaring, he didn't let go of her hand. "Please, sit down. You've done enough. Anandur is perfectly capable of making coffee and serving it."

Bossy little fucker, but he was right, and it wasn't as if Anandur could tell him to do it himself. Brundar was taking advantage of his temporary disability.

No matter. Payback was a bitch. Once he was back on his

feet, Anandur was going to make him wash dishes and serve coffee for weeks.

"I'm all rested." He pushed his chair back. "And I'll bring cookies."

Calypso chuckled. "I thought you said you were full."

"I am. So what? There is always room left for dessert." He headed for the kitchen.

A loud knock on the door startled all three of them, freezing them in place.

"Fuck." Anandur rushed back. "You need to hide," he whispered as he caught Callie's elbow, helping her up.

This time Brundar didn't pull her back.

Where could he stash the girl so whoever was on the other side of the door wouldn't hear her heartbeat? Given the cooking smells permeating the apartment, her scent was less of a problem.

"The balcony," he whispered in her ear as he propelled her toward the sliding glass doors.

"Give me a moment!" Brundar called out to stall their visitor. "I'm in a goddamned wheelchair!"

Anandur slid the balcony door open and pointed to the farthest corner. "Stand flush against the wall."

She nodded and did exactly as he'd instructed. Anandur closed the door and pulled the curtains closed.

Brundar motioned for him to duck into the corridor, then continued wheeling himself clumsily toward the door while banging into everything in his path to make as much noise as possible.

In his room, Anandur went a step further, going to the bathroom and flushing the toilet.

"Kian," he heard Brundar say.

Fuck. Out of everyone in the keep, Kian was the last person Anandur wanted to see this evening. He'd thought they had made it through the weekend, and that later tonight he would sneak Calypso out of the keep with no one any the wiser.

Yeah. Neither he nor Brundar were that lucky.

"How are you doing?" Kian asked.

"Have been better," Brundar grumbled.

"Aren't you going to invite me in?"

"Yes, of course. It's hard to maneuver this damned thing. I can't wait to be out of it."

Anandur walked into the living room as Brundar pushed himself back, letting Kian in.

Fuck, fuckety fuck. The dining table was set for three.

Anandur moved to block it with his body, leaning against the table and motioning for Kian to take the couch.

"I heard you were injured. How come you didn't report it to me?"

"It wasn't in the line of duty, and I didn't want to bother you on the weekend."

Kian lifted a brow. "What happened?"

Anandur crossed his arms over his chest. "Brundar decided to play the hero and rescue a damsel in distress."

Kian ignored him, focusing his intense eyes on Brundar instead. "Care to elaborate?"

"I do not. It's a private matter."

"When my best fighter is put out of commission for two weeks, I think I'm entitled to an explanation, and for your sake, I hope it's a good one, like saving a bus-load of school children from certain death."

Brundar returned Kian's glower with one of his own. "The life of a friend was on the line. In my book that's a good enough reason."

Kian glared for a few seconds more, then took in a deep breath and let his shoulders relax on the exhale. "I can't argue with that. Especially since I would've done the same thing."

He rose to his feet. "I'm sorry for interrupting your dinner. I'll let you guys go back to it." He took a sniff. "Something smells amazing. Where did you order the food from? Syssi and I should give it a try."

Anandur was about to come up with a lie when Kian peeked at the table behind him, immediately noticing the three place settings.

"Who is your guest?" He took another sniff. "You have a woman here?" His chest inflated with anger. "How many times do I need to repeat that no one is allowed to bring their hookups up here?"

Anandur let out a quiet breath. Kian's assumption would make this much easier to explain.

"I'm sorry, boss. My bad." Anandur took the blame. "When she offered to cook for me, I couldn't resist." He inhaled deeply. "Can you blame me? The girl is a wizard in the kitchen."

Kian didn't smile. "Where is she? Where are you hiding her?"

"Come on, boss. No need to scare the panties off the little thing. Right after dinner, I'm going to take her home and scrub her memories. She doesn't need to see you."

"If you care for her feelings, bring her out from wherever you've stashed her before I do. And just so we are clear, Monday morning I want you in my office for a formal reprimand. You're not getting away with harboring a human without penalty."

"Yes, boss." Anandur inclined his head in acceptance but didn't move toward the balcony. Maybe now that Kian had huffed and puffed he would leave.

"I'm waiting. Bring. Her. Out."

Fuck. He was going to smell Brundar all over Calypso and know that she wasn't Anandur's. Unless he held her close. It would be hard for Kian to tell where Brundar's scent was coming from. After all, he was right there with them.

Anandur walked to the door, slid it open, and stepped out

onto the balcony. He found Calypso shivering from the cold, her arms wrapped around herself.

Damn. For a human, it was way too chilly and windy to be standing outside in a T-shirt.

"I'm sorry, love. Come here, and I'll warm you up." He winked and tilted his head toward the inside, urging her to play along, then wrapped his arm around her and walked her in.

"Kian, this is Calypso. Calypso, this is Kian."

Kian's angry expression turned furious. "Who did this to you?" He pointed at her face.

Fuck, Anandur felt like such an idiot. He'd forgotten about Calypso's bruises.

As opposed to just playing along, she huddled closer to him, seeking shelter from Kian's anger.

Brundar growled and wheeled himself between Kian on one side and Anandur and Calypso on the other. "Enough. Come to me, Calypso."

He extended his hand, and she took it.

Pulling to bring her close against his side, he turned his head to look at Kian. "Calypso is with me, not with my brother."

Kian kept glaring.

"Her ex-husband did this to her." Brundar pointed at her bruises. "And he would've done much worse if not for Anandur's and my intervention."

Kian looked at Calypso's battered face, then pinned Brundar with a hard stare. "Is he dead?"

"Yes."

"Good."

13

CALLIE

*I*t wasn't often that Callie felt so grossly intimidated. Brundar's boss had a commanding presence, saturating all the air in the apartment with his anger.

He was blindingly beautiful, and usually she would have been attracted to a guy who was that good-looking, and who exuded such a powerful vibe, but all she felt now was fear.

As Donnie had said, the devil was beautiful because he used to be an angel. From now on, whenever Callie thought of the devil, he would be wearing this guy's stunning face.

You're being silly, the voice of reason in her head whispered. She had experienced evil. He had left ugly, painful marks all over her body. This guy was intense, but she was willing to bet that he'd never in his entire life hit a woman.

As he turned to look at her face again, Kian's expression softened and he raked his fingers through his hair, which she suspected was a nervous habit. "Are you okay?"

She nodded, not trusting her voice not to quiver.

"I'm sorry for what happened to you, but I can't allow you to stay."

"Why?" She managed a tiny whisper.

"I don't need to share my reasons with you." He said it matter-of-factly, not in anger, or in any way condescendingly.

"Can I come visit Brundar? I mean while he is recovering and can't drive?"

Kian shook his head. "I'm sorry, but no."

Evidently, Brundar hadn't been lying about his boss's eccentric demands.

Tears pooling at the corners of her eyes at the thought of not being allowed to see Brundar, Callie nodded in resignation. She was going to miss him so much. Maybe she could convince Anandur to drive him over to her apartment.

"Do you have somewhere to go?" Kian surprised her.

Would he let her stay if she said no?

"I can arrange an apartment for you until you get back on your feet."

So sweet of him to offer. Callie felt guilty for comparing him to the devil. "Thank you, but that won't be necessary. I have my own apartment and a job that pays the bills." She knew better than to add that she had those things thanks to Brundar.

"Good. I'm glad to hear that." He turned to Anandur. "Take Calypso home today, and make sure to do whatever is necessary to help her get settled."

"It will be done, boss."

For some reason she had a feeling there was a double message in Kian's command. Why would he tell Anandur to help her get settled in her own place? She had the absurd notion that Kian was telling Anandur to get rid of her.

Permanently.

Crap, she'd been reading too many crime novels.

Kian inclined his head in her direction, then turned on his heel and walked out without saying goodbye or any of the other conventional niceties.

As soon as the door closed behind the guy, Anandur

plopped down on the couch. "Do you think he is going to invent some new creative torment for me as punishment for aiding and abetting?"

Brundar shrugged, appearing significantly less rattled by Kian's unexpected visit than his brother was. Anandur looked like he'd been in a boxing match and lost. "You know him. Kian gets all riled up and then calms down after letting the steam out."

Callie sat on the couch next to Anandur. "I don't know how you can stand working for him. It must be like holding a live wire in your hands for hours every day. So draining."

"Nah. Kian is okay. Most of the time his electrical hum is low and steady, and when it gets a bit intense it is usually for a good reason," Anandur said.

She cast him a sidelong glance. "A bit intense? Are you serious? It's like calling a woman giving birth a bit pregnant."

Anandur laughed. "The lass has a sense of humor. Tell me, Callie, how can you tolerate that dry stick over there?" He pointed at Brundar.

She wasn't about to allow anyone to belittle her guy. Not even his brother, and not even as a joke. Lowering her voice, she waggled her brows. "Brundar compensates in other areas."

Brundar cleared his throat as if he was uncomfortable with their banter. Funny, as a part owner of a kink club this little sexual innuendo shouldn't have bothered him.

"We need to figure out what to do. I have no intention of being stuck in this apartment until I can walk again."

"You can come stay with me," she offered on the remote chance that he would agree.

"Not a good idea," Anandur said. "You can't lift him or hold him up in the shower."

If that was the only objection, she'd already won the argument. "There are handicap attachments we can install next to the toilet and in the shower. The shower in my apartment is big. We can fit a sturdy chair in there."

Anandur threw her an amused glance. "What's all that about, we can do this, and we can do that? Are you handy with a drill?"

"We, as in a joint effort. I'll buy the accessories, and you'll install them."

"I was just teasing, lass. I'll get the stuff and put it in."

That was good because Callie wasn't sure what to get and where, and she was very glad to fob it off on the big, strong guy sitting next to her. Her style of feminism wasn't about doing everything herself to prove she didn't need men for anything. Of course, she could do that, but why should she, when she could utilize them to do the things they were good at, like lifting heavy stuff and tightening screws.

Good managers delegated, they didn't do everything themselves. Not only that, though, they put the task on the schedule to make sure it was going to get done, and then inspected the completed product.

"When? Can you do it tomorrow?"

"The sooner I do it the better. With Brundar staying at your place, I can go back to work." He glanced at his brother. "First, though, you need to go see Bridget and ask her if it's okay."

"I'll do it later after you take Calypso home."

She was a little sad that he wasn't coming home with her tonight, but knowing he would be there tomorrow or the day after to stay, at least until he got better or maybe longer, was good enough.

Maybe she could keep him there. Tie him to her bed.

Callie smiled at the thought.

There was just one problem with her pleasant fantasy. "What about Kian? He is not going to approve."

Brundar shrugged. "He can kiss my ass. What is he going to do, fire me?"

Anandur's eyes peeled wide. "You're willing to leave everything behind for the lass?"

God, what a lack of sensitivity. With that remark, Anandur was putting them both on the spot.

"Slow down." She lifted her hand. "No one is firing anyone, and no one is quitting either. How about we take one day at a time and see what happens?"

Anandur shook his head. "What's going to happen is shit hitting the fan. But then it wouldn't be our first shit storm. I'll get my umbrella ready."

BRUNDAR

*T*he quiet in the apartment felt oppressive. It hadn't been even half an hour since Calypso had left with Anandur, and Brundar was missing her already.

If he were out in the field, the separation would've been tolerable, but sitting in the damned wheelchair in the middle of the living room and staring at the wall was making it worse. Much worse.

Being alone had never bothered him before. On the contrary, he used to enjoy the quiet whenever Anandur was out and he had the apartment all to himself. He would put on some classical music and read.

Not that he'd done either lately.

Brundar had no time to indulge in leisure activities. Since buying into Franco's, those moments had become scarce.

The thing was, right now he didn't feel like listening to music or reading. He craved what he'd had for the last two days.

Calypso.

How the hell was he going to make it until tomorrow?

Come to think of it, there was no reason to wait. He could go see Bridget right now.

Damnation. The doctor wouldn't be in her office on a Sunday night. Bridget was probably partying somewhere. He could call her and complain about something. She would drop everything and come check up on him.

Brundar chuckled. If he told her his heart was acting up and his blood flow was all screwed up, he wouldn't be lying.

Where the hell was his phone?

Did he have it on him when they'd gotten home Friday night?

Damn. It was probably in the pocket of the jeans Bridget had cut off him. Hopefully, she hadn't tossed the pants with the phone in the trash.

Brundar wheeled himself to the kitchen counter, grabbed the house phone, and dialed the clinic's number. It was worth a shot. If there was no answer, he would call her apartment. Her cell phone number was programmed into his shortlist of favorites, but he didn't remember it.

She answered after a few rings. "Bridget here."

"What are you doing in the clinic on a Sunday night?"

She chuckled without mirth. "Research. Whenever I'm in a shitty mood I dive into my research. What can I do for you? Are you in pain?"

"I don't remember if I left my phone in the pants you cut off me. Did you throw them away?"

"I put them in a zipped plastic bag in case you wanted them as a memento."

"Could you check to see if my phone is in one of the pockets? After that burn them."

"Not a sentimental guy, are you?"

"Did I ever give you the impression that I was?"

He'd spent most of his life trying to forget things, not remember them. Most of his experiences had been of the kind better forgotten, but then some he needed to keep as a reminder of what not to do next time in similar situations.

"Hold the line while I check your pants."

He waited, listening as Bridget opened a drawer, then the rustle of plastic and the whoosh of unzipping, until she picked up the receiver again. "It's here. Do you want me to bring it up to you?"

"I can come down. Anandur got me a wheelchair."

"That's okay. I will come to you. I need a break anyway, and I'll check your knees while I'm at it."

"Thank you."

He'd been looking forward to wheeling himself out and into the elevator. It would have given him something to do other than staring at the walls. Now he was going to pass another ten minutes or so in inactivity.

The next two weeks were going to be hell. Even when he finally replaced the wheelchair with crutches, he would still be stuck doing nothing.

An injured Guardian was worthless.

Maybe he could dedicate this time to focusing on Franco's.

In fact, if he stayed at Calypso's she could drive him there and back, and it would be nice to spend his days and nights with her. It would sure make the coming weeks more tolerable.

Would she tolerate his presence twenty-four-seven?

Brundar knew he was going to love every minute of it. But that was because Calypso was all sunshine. In contrast, he was the dark cloud to dim her light. She might soon get tired of him.

The thought obliterated the temporary spark of good mood.

Brundar was glad to hear the knock on the door announcing Bridget. For the next few minutes, he would be too busy to brood.

"Come in. It's open."

Bridget entered, holding her old-fashioned doctor's bag. She pulled his phone out of her pants pocket. "Here you go.

Nothing broken."

"Thank you."

"Let's see those knees of yours. Can you wheel yourself next to the couch?"

He nodded and followed her.

"You're doing as well as expected," she said when she was done. "Tomorrow, you can start putting a little pressure on them. Not walking, but you can put your feet down on the floor while bracing most of your weight on your arms to move from the wheelchair to the bed or the sofa."

"That's good to hear because I'm moving in with Calypso until my knees heal completely. We don't have enough Guardians for Anandur to play nurse to me."

"That's a big mistake, and you know it. It was semi-okay to pretend like this was going to work before your injury. Callie saw your knees get shot to pieces, and she is not stupid. Even with my bullshit explanation, she would know no one can recover from an injury like that in two weeks. What are you going to do when there is no trace of it? Keep your pants on so she won't see your perfectly healthy knees?"

Brundar's lips curved in a smirk. "I got that part covered."

Bridget frowned. "How?"

"I have my ways."

"Oh, yeah." She blushed. "So the rumors are true? You're into that bondage thing?"

He'd been hiding it for so long and for no good reason. There was no shame in what he did. But then it was no one's business how he liked things in bed. However, he could make an exception in Bridget's case. It would ease her mind to know how well he was hiding his nature.

"A blindfold is a great tool for an immortal male. I don't need to worry about my eyes glowing or my fangs showing. And now I can add perfectly healed knees to that."

She shook her head. "I agree that it's an excellent cover. In fact, you may suggest it to some of the guys who need help in that department. But the more time you spend with the girl, the stronger the emotional entanglement will become. You're sentencing both of you to misery. And don't forget the addiction part. It can happen with a human female as easily as with an immortal. Think how difficult it would be for her once you leave."

What did she think? That he hadn't gone through all those scenarios in his head already and still felt powerless to resist?

Maybe he was losing his ever-loving mind, but he was willing to sacrifice everything for a few good years with Calypso until he could no longer hide the fact that he wasn't aging.

Except, he was not ready to challenge the clan yet. There was time for that. In the meantime, he was going to lie.

"It's just until I'm healed. I'll end it then."

Given the doubtful expression on her face, Bridget wasn't buying it. But she wouldn't go as far as accusing him of lying. Most likely, she thought he was delusional.

"I want to see you tomorrow before you put any pressure on your knees. If everything is okay, I'll give you a different kind of braces that allow for more movement."

"What time do you want me here?"

"Late afternoon or early evening. Do you have a way to get back here?"

"I'll have to ask Anandur to pick me up."

"He might be busy. Give me Calypso's address, and I'll come to you."

He shook his head. "I don't want you to get in trouble because of me. Kian knows that we snuck Calypso in. He caught us. But I'm not going to tell him I'm staying with her. If I'm lucky, he won't know until the two weeks are up."

Bridget put a hand on her hip. "I'll keep your secret, Brundar. He is not going to hear it from me."

"I know. But if he finds out, you'll get in trouble."

She waved a hand. "I'm not scared of him. He is all bark and no bite. What is he going to do? Fire me?"

Brundar smiled. "Funny that you should say that. That's my stance as well."

Bridget put her hand over her heart. "Oh Fates, Brundar, are we talking mutiny?"

"We are a family, Bridget, not a ship crew. We cooperate because it's in our best interest. Sometimes, though, it is not."

15

RONI

*R*oni looked at the cuff William had secured around his wrist and grimaced. "It looks like women's jewelry. Don't you have anything more manly?"

William snorted. "Dalhu and Michael didn't complain, and those two are as manly as they come."

Roni shook his wrist from side to side, testing the cuff's fit. "I don't know those guys, but I'll take your word for it. What happens when I gain weight? Can you adjust it?"

"I'll make you a new one."

"If I never take it off, how am I going to clean the skin under it? It's going to get gross."

William sighed and gripped Roni's arm. "Look, it's loose enough so you can push it up for washing. Do you always complain this much?"

"Yeah, I do. It's a good strategy. The squeaky wheel gets the grease."

"And gets annoying, but what do I know?" The guy shrugged. "I'm not so great with people either. I talk too much. They get bored and scurry away."

William talked fast, but Roni didn't mind. Everything the guy had told him was fascinating. "That's because they are a bunch of morons who don't understand half of what you're talking about, and even if they do, they can't follow because you talk so fast. You're too smart for them, man."

William cracked a smile. "Thank you. Let's see how you're going to talk after working with me for a couple of weeks. Kian told me to make room for you in my lab."

That was the best news Roni had had in a while. "Are we going to work together?"

"Yep. Side by side." William collected the tools he'd brought with him to cuff Roni and put them back in a blue fabric pouch.

"Can I come see the place?"

"Do you feel well enough?"

"I'm much better, thank you for asking." For some reason, Roni felt like being polite to the guy and curbing the snarky attitude he treated almost everyone else with. Not because William was a good guy, and not because he was inviting Roni to share his kingdom, but because he sensed vulnerability in him.

Most of the time Roni was too self-absorbed to notice other people's emotional states, but William's eyes had a haunted look to them that bothered Roni. He had a feeling it was something that happened recently because everyone who mentioned William had commented what a cheerful and friendly guy he was. The dude was friendly for sure, but he was far from cheerful.

"Then let's go. Now that you have the cuff, I can have your thumbprint programmed into the scanners."

"Right, I was wondering when I'd be allowed out of this apartment." Not that he was going anywhere.

Roni's computer equipment was right there, and Sylvia made sure he had food in the fridge. Other than work and necessities, the only reason to leave would be to go visit someone, but he knew only a few people: Andrew, who still kept his distance; Kian, who Roni wasn't going to visit unless his life depended on it; and Jackson and Tessa, who didn't live at the keep. And William, of course.

Sylvia had told him about the gym and the movie theater, but he was still too weak for exercising, and watching a movie all by himself in an empty theater was as appealing as telling jokes to himself in the mirror. Some things had to be done in company. Even a loner like him knew that.

The first thing that struck Roni as odd was that the door to William's lab was unlocked. Apparently, the guy trusted his fellow clan members not to sabotage his work.

"You should lock the door when you leave the room," he said as he followed the guy inside.

"It's safe down here."

"Yeah, until it's not." Roni took a look around, underwhelmed by what he saw. It was a disorganized mess of epic proportions. How the hell did the guy work in a dump like that?

William frowned. "What do you mean? Only family is allowed in here."

"And you trust every one of them implicitly? There are bad apples in every family. Imagine if someone holds a grudge for something and decides to retaliate by sabotaging the keep's brain, which I assume is all in here."

"It is." William pushed his glasses up his nose. "I never considered the possibility, but you're right. It's not like it couldn't happen."

"Exactly. Put in a retina scanner. Those are impossible to trick. Better than thumb scanners."

William's lips lifted in a crooked smirk. "I can do better than that. I can use my facial recognition program to grant entry only to those who need to be here, and I'll have a record of everyone entering the lab."

"Perfect."

William walked over to his messy station. "So, what do you think? Nice setup, right?"

Roni liked the guy, but it didn't mean he was going to lie about something as important as his future working environment to spare his feelings.

"It's a dump. Your equipment is good, but I don't know how you can work here. First of all, all those cables lying around on the floor are a safety hazard. This super expensive equipment is piled up like it's a junkyard. Then there is your desk and your chair. No considerations at all to ergonomics. I know that you're an immortal and that you heal fast, but sitting in that crappy chair all day must do a number on your back. I'm sure it hurts."

William glanced around his domain, once, then again, as if he was trying to see it through Roni's eyes.

"There are no pictures on the walls, either," he added to Roni's list of things that needed improvement.

Roni nodded. "The walls could use a fresh coat of paint before you hang pictures on them. Look at the smoke stains over there. Did something catch fire?"

William rubbed his neck. "Yeah, I had a small accident a couple of years ago."

"Wow. Your maintenance crew sucks, man. You should hire a new one."

"We have no maintenance crew. We have my ramped up Roomba, but because of the wires I can't let it loose in here."

"You don't hire maintenance people because of the secrecy?"

"Naturally."

"How about your own people?"

"No one wants to do a job like that. We each clean and perform upkeep on our own work spaces. Except for Kian, that is. He has a butler that does it for him. But then Kian is the hardest working person in the keep."

Roni glanced around. "I'm sure not everyone does a good job of keeping things clean."

William cast him a sheepish glance. "Any ideas on how to

improve things? From what Andrew tells me, you worked in the heart of hearts of the government's computer network."

"I did. Anything I wanted I put in a request for, and it was delivered or done. I called it my throne room and treated it as such."

"I like it. A throne room. In here, if the procurement requires serious funds it goes through Kian. I'm authorized to spend up to twenty thousand a month at my own discretion. Usually, it's enough."

It was Roni's turn to look uncomfortable. "I can make a list of what we need to transform this place, but I have no clue how much it's going to cost. I worked for the government. Our department had unlimited budget."

"Let's start with that list and go from there."

16

ANANDUR

*A*nandur wiped the drill shavings from the bathroom floor with a wet rag, then stood back to examine his work. If Kian ever kicked him out of the Guardian force, he could have a career as a handyman.

Installing the special handicapped rails and supports hadn't been a complicated job. If he could do that with no training, after watching two YouTube vids, he could learn how to do other things just as quickly. It boiled down to having the right tools and figuring out how to use them.

As the idea took on a life of its own, Anandur grinned at his reflection in the vanity mirror. He could imagine himself with a tool belt, fixing things for lonely ladies in need of small home improvements and big orgasms.

He could be known as the fixer-upper gigolo. He'd charge for the improvements and throw in the orgasms for free.

"What are you smiling about?" Calypso asked, handing him a tall glass of lemonade.

"A job well done." He moved back so she could inspect his work.

"Looks awesome. I'll tell Brundar to come give it a try."

Last night, his stubborn brother had made Anandur take

him to Calypso's even though her apartment wasn't ready for him and his special needs. The guy had it bad, or good, depending on which end of the prism one chose to look through.

"You'll have to clear the bathroom," Brundar said from the entrance. "It's not that I'm modest, but there isn't enough room for you and me and my wheelchair."

Anandur stepped out, and Calypso followed.

Brundar wheeled himself inside, maneuvered the chair next to the toilet, grabbed the bars and hoisted himself up. "Okay, going in. Now let's see if it works the other way around." He hoisted himself up again and sat back on the chair.

"Dude, you need to check if you can take your pants down as well."

Brundar ignored him and wheeled himself toward the shower, where Anandur had put in a sturdy chair designed especially for that purpose. With his brother's upper body strength, it was really no challenge, but Anandur wondered how injured or paralyzed humans handled situations like that. They probably couldn't do it at all without assistance.

"Thank you," Brundar said as he got himself back into the wheelchair. "I owe you."

"No, you don't. I did it for me as much as for you. I want to get back to work knowing you can manage on your own."

Brundar nodded. "Still, it's appreciated."

Calypso nudged Anandur's arm. "I'm making lunch. Wash your hands and come join us."

He would've loved to, but he'd already spent the entire morning on the installation and needed to get back to the keep before Kian decided to pay them another visit, finding no one home.

"I wish I could. But I have to get back to work." And whatever torment Kian had planned for him.

"I'll put the cutlet inside a sandwich so you can eat it in the car on the way."

"Thank you. That would be great."

Anandur was falling a little in love with his brother's woman. Not romantically, but as someone he was happy to know. Calypso was awesome. Pretty, funny, feisty, and a goddess in the kitchen. But most importantly, she made Brundar smile.

After collecting his new tools and washing his hands, Anandur walked out the door with a kiss on his cheek and a sandwich packed in a paper bag.

He could get used to that. Would his brother mind if he moved in with him and Calypso?

Yeah, he would.

Bummer.

Even though Brundar's knees were busted and he was in a wheelchair, the guy looked happy for the first time since he was a little kid. Anandur was adamant about keeping it that way. If need be, he would slay dragons and fight Kian, or the other way around, to guard Brundar's little slice of happiness.

His brother deserved it.

Back in the keep, Anandur headed straight for Kian's office to report for duty. As far as he knew, Kian had no outside meetings scheduled for today, but things often changed.

He knocked on the door and walked in. "I'm back and reporting for duty."

Kian lifted his head and cast him a hard look. "Who is taking care of your brother?"

"He is doing fine by himself. A few grab bars solved the bathroom problem." He wasn't lying, he just wasn't being specific. Kian didn't need to know that the grab bars were not in Anandur and Brundar's apartment.

"What about the girl?"

"She is back at her place." Again, not a lie.

Kian shook his head. "What are you not telling me, Anandur? I can smell your guilt."

Damn. He'd forgotten about Kian's super-nose. His sense of smell was superior. Perhaps because he was as close genetically to the gods as it got, or maybe it was his special talent, but the guy could differentiate between the slightest nuances.

"Brundar has feelings for the girl. You know him, you know how closed off he was, pushing everyone away, including me. He was living on autopilot, like a zombie. I'm sure you realize what a breakthrough this is for him."

"I do. But it changes nothing. Even if he decided to run off with her, what would happen in a few years when she ages, and he doesn't? He would have to leave her, and it'd destroy him. I've been in that movie. The pain I carried with me for years was much worse than if I had given the girl up right at the beginning."

"I like Calypso."

"I'm sure you do, but it has nothing to do with anything."

"But it does. Amanda has a new theory about immortals and Dormants feeling affinity toward each other. Maybe Calypso is a Dormant?"

"If she were, she would've transitioned already. I'm sure Brundar hasn't kept their relationship platonic. He is behaving like a mated male."

Yeah, there was that. Anandur suspected Brundar had been involved with Calypso for a long while. All that secrecy, all those days and nights he would disappear from sight, not telling anyone where he was going.

No doubt some of it had to do with the club he'd acquired, but not all. Kian was right. Brundar and Calypso acted like a mated couple.

And yet, Jackson and Tessa were another couple in a similar situation, and Kian was allowing them to be together. Not only that, he let Tessa live away from the keep, free as a bird while privy to all their secrets and its location.

It wasn't right, and Anandur was going to confront Kian about it even if it got him in deeper shit than he already was. "How come you went out on a limb for Tessa and Jackson, a teenage boy and a human girl with no Dormant indicators, but you're refusing to do the same for Brundar? A man who has served you faithfully for centuries?"

Kian's eyes started glowing dangerously. "I have my reasons, and I don't need to share them with you."

Anandur should have known to back off, but he was too riled to back down. "You're playing favorites, Kian, and not for the right people. I don't care what your reasons are. If anyone deserves happiness, it is my brother."

"Get out," Kian hissed from between tight lips, his fangs getting so long they were protruding below his upper lip. "You chose a bad day to question my leadership and show disrespect for my authority."

As if there were ever a good day for that.

Anandur rose to his feet. "I'll be in the gym if you need me." He still had a duty to perform, even if his boss was a monumental jerk with a God complex.

Well, he happened to be an actual demigod, but that was beside the point.

It took all of Anandur's self-restraint to walk out of Kian's office without throwing a punch into one of the walls and to not slam the door behind himself.

Imagining the punching bag in the gym helped.

Alone in the elevator, Anandur let out the growl he'd been holding. It shook the small cabin. A disembodied voice came through the loudspeakers. "Is there a problem?"

The shaking must've alerted security.

"No problem. I was just releasing some steam."

The voice chuckled. "Is the elevator still in one piece?"

"Yeah, no worries."

"I'll take your word for it, Anandur."

Damn it. Everyone working in security knew him, but Anandur hadn't expected his voice to be so easily recognizable.

As the elevator came to a stop at the gym level, Anandur stepped out and walked straight into Amanda. He caught her shoulders, steadying her.

"Sorry, princess. Are you okay?"

"It's my fault. I was checking messages on my phone and not paying attention. What's going on? You look flustered."

"Do I?" Anandur touched his hand to his cheek. It was warm. One of the many disadvantages of being a redhead was that cursed fair skin that became ruddy with every heightened emotion and after a couple of drinks.

"You do. Is it about Brundar? I heard what happened to him. In fact, I came home for lunch with the intent of paying him a visit."

Anandur closed his eyes. The plot was thickening. Pretty soon every goddamned clan member would want to come visit poor injured Brundar, only to discover that he wasn't there.

"Brundar doesn't want to see anyone. You know how proud he is. Getting bested by a human is not something he wants to talk about. He wants to forget it ever happened."

Amanda put her hand on her hip. "That's the thing. No one knows what happened. Or how. I want details, Anandur."

"I'm sure you do."

17

AMANDA

"I'm going to talk to Kian," Amanda said after Anandur had filled her in on what was going on. She'd practically muscled him into one of the empty classrooms and forced the story out of him.

It was so much bigger than Brundar getting shot. The ice prince was in love. Not that Anandur had mentioned the word love, but the words fate and mate and affinity had been thrown into the mix of his otherwise matter-of-fact account.

"Don't. And please, for the love of everything that's dear to you, don't spread the story. Especially since it is not my story to tell. You trusted me with yours way back then, and I'm trusting you with this."

"You're not the only one who needs to fight for Brundar. I'm going to fight for him too."

"I appreciate the sentiment, I really do. But your brother is in one of his shite moods today. He told me to get out when I dared mention Tessa and Jackson and the leeway he is allowing them. He will just blow up at you."

"Tessa and Jackson have nothing to do with Brundar and his girl. Each story is different. It was a strategic mistake on your part to bring them up."

"In hindsight, yes. But I don't understand why."

Amanda re-crossed her legs in an attempt to get comfortable on the desk she was sitting on. "Tessa is like Eva's daughter. She would never do anything to betray the woman who saved her life and raised her as her own."

Anandur tilted his head. "That's a story I would like to hear."

"I bet. But it's not my story to tell."

"I told you Brundar's."

"Nice try. It's not the same. I barely know Tessa, while Brundar is your brother and you're trying to build a team to fight for him."

"I am?"

"Sure you are. That's why you told me his story. You want my help."

"Honestly, I wasn't thinking in that direction at all. I just needed someone to hear me out, and as I said before, I trust you."

"And I owe you. Don't think I've forgotten what you did for me when I was fighting for my right to be with Dalhu."

Anandur let out a sigh. "Why is your brother such an ass?"

"He is not an ass. He is stressed out and overworked, and he needs to take time off. I think he is nearing a breaking point. He snaps at everyone, except Syssi, that is. She is the only one who can calm him down."

"In that case, we need her on our team."

"We need my mother."

Anandur crossed his arms over his chest. "I don't know about that. You are her daughter, so naturally, she was inclined to assist you. But Brundar is just one more clan member, no more special than the next. She will not go against Kian for him."

Amanda smirked. "Men think so linearly. I will not ask her to come here for Brundar. I'll ask her to come to help

Kian. He needs a vacation, and she is the only one who can force him to take one."

Anandur looked doubtful. "And who is going to run things when he is vacationing?"

"I can take time off from the university and run things for him while he is gone."

Anandur tried to stifle his snort but failed. "With all due respect, Amanda, you're a smart and capable woman, but you can't fill Kian's shoes. He's been running this conglomerate since its creation. You wouldn't know where to start."

"True. But contrary to what Kian believes, the world will not come to an end if he is not holding it up on his shoulders twenty-four-seven. Our business empire will not crumble during the two weeks he is gone, and World War III will not start because he abandoned his watch."

"Dream on, princess. You'll be lucky if he takes the weekend off. Don't even mention two weeks if you want your head to stay attached to your shoulders."

She shrugged. "I'm not afraid of him."

"Yeah, that's why you're thinking of pulling out the big guns, meaning your mother."

"It's not because I'm afraid, but because I know she is the only one he is going to listen to. He has no choice."

Anandur sighed. "I have a feeling we are getting carried away. Conspiring against Kian, asking Annani to come, it's like we are preparing for war. I don't want that."

Amanda put a hand on his bicep. "I was meaning to ask my mother to come and stay with us for a while even before you told me about Brundar. Andrew and Nathalie are dragging their feet about taking little Phoenix up to Annani's sanctuary. They are leaving that child vulnerable for no good reason. So instead of harping on at them to take their daughter up there already, so the goddess can induce her transition, I figured Annani can come for a visit and spend time with the baby, which she loves doing. Phoenix can transition right here without leaving the keep."

"I like it. It will look less like a conspiracy if Annani comes for the baby, but then notices that Kian is at the end of his rope and needs a vacation."

"Exactly."

"You are a deviously brilliant woman, Amanda."

She lifted an eyebrow. "And that's news to you?"

He chuckled. "No, not really. But I keep forgetting that you are so much more than your gorgeous face."

"A mistake a lot of people live to regret."

"So let me get this straight. The goddess comes and forces Kian to take a vacation. How is it going to help Brundar's cause?"

Amanda rolled her eyes. "Darling, did you forget already that Kian needing a vacation is only the excuse I'm going to use to lure her in?"

He frowned. "I thought it was the baby."

"Both. She will ask what's going on with Kian, and I'll give Brundar's situation as an example of Kian being unreasonable. Annani is a sucker for romance. She will intervene on your brother's behalf."

Anandur crossed his arms over his chest. "I'm not sure you're right. She might be a sucker for romance, but she is the one who made the rules about staying away from humans. Not that she wasn't absolutely right to do so. I happen to believe that an exception needs to be made in Brundar's case because it is crucial for his mental health, but I'm not sure Annani will share my opinion."

"That might be. But do you have a better idea?"

"Can't say that I do."

"That's what I thought. We will do the best we can, while praying to the Fates to smile upon us. It is better than doing nothing and hoping everything will turn out fine on its own."

"True."

18

CALLIE

*C*allie applied another coat of makeup and took a step back to examine her face. The bruising was still visible. But maybe in the club's dim light no one would notice.

As much as she enjoyed spending all day with Brundar, she needed to get back to work. The thing was, customers didn't want their waitress to look as if someone had used her face as a punching bag. Franco would take one look at her and send her home.

"No one expects you to go back to work yet," Brundar said from behind her.

She turned and smiled at him. "Maybe so, but I need to go grocery shopping. I have nothing to make dinner from."

"We can order takeout."

Callie put a hand on her chest. "Blasphemy. Do not utter the word takeout in this house." She tried to sound stern.

"Takeout," he deadpanned.

Frowning, she waved a finger at him. "You're not a God-fearing man."

"I'm not. I worship a different deity, and its temple is the Golden Palace."

"Chinese food?"

He nodded.

"Does your brother know that you actually have a sense of humor?"

Brundar's lips lifted in a crooked smile. "I'm experimenting with it. Am I doing it right?"

Callie giggled. He reminded her of a cyborg in one of her sci-fi romance novels. Part machine part man, the guy was trying to assimilate into human society by attempting humor and slang.

Was that what Brundar was trying to do? Assimilate?

"You're doing it perfectly. I like dry humor. I think jokes that are told with a straight face are the funniest."

"Then you must find me very funny."

"Not yet. But you're getting there." She leaned to kiss his cheek.

Ever since Brundar's injury, Callie had been sneaking a little touch here, a kiss there, and gauging his responses. He was either not noticing them, or humoring her. In either case, it was progress she was very pleased about.

"Are we ordering Chinese?" he asked.

"Fine. But don't get used to that. Tomorrow morning I'm going grocery shopping, and you're going to eat what I make for you—healthy food your body needs in order to heal. Not crap that is loaded with MSG and oil."

"Yes, ma'am."

She liked it when he obeyed so nicely. In some small way, it evened the score between them a little.

Callie loved submitting to Brundar sexually, but despite all her self-talk and the famous *love as thy wilt* that she'd adopted as her mantra, it still bothered her on some level that she did.

That was why hearing him saying 'yes, ma'am' felt so good. It made her feel better about saying 'yes, sir' during their play time.

"Do you have their number?"

"On speed dial."

She waved a hand. "Then dial away."

"What would you like?"

She shrugged. "I don't know what's on their menu, and I'm not a big fan of Chinese food. Order what you like, and I'll nibble."

"I can order from somewhere else."

"No. If you find their food worth worship, I have to check it out. Just make sure there are some veggies in there, not only meat."

Brundar cast her an amused glance. "Why don't you go online and check out their menu and decide what you want?"

She sauntered toward him, braced her hands on his wheelchair's armrests and leaned forward, giving him a good glimpse of her cleavage. "I want you to order for me, and later order *me*."

"Order you what?" His tone got deeper.

"Order me to strip, order me to pleasure you with my mouth or my hands, or both. You decide."

His hands closed on her ass and squeezed. "I would like to reverse the order."

"You would?"

"You first, Chinese later."

"Hmm, that's not a bad idea. We can work up an appetite."

"Are you ready for your first order?"

"Yes, sir."

"Get the blindfold and bring it to me."

Crap. She'd been hoping he would forget about the damn blindfold for once. Not that it wasn't a turn-on for her, it was, but she wanted to see Brundar's face while he climaxed, at least once. After that, he wouldn't even have to remind her to put on the blindfold.

He followed her to the bedroom, watching as she pulled out the scarf from the nightstand's drawer. The condom packets peeked at her from under the other scarves. Callie reached for one then paused.

It hadn't been a week yet, and Brundar hadn't provided her with a clean bill of health like he'd promised, but she'd seen the doctor treat him without gloves. If Bridget deemed his blood safe to handle with her bare hands, then she must've known he was clean.

She could still get pregnant, though, and as someone who'd experienced an unwanted pregnancy and its consequences, Callie knew better.

With a sigh, she closed her hand around the packet.

"What's the matter, sweetling?"

"Nothing." She turned around with a smile and handed him the scarf, then dropped the packet on the bed where he could see it and remember to use it.

Brundar's eyes followed the plastic square. "Right. I don't know why I keep forgetting to ask Bridget for that letter."

"I'm not worried about that. It hasn't been seven days yet. I can still get pregnant."

He looked like he was about to say something but then changed his mind. Brundar did that a lot, and she always wondered what he was about to say and why he decided not to.

If only she could read minds.

Yeah. Life would've been so much easier.

She would've known not to marry Shawn despite the pregnancy. It would've been infinitely better to be a single parent than to tie herself to a monster.

If she were a mind reader, she would know what Brundar was hiding from her and maybe avoid making another catastrophic mistake. In her gut and in her heart she knew Brundar was a good man, but Callie didn't trust her instincts. Not fully. Not after they had led her astray before.

Well, that wasn't exactly true. Her instincts had screamed

at her not to marry Shawn, but she'd chosen to ignore them and do what everyone had expected her to.

It seemed her heart and her gut were better judges of character than her mind because they didn't have the capacity to come up with excuses and lies.

"Bed or couch?" Brundar asked.

"Bed."

19

BRUNDAR

*A*fter three days in the damned wheelchair, Brundar was a pro at getting himself out of the thing and onto the bed.

That didn't make it any less of a turn-off, though, for him as well as for Calypso. His usually graceful movements were clumsy and laborious.

Regrettably, he couldn't blindfold her yet to keep her from watching him perform those maneuvers. It would've been counterproductive to do so while he still needed her help to pull off his pants.

Everything had to be done with utmost care not to disturb his knees—a task impossible to do blindfolded. Hopefully, when Bridget got there later, she would approve more freedom of movement for him and replace his knee braces with ones that were more flexible.

Sensing his discomfort, Calypso got busy taking off her clothes, letting him watch her instead of her watching him.

And what a sight she was. Even battered and bruised, she was perfection.

Thankfully, the pain was keeping his arousal at bay. Without her blindfold on, he had to be mindful of his eyes starting to glow and his fangs starting to grow, which was difficult while watching Calypso's beautiful, nude body.

He removed his shirt and folded it on the nightstand beside him, then popped the button on the wide, carpenter-style jeans Anandur had gotten for him from Walmart, of course, and lowered the zipper. When Calypso got in position, he braced on his arms and lifted himself off the bed a couple of inches, while she carefully pulled his pants and boxers down to his thighs.

Her eyes lingering on his shaft, she paused. It twitched in greeting, lifting away from his belly.

"I love this sight," she said. "Do you realize that this is the first time you let me see it? I always had a blindfold on before." She smoothed a finger from the tip down to the base. "Perfect, like the rest of you."

Damnation. Having her look at his shaft with such admiration in her eyes was hotter than hell, but if he didn't blindfold her in the next second, she would get an eyeful of much more than his dick.

He could just imagine the horror replacing that reverent expression.

"Come closer," he commanded, lifting the scarf.

Calypso wasn't happy about that, her beautiful, expressive face showing her disappointment, but she obeyed.

"Can I at least touch you?" she asked when he finished tying the scarf around her eyes.

"You may." It would be a first for him. No woman had ever touched his manhood with her hands or her tongue. To allow it required trust he hadn't felt toward anyone.

But he trusted Calypso, deeply, implicitly. In fact, he couldn't wait to feel her hands and her mouth on him. Should he tell her that she was going to be the first?

He fisted his cock. "No one but me has ever held it. No one has tongued it either. You're the first." He wanted to add that she would also be the last, but she wouldn't believe him.

92

For a moment, Calypso remained speechless, but then she smiled. "Good, because with no one to compare me to you'll think I'm amazing."

"You are incomparable."

"I hope so." Starting from his thigh, she smoothed her palm up to his groin.

He let go of his erection, relinquishing control.

She cupped it gently. Her palm soft and warm on his skin, she leaned down from her kneeling position at his side and gave him a tentative lick, then another, and another. Emboldened, she swirled her tongue around the bulbous head, pulling a ragged groan from his throat.

It felt good. Better than good, but the taste she'd given him only whetted his appetite for more. Cupping the back of her head, he pulled her a little lower.

Calypso didn't need any further encouragement. Taking him into her mouth, she sunk lower to envelop as much of his length as she could before retreating back up and swirling her tongue around the tip.

His eyes rolled back in their sockets. He threaded his fingers in her hair, fanning it out so he could watch his cock going in and out of her hot, wet mouth. The sight was so erotic he could've climaxed just from that. But he didn't want it to end, not yet.

Unhurried, Calypso bobbed her head in a steady rhythm, prolonging his pleasure and not pushing for his release. Did she love pleasuring him with her mouth as much as he loved eating her up?

Given the intensifying scent of her arousal, she did.

Which was good, because he never wanted her to do anything just to please him. If she didn't find pleasure in whatever he wanted to do to her, or her to do to him, then he couldn't find pleasure in it either.

"This is so good, sweetling."

She moaned around him, sending another electrical pulse

through his nervous system, priming his balls and his venom glands for action.

Brundar didn't want to come in her mouth, and he definitely didn't want to come before she did.

He cupped her cheek. "That's enough, love."

She let his cock slip out of her mouth. "Did I do something wrong?"

"No, you were perfect. But I can't wait any longer to have my mouth on you. Turn around and straddle me, then bend down and lift your sweet ass up so I can eat you up."

She smiled. "I like the way you think."

Careful around his knees, she did exactly as he'd asked, but the moment her ass was in the right position, she leaned down and took him back in her mouth.

He chuckled as he clamped his hands on her butt cheeks, his thumbs seeking her entrance. "I like the way you think even better."

She was drenched as if he'd been the one pleasuring her and not the other way around. He was one lucky bastard to have a woman who enjoyed giving as much as she enjoyed receiving. In that, they were perfectly matched.

He squeezed her buttocks and pulled her closer to him, so he could lap all that nectar up.

She moaned against his shaft again.

If he didn't hurry, Calypso would have him climax before she did, and that was unacceptable.

It was a catch-22. The more excited Calypso became, the more she moaned, and the more she moaned, the more excited he became. If he weren't injured, he would've flipped her around and fucked her, but that was not in the cards.

Shite. He couldn't pull on her hair to let go of him either because her scalp was still very sensitive. The only option was to grit his teeth and hold back while giving it all he had so she could reach the finish line first.

LOSHAM

*L*osham paced the spacious living room of his hotel suite, listening to his assistant's report while his mind was racing ahead.

"Any news from Grud?" he interrupted Rami.

"No, sir. He is still MIA."

That wasn't good. First, the human they had chosen to lead their so-called cult hadn't shown up to a meeting, and then the next one, and he wasn't responding to phone calls either.

Now one of his men had gone missing too.

No one had heard from Grud since he'd gone out last night to search for a suitable victim.

Grud was a good man, not the type Losham would have suspected of desertion. Not that any Doomer was stupid enough to attempt it. The warriors' lives might not have been perfect, but they were much better than what they could've hoped for on the outside.

Besides, the men knew they would be hunted until found and then tortured horrifically and publicly as a deterrent to others.

No. Doomers didn't desert. Something must have happened to Grud. Somehow he had met with misfortune.

Since fangs were all that was needed for the nightly missions, the men didn't carry firearms with them. Grud could have succumbed to a group of humans. But unless they had shot him execution style, emptying a chamber straight into his head or his heart, he wouldn't have died.

Besides, without a body, Losham couldn't be sure the guy was dead.

Had he been captured?

Was he being held by Guardians and tortured for information?

Again, it was a remote possibility. But not one that Losham could ignore.

"We need to move the men to a new location and rent a new warehouse for our meetings."

Rami lifted his head from his tablet. "You think Grud was captured?"

"It is a possibility we need to consider." Losham was glad about choosing to lodge separately from his men. His decision had been motivated mainly by costs and in deference to his status, but it had proven to have strategic value as well.

"I'll get right on it."

"Yes. Time is of the essence."

The human wasn't as important as Grud. He didn't know anything about Losham or his organization. Whatever misfortune he'd met with was regrettable only in the sense that they had wasted ten thousand dollars on the drunkard and would now need to search for a new candidate.

A setback, but a minor one. No operation ran smoothly from start to finish. There was always something to contend with. A smart leader didn't allow those small annoyances to distract him from his goal.

Except, Losham's analytical brain abhorred unsolved mysteries and unlikely coincidences. The human disappearing could be explained in a lot of ways, but not Grud's, and not the fact that they had happened only several days apart.

As much as his mind raced and churned trying to come up with plausible scenarios, Losham was coming up with nothing.

Obviously if the answer eluded him, a mastermind, he was missing vital information.

Perhaps the human's disappearance was worth investigating after all.

BRUNDAR

"When is the doctor coming?" Calypso asked.

"She should be here any minute." Brundar glanced at his watch. "Bridget called around four o'clock and said she'd be here within an hour."

"I'll set up the table for three."

After an epic afternoon of lovemaking, they had worked up quite an appetite. He was hungry, and the food smelled delicious. Brundar wanted to dig into the boxes right away and not wait for Bridget. "It will get cold by the time she gets here. Let's eat."

"You said she would be here any minute. How would it look if she gets here and we are munching away and not inviting her to join us?"

"Like we are hungry and she is not a dinner guest."

Calypso put her hands on her hips. "If you want to be rude, do it while you're not with me."

"Fine. Just give me one of the boxes to tide me over. You can't deny a hungry, injured man food."

"I can do that." She looked at the labels until she found the beef dish. "Here you go." She handed him the box. "Chopsticks or fork?"

"Chopsticks."

She pulled out a pair from the delivery bag.

Brundar opened the box and picked a piece, but it felt wrong to eat while Calypso didn't. He knew she was hungry too.

"Come here." He beckoned with the chopsticks. "Open your mouth."

She hesitated for a couple of moments but then bent down and took the piece he was holding up for her. The next piece went into his mouth, and then another one because she was still chewing.

"Hmm, it's really good," Calypso said.

"Told you. Here, take one more." He held out another piece.

She ate that one as well, but then refused the third. "You can finish the rest."

He wanted to argue, but the buzzer went off, announcing their visitor.

Calypso buzzed Bridget in, then opened the door and waited for her to exit the elevator.

"Hello, guys." The doctor walked in, holding her black bag in one hand and a big plastic one in the other. "It smells good in here."

"We were just about to sit down for dinner. Please, join us." Calypso motioned for Bridget to take a seat at the dining table.

Bridget shook her head. "I should check on my patient first."

"The food will get cold. Let's eat first."

Bridget didn't need more convincing. "I would have loved to politely decline, but I'm hungry, and I love Chinese." She took the seat Calypso pointed to.

"Brundar ordered enough to feed a small village. Dig in."

"Don't mind if I do. But I'm going to stick to the fried rice. I don't eat meat."

Calypso opened all of the boxes and pushed some toward Bridget. "There is also an eggplant dish, and one with green beans and tofu."

"Fantastic."

Brundar dumped his empty container in the trash and wheeled himself to the table, where Calypso had already prepared a plate for him, heaped with an assortment of different dishes, including the green bean one and the one with the eggplant.

"*Bon appetit*," Bridget said and dug into her plate. For a small woman, the doctor sure had a big appetite.

"Your face looks much better," she commented as she refilled her plate.

"Makeup does wonders. I'm going back to work tomorrow."

"What do you do?"

"I'm a waitress at a nightclub."

"Then I would advise you to stay home for one more day and rest. If you had a desk job, it would've been okay to go back to work. But you're not ready for a job that keeps you on your feet for hours."

Brundar wiped sweet and sour sauce from his chin. "That's exactly what I've told her. Maybe she will listen to you because she sure doesn't listen to me."

Bridget grinned from ear to ear. "Good for you." She winked at Calypso but then wagged a finger at her. "This time, though, I have to agree with Brundar. One more day of rest. Doctor's orders."

"Is everyone in your family bossy?" Calypso grimaced, and he knew they would be arguing about it later.

Bridget smiled. "Yep, pretty much."

"How do you manage not to kill each other?"

"With difficulty and a lot of love." Bridget winked.

When they were done, the doctor stood up and lifted her

plate. "I'll help you clear the table and then check up on Brundar's knees."

"Leave it." Calypso took the plate from her hand. "Go check up on Brundar. I'll take care of the cleanup."

Bridget shook her head. "And you call us bossy."

Fifteen minutes later the table was clean, and the doctor was done adjusting the new braces she'd brought for him.

"Tell me again what I can and can't do with these."

"Keep using the wheelchair and brace on your arms when you want to sit on the couch or go to bed. But it's okay to put your feet down and put a little pressure on them. In two days you can go to the bathroom using crutches. But nothing longer than that. After a week, you can walk with the crutches, but, again, only short distances around the apartment."

"Got it."

Brundar's phone rang where he'd left it to charge on the kitchen counter. Calypso disconnected it from the wire and brought it over.

Glancing at the display, he frowned. What the hell did Amanda want from him? Hopefully not to pay him a visit.

"Amanda," he answered.

"Syssi and I are coming over, and don't you dare say no to us. We are bringing pastries."

"I'm not feeling up to it."

"We don't care."

He rolled his eyes. "I'm not home."

"I know. I got your girlfriend's address from Anandur."

He was going to strangle his brother. The idiot was supposed to keep quiet about Brundar staying with Calypso.

"Is there any way I can convince you not to come?"

"Nope. I called just to let you know we are coming. Not to ask your permission."

Brundar groaned as he clicked the call off.

Bridget patted his shoulder. "Don't worry about that. They are on your side."

He lifted his eyes to her. "Why? Did you hear anything?"

She shrugged. "No. But I know those two, and I bet they are up to something. It's good to have powerful allies, Brundar."

Yeah. The question was whether they were really on his side or not. If they were coming to try to convince him to leave Calypso, he was going to throw them out.

CALLIE

"*I* should leave." Bridget picked up her things.

"What's the hurry? We are going to have a fucking party here," Brundar grumbled.

"Stay." Callie put her hand on the petite doctor's arm. "It's going to be fun." She winked. "Four girls and one poor Brundar, no wonder he is not happy about it. Maybe we should call Anandur and ask him to join us?"

"He is on rotation tonight," Brundar said.

Bridget put her bag back down. "Okay, I'll stay. I'm curious to hear what those two are planning."

"What do you mean?"

The doctor regarded her as if she was dim-witted, which rankled. "Kian's sister and his wife are paying you a visit after he kicked you out. Why do you think that is?"

"They are curious? They want to check out Brundar's new girlfriend?"

"Yes, but not only that."

"What else?"

Bridget winked. "That depends on whether they like you or not."

Great, now she wasn't as happy about the visit as she was a moment ago. What if they didn't approve?

Callie touched her face. "Tell me the truth, do I look horrible?"

"No, Callie, you're a beautiful girl who was criminally assaulted. After five minutes with you, Amanda and Syssi will forget all about the bruises. They are going to like you."

"How can you be sure?"

"Because I am. What's not to like?"

Callie could think of a thing or two or three, but she wasn't going to spend valuable time convincing Bridget that she was far from perfect. "If you excuse me, I'm going to freshen up a bit."

She practically ran into the bedroom. Was there time to curl her hair? When it was all puffed up, it could hide some of the bruising. It would also make her look a little bit older and better put together.

Hot iron on dry hair could do only so much, but she managed to give herself a little bounce. Another layer of foundation helped hide some of the hideous coloring, and she framed her eyes with a dark green pencil, hoping to draw attention to her best feature and away from the ugly bruises.

She'd already put on her best pair of jeans and nicest T-shirt before Bridget came, so there was no need to change clothes. Maybe she could put on her black pumps? They made her legs look longer and her butt look tighter, but then she would look as if she was trying too hard. In the end, she chose to keep her flip-flops on.

So what if her toenails weren't painted.

The buzzer went on in the living room, and Bridget answered, letting the two women come in.

Callie opened the door and took a deep breath, waiting for the elevator doors to open.

A stunning, tall brunette and a much shorter beautiful blond came out of the lift. The brunette smiled like a movie star and extended her hand. "Hi, I'm Amanda. And this is Syssi, my sister-in-law."

"Nice to meet you both. I'm Callie." She shook Amanda's hand and then Syssi's.

Amanda looked like she wanted to give Callie a hug but then reconsidered. Which meant that the bruising was still visible despite her best efforts to hide it.

"We brought pastries. I hope you have coffee." Amanda walked in and put the box she was carrying on the counter.

"Bridget, what a nice surprise." She pulled the tiny doctor into her arms and gave her a big hug. "I'm so glad you're here. We are recruiting if you care to join us."

"Are we planning a war?"

"No, just a friendly takeover. " She winked.

"Oh, my."

"Where is our injured hero?"

Just then Callie noticed that Brundar wasn't in the living room. Where had he escaped to?

A flutter of curtains gave his hiding place away.

"I think he is on the balcony, getting a breath of fresh air."

"More like hiding from us, but that's okay. We are here mainly to see you."

"Well, in that case, please take a seat."

"In a moment. First, I need a plate for the pastries, and second, where is your coffeemaker?"

"I'm in charge of the coffee," Syssi said.

It was strange how the four of them felt comfortable with each other as if they had been friends for years.

Amanda was even more blindingly beautiful than her brother and had the confidence to match. She was dressed simply, but Callie could tell it was all very expensive stuff. And yet she wasn't off-putting or intimidating. Her high energy was infectious.

Syssi was beautiful too, but in a more approachable girl-next-door way. Less outgoing than Amanda, and definitely not as dramatic, she was sweet and friendly and exuded a sort of calm that was soothing. How could she stand being married to Kian? The guy was all pent up anger and frustration.

An ogre of a man, only gorgeous instead of green and ugly.

But then Brundar wasn't a cheerful cherub either, and still, Callie would not have traded him for anyone. Maybe Syssi was the cool water to Kian's inferno, the soothing balm on his rough edges.

The redheaded doctor was somewhere in between the two. Confident, but not at all dramatic, beautiful and curvy in all the right places, but not as stunning as Amanda. No woman was. Callie wondered what Kian and Amanda's mother looked like. Was she even more beautiful than her children? Was it even possible to outdo perfection?

Next to these women, Callie felt quite plain. And yet, not uncomfortable.

"Coffee is ready," Syssi said. "Let's take everything to the living room."

Brundar was still out on the balcony, and Callie decided it was time for him to stop playing chicken and get inside.

"Come on, Brundar, please come back. You're being rude."

He shrugged. "They are used to me being like this. They don't expect anything else."

"That's not an excuse. Those are your relatives, and you're leaving me alone to entertain them."

That finally got to him, and he wheeled himself inside. "Amanda, Syssi, how nice of you to drop by." He sounded as sincere as a used car salesman.

Bad analogy. Shawn was a car salesman. Or rather had been. She shivered, remembering the terrible hours that had led to his death.

As always, Brundar noticed everything. He turned his wheelchair around and closed the balcony door, probably thinking she was cold. "Do you want me to get you a sweater, Calypso?"

That was so sweet of him to offer, especially since he was the one with limited mobility.

"Thank you, but I'm okay." She lifted a cup of coffee off the table and handed it to him. "Which pastry would you like?"

"I'm good. The coffee will do."

"So, Calypso, or is it Callie? Tell us how you and Brundar met."

Callie glanced at Brundar, who retreated into his impassive mask. He shook his head slightly, letting her know not to tell them their story. But which parts?"

"Calypso is my given name. My friends call me Callie, but Brundar prefers Calypso."

"I like Callie," Amanda said. "I'm so curious to hear you guys' story."

"We met at a nightclub," Brundar said.

"And when was that?" Amanda kept pushing.

"About a year ago," Callie said, sneaking a glance at Brundar.

He shrugged.

"You've been together for an entire year?" Syssi asked.

"No. We met a year ago in passing. Then again about a month ago."

Please let them be happy with that and not ask more questions. Perhaps she could turn the tables on them.

"What do you do, Amanda?"

"I teach at the university."

Callie's eyes widened. "I want to be a teacher too, but not in the university. I want to teach kindergarten, maybe go into special education. I have not decided yet. I'm starting UCLA in the fall."

"That's marvelous," Amanda said.

Did she mean it, though? On top of the way she looked,

she was also a freaking professor? How many gifts could one woman have?

Unfair.

Syssi put her coffee cup down. "You must love children."

"I do."

"I do too."

"Do you have any?"

Syssi's eyes looked sad, but she put on a smile. "Not yet. Working on it, though."

Amanda snickered. "That's the fun part."

Callie couldn't imagine Kian as a father. He would terrorize his kids just by looking at them. "Well, I wish you good luck. In the meantime, though, have fun practicing."

Syssi blushed.

Amanda chuckled. "I like this girl."

"Me too," Bridget said.

BRUNDAR

"*I* had a really good time. I hope we can do this again sometime." Calypso hugged Bridget and then Syssi.

Amanda was the last one at the door. She pulled Calypso into a gentle embrace and kissed her forehead. "I would've kissed your cheek, but I didn't want to hurt you. The forehead seemed like a safe place."

"Yeah, it's probably the only spot on my face that is not damaged. Thank you for coming. It was fun."

"Thank you for having us. Good night, Callie." She looked over Calypso's head and waved at him. "You too, Brundar. Don't overexert yourself." She winked.

"You have a very nice family," Calypso said as she closed the door.

"Busybodies."

She started picking up cups and plates from the coffee table. "Maybe, but they mean well."

"They are annoying."

She put the dishes in the sink and returned with a rag to wipe the table. "And you're grumpy."

He grunted in agreement.

"I would love to hang out with them some more, also with Anandur. Are Bridget and Amanda married?"

"Amanda has a mate. Bridget doesn't."

Calypso threw him a puzzled look. "A mate? What does that mean?"

A slip of the tongue, but easily corrected. Calypso didn't expect him to express himself clearly or correctly, which worked to his advantage in situations like this. "She has a life partner whom she didn't marry in an official ceremony."

"A live-in boyfriend."

"No. A boyfriend implies a temporary arrangement. Amanda and Dalhu's is permanent."

Calypso sighed. "Nothing is permanent, not even marriage."

"In their case it is."

"You're awfully sure of that. What if you're wrong?"

Damnation. The woman was impossible. He would have to either lie or tell her that the discussion was over.

Unless he managed to deflect again. He was becoming an expert at it. "You can call your father now and let him know you're no longer in danger."

Calypso plopped down on the couch, flipped off her flip-flops and put legs on the ottoman. "I almost did, but then thought better of it. I don't know if Shawn's body's been found yet. I can't call my dad and tell him Shawn committed suicide because how am I supposed to know that, right?"

"Good point. I'll call my contact in the government and have him check if it was reported. Not every suicide makes the news."

"You mean Andrew, Syssi's brother?"

"Yeah."

He didn't know what game Amanda and Syssi were playing. They had blabbered freely as if Calypso was one of them and had divulged too much information. If he were ever forced to thrall away Calypso's memories, it would be one hell of an impossible job. As long as he was the only one she remembered, the clan's secret was safe. She didn't know he was different, and Brundar wasn't about to let her find that out. But his connections to Amanda and Andrew were like a trail of breadcrumbs. Someone determined enough could find where a professor named Amanda taught. Cross-referencing it with a government employee named Andrew would narrow the search.

"If your cousins and your tough boss's wife can tell me people's names, I'm sure you can too."

"Not really. One is his sister, the other is his wife. I don't hold the same sway over him."

"Could be. But you no longer need to talk in code about things they already told me."

That was true, but old habits were hard to break, as was remembering what she already knew and what not. The safest thing for her and for his clan would've been to keep them separated and for Calypso to know nothing about them. She already knew too much.

Tomorrow, he would ask Anandur to drive him back to the keep so he could have a talk with Amanda and Syssi. They meant well, but those good intentions might lead straight to hell.

"Did you call the steakhouse and tell them that you're not coming in to work?"

"No, I didn't. Why would I? They don't expect me for another week."

"Now that you no longer need to hide, you can keep working at Franco's."

"You're right. I didn't think of that. It's a hard decision, though. I like the people at Franco's, and I don't know anyone at the new place, but the pay is going to be a little better and so will the hours. I wouldn't have to work late nights anymore. What will happen once the school year starts and I have early morning classes? On the other hand, a late shift means I have all day for studying."

"You're forgetting one thing. At Franco's you have me."

Calypso huffed and crossed her arms over her chest. "Yeah, right. You disappear into that basement, and I'm lucky if I get to see you after closing time."

She had a point. Brundar wheeled himself closer to the couch, and using the armrest and coffee table to brace most of his weight, hefted himself to sit next to Calypso.

"What if I promise to come see you at least once during your shift?"

She shrugged. "Not good enough. Besides, I have my hearing to think of. I'm sure I've already done enough damage."

"That's what earplugs are for." He wrapped his arm around her and pulled her closer to him.

"I tried. But I can't take drink orders when I can't hear the customers."

"There are special earplugs that filtrate certain wavelengths. You can still hear people talking, but the ambient noise is reduced."

"Earplugs are uncomfortable."

Calypso was proving to be a tough negotiator. There was something she was hoping to get out of it. Was it a raise? More shifts?

"Tell me what would sweeten the deal for you, and I'll make it happen."

Her triumphant smile proved that he'd been right. "I want to participate in the classes and demonstrations you guys hold down in the basement. I'll schedule my breaks accordingly."

"Only watching, nothing more."

"That's what I want." She snorted. "I don't want to be the test dummy for your whip."

"I might allow it as long as you sit quietly and don't ask any questions. I don't want the club members to notice you."

She narrowed her eyes at him. "Why? Are you embarrassed by me?"

Silly girl. "No, I'm proud of you. More than you can imagine. But I don't want any members to get ideas about you. I don't want them to look at you and imagine what they would like to do to you. If I catch them leering, I'll have to kill them, and their blood will be on your hands."

He'd meant every word, but Calypso thought he was joking.

"I wouldn't want that. I promise to be as quiet as a mouse. I'll slink in after the class or demonstration begins, sit in the back, and then slink out before it ends. No one will see me."

He smiled and offered her his hand. "It's a deal. You stay at Franco's, and I'll allow you to sit in on the classes and demonstrations but only if you keep your presence unobtrusive."

Calypso squealed happily, wrapped her arms around his neck and jumped on him, brushing against his knees as she straddled him.

Brundar winced.

Her face fell. "I'm sorry. I forgot about the not touching rule." She dropped her arms to her sides.

"It's not that." He lifted her arms and put them back around his neck. "You brushed against my knees."

Her eyes widened in horror. "I'm so sorry. It was so careless of me. What can I do to make it better? Do you need an ice pack? Painkillers?"

He shook his head. "Your lips will do." He pulled out the scarf he stashed in his pocket just for such occasions. After their afternoon lovemaking session, he'd been struck by the brilliant idea of always having it with him. "But first, the blindfold."

RONI

"*D*o you really need me in there?" Roni asked William.

William patted Roni's shoulder. "Don't worry. He is not going to eat you for breakfast. You're too skinny."

"And sour. He is going to eat you first."

William laughed.

Kian wasn't on Roni's list of favorite people. Not that the dude was evil or anything. Roni had met his share of self-entitled pricks, and Kian wasn't like them either. But he made Roni feel like a nuisance.

Maybe he was like that with everyone, but that didn't make Roni any happier about having to sit in front of the guy again.

No one had treated him like a nuisance in his previous job. They might have not liked him, and some had resented a teenager holding so much power, but everyone had respected him and vied for his services.

He was one of a kind, goddamn it, an irreplaceable asset any organization would have killed for, and he deserved to be treated as such.

William knocked on the door and then pushed it open

and walked in. Roni followed behind him.

This time Kian wasn't alone in his office. A tall, gangly guy was sitting at the conference table with several files spread out in front him.

"Hi, Shai." William and the guy clapped hands.

Kian pointed at the two chairs in front of his desk. "You have two minutes. Talk."

William took a seat and looked at Roni.

Damn it, he'd been hoping William would do the talking. He was older, loved to talk nonstop, and he knew Kian better. Maybe that was why he wanted Roni to present their request. He knew Kian was going to be nasty about it.

Roni pulled out the list of supplies he needed and handed it to Kian. "William's lab is a mess and a health hazard. He's also missing some components. This is the list of what I need to transform it into a decent workspace. At the bottom is a rough estimate of how much it is going to cost." His presentation had taken about thirty seconds.

Kian took the list, skimmed through it, and then handed it back. "Approved. Shai is going to take care of the rest. Good day, gentlemen."

"Thank you."

Well, that had gone well. Kian had been curt, but he'd approved the acquisition request, and that was what they had come for—not to socialize over coffee and canapés.

As they stood up and turned to Shai, William cast Roni an appreciative look, but it wasn't until they were done with Kian's assistant and on their way back to the lab that he commented on Roni's performance. "From now on you are in charge of dealing with Kian. He likes you."

Roni snorted. "If that's how he treats people he likes, I don't ever want to get on his shit list."

William rubbed his chin. "He is not always like that. When he is not so stressed, he even jokes around. But there is a lot going on right now."

"The move to the new place?"

"Yes. It's a very complicated project, and it's taking longer to complete than Kian would've liked. Then there are the murders that are keeping the Guardians busy. Other than that he still needs to run the business side of things, and one of the two people he hired to manage parts of it couldn't handle the pressure and quit."

Roni shook his head. "I feel for him, but you know that it's all in his head."

William gave him one of those condescending looks adults tended to throw at him before realizing that Roni wasn't a typical teenager. "Those are real problems, Roni. He is not imagining them."

"What I meant wasn't that the problems do not exist but that the urgency is in his head. He can slow down on everything except the murders. Nothing will happen if the village is completed a month later than scheduled. And all the corporate crap can be done at a slower pace as well. Other than that, he should wait with further expansion until he has the current business running smoothly with good people at the helm."

"Good advice, kid. But not so easy to implement. Good people are hard to find. But you are right about one thing. Kian is a perfectionist, and a lot of the stress he is under is his own doing. I wish I could help. I can design programs that would make his life easier. But to do so I need his input, and he doesn't have the time to spend."

"What about his assistant, Shai? The dude probably knows everything that's going on."

William stopped and turned to Roni. "Why didn't I think of that? It's such an obvious solution. I can have Shai explain how they do things and work from that."

Roni felt incredibly smug but covered it up with fake modesty. "Sometimes it takes an outsider to see things those on the inside are blind to."

KIAN

"What's new with the murder investigation?" Kian opened the Guardian meeting by addressing Onegus.

"There were no new murders in the past week."

Interesting. It wasn't because the Guardians were patrolling the streets, because they weren't. They were waiting in a central location for the command center to alert them to suspicious activity caught on the surveillance cameras.

But there had been several false alarms. Two involved street-walkers getting into an argument with clients, and the rest were drunk couples making out on the streets. Could the murderer have seen a Guardian arrive at the scene?

Not likely.

Something else was going on. But what?

"Let's keep the rotations for another week. If nothing happens, we can assume that's the end of it."

"What if it is not?" Onegus asked.

"We can't keep it up forever. We knew that at some point the rotations would have to stop. I just hoped we would catch the murderer first."

The guys looked grim. With Brundar out of commission, they'd each had to take on more hours. Anandur had volunteered to do both his and Brundar's shifts, but Kian had forbidden it. Everyone shared the burden equally.

He needed more Guardians.

The thing was, when nothing was going on, there was barely enough work to keep the seven he had busy. But then when something happened, they were short on warriors. The retired Guardians would not come for anything less than a full out war or a rescue operation. Kian had had a hard time convincing them to come in for one week of training a year to keep up their skills.

He needed more Guardians on a permanent basis, and if they had nothing to do, so be it.

"Onegus."

"Yes, boss."

"I want you to stay after the meeting."

Onegus nodded.

Later, when everyone was done reporting and had filed out of his office, Kian walked over to the fridge hidden behind the wooden doors of the buffet and pulled out two beers.

Onegus took one with a raised brow. "Beer for breakfast?"

"Are we Scots or are we not?"

"Aye, we still are." Onegus took a swig.

"I want to get at least two more permanent Guardians. Any ideas on who might be open to negotiation? I'm willing to pay handsomely."

"You can't pay them more than you pay the other Guardians. It wouldn't be fair."

"So I'll pay everyone more. What else?"

"More vacation time. Especially after weeks of rotations."

"If we have more people, then they can take vacations whenever they want. Unless there is a crisis, that is."

"How many do you want?"

"As many as I can get, but I'll settle for two. Give me names of possible prospects."

Onegus regarded him with a frown. "Don't tell me you want to make the phone calls yourself."

"I'd be more than happy to leave that job to you."

"Good, because you're too grumpy to convince anyone to join."

"What's that supposed to mean?"

Onegus scratched his head. "If anyone needs a vacation it's you."

"If you can find someone to do my job, I'll gladly take one."

BRUNDAR

Fucking crutches. Brundar dropped his butt on the couch and threw them on the floor in disgust. He'd thought they would make moving around more manageable, but they were a nuisance and made him feel even more disabled than the wheelchair had. Sitting in one was not so much different from sitting in an office chair with wheels.

Not really, but he could pretend.

It wasn't only that. The inactivity was getting to him. For a man who was used to long grueling days, doing nothing was maddening.

So yeah, he'd made love to Calypso four times yesterday and then had felt guilty as hell because it was too much for a human girl to take, especially one who was recovering from an ordeal herself.

She hadn't complained, but that didn't mean it had been okay to exhaust her like that.

He should've asked Anandur to bring him a book. Except, Brundar was too agitated to focus on anything. Even the stories of epic battles that he usually enjoyed reading would probably not hold his interest. It was an activity reserved for the end of a satisfying day in the field. That left the television, which was the only form of entertainment in the apartment, and he hated the thing. He couldn't find anything worth watching. Even the news reported nothing of substance. It was mostly sensationalized nonsense.

Calypso emerged from the bedroom, her hair wet from the shower. "I called Franco and told him I'm coming back to work today."

Brundar couldn't blame her for wanting out of the apartment. "I'll come with you."

She put her hands on her hips. "Bridget said not to overdo it with the crutches."

"I'm going to sit in the wheelchair with a beer in my hand, watching your sexy bottom as you run around serving drinks."

Calypso sauntered closer and leaned over him, her ample cleavage on display in the flimsy, low-cut shirt she had on. "It's been a week."

"It's only Wednesday." His injury had happened Friday night.

"I'm not talking about that. I'm talking about the birth control. We can throw the condoms away, or donate them to a worthy charity." She winked.

His male anatomy responded with enthusiasm, but his male ego not so much. The first time he made love to Calypso without a bloody rubber between them, he wanted her under him, which was impossible at the moment. On the other hand, he didn't want to wait another week and a half either.

Her smile wilted. "Why are you frowning?"

"It doesn't feel right to celebrate our first time while I'm like this." He waved a hand over his knees.

"Oh, baby." She cupped his cheek and kissed him.

It hadn't escaped Brundar's notice that each passing day

she was touching him more and more, or that he was getting more and more comfortable with her doing so.

In fact, he craved her touch.

That didn't mean that he wouldn't tie her up as soon as he was back to normal, but it would be for fun, not because he couldn't do it any other way.

Calypso was healing him.

Without breaking the kiss, he wrapped his arm around her and pulled her to sit next to him. She moaned, and he pushed his hand under her shirt and cupped her breast, thumbing the stiffening nipple.

Eyes hooded with desire, Calypso arched into his hand. "It would be silly to keep using condoms until you get better," she said when he let go of her mouth.

It was. But the only way they could have sex now was with her straddling him, and they both craved more than that.

"I know."

"We will make it special in some other way." She waggled her brows. "Missionary position is not a prerequisite."

"What do you have in mind?"

"I'll think about it while you are in the shower."

Trying to imagine what Calypso could possibly come up with, Brundar let the water pelt him as he sat on the shower bench. Whatever it was, they were still limited to the one position of him either sitting or lying, and her straddling him.

He was just about finished when Calypso walked into the bathroom and opened the shower enclosure, holding a large towel in front of her. "Are you done, your lordship? I was sent to towel you dry."

Brundar cocked a brow. What kind of a game was she playing?

"By whom?" he asked.

"The head maid, of course. May I turn the water off and pat you dry with this big, fluffy towel?"

With a smile curving his lips, Brundar leaned against the shower wall. "You may."

"Thank you, my lord." Still holding the towel in front of her, Calypso curtsied.

She was hiding something. Was she naked? Waiting for her to come closer, Brundar yanked the towel out of her hands.

Wow. The girl was sure creative. She had taken her plain black cooking apron and fashioned a tiny French maid one out of it. The front was cut in the shape of a heart and barely covered her nipples, and the bottom was cut in an arc, with its lowest point barely covering her mound.

Sexy didn't begin to describe it.

Tossing the towel on the bench, he reached for her and cupped her ass. She had nothing on other than the apron.

Playacting wasn't his strong suit, but he was going to give it his best because Calypso's idea was brilliant. His injuries limited the physical possibilities, but there was no limit on imagination.

"You are a naughty, naughty maiden. Did you come in here to try and seduce your master?"

Calypso lowered her head in pretend shame and nodded. "Are you disappointed in me, my lord? Do you think I deserve punishment for my presumptuousness?" Worrying her lower lip, she peeked at him from under her long eyelashes.

Aha, so that was where she wanted to take this. It hadn't crossed his mind to spank her, even playfully, while she was still bruised and hurting. But apparently, Calypso was ready for some play. He should be able to satisfy her wish while being very gentle. After all, it was all an act, the excitement having more to do with the mindset than the physical sensations.

"Turn around, young miss. And present your bottom."

Calypso barely managed to stifle her smile as she pretended remorse. "Yes, my lord."

She turned around, braced her hands on the shower wall, pushed her lovely bottom out, then gave him a sexy come-hither look over her shoulder. "Is that how you want me, my lord?"

Oh yeah, he did. Calypso assumed the perfect position for him to reach her bottom from where he was sitting. The minx had thought of everything.

He rubbed her left butt cheek first, then the right. "You have to keep your eyes closed tight. If I catch you peeking, you're going to be a very sorry young lady. Is that clear?"

"Yes, my lord," Calypso breathed.

"You are going to keep your eyes closed until I tell you to open them."

"Yes, my lord. I swear I'm going to obey your commands."

Even though it was pretend-play, he knew her promise was sincere. Calypso was trustworthy. She wouldn't open her eyes until he told her it was okay.

"Good girl." He caressed her butt cheeks. They were soft and smooth and so small that he could cover both with one hand, but it didn't make her shape any less feminine. Her narrow hips tapered into an even narrower waist, giving her a beautiful hourglass form.

"You are a very beautiful girl, Calypso."

"Thank you, my lord. Does it mean you forgive me for coming in here with illicit intent?"

"I do. But I'm going to spank you anyway because you need to be taught self-discipline."

"Thank you, my lord. I'm looking forward to your correction."

CALLIE

*C*allie was having a blast. When she'd concocted her plan, she'd been worried that Brundar was too rigid to enjoy playacting, or even to participate, but her guy was full of surprises.

He was doing great.

It was like he was reading her mind and doing everything exactly as she'd envisioned it.

What a turn-on.

The first smack shocked her, not because it was hard or painful, it was neither, but because of the magnifying effect of the shower enclosure creating an echo chamber. The gentle slap had sounded like a thunderclap.

It was good that her next door neighbor was out of town again, or she might have imagined the worst and called the police.

"It's very loud in here," Brundar said, probably worried about the neighbors as well.

"There is no one in the adjoining suite of rooms, my lord. No one can hear you disciplining me."

He rubbed the spot he'd slapped. "In that case, I shall continue."

"If you please, my lord."

A volley of light smacks ensued, warming her behind and delivering just a smidgen of a sting. It was exactly what she wanted. Nothing overly taxing or intense, just playful.

"As this is your first offense, young lady, I think it is enough. Have you learned your lesson?"

Callie hesitated. Did she want more?

Yeah, she did. He hadn't spanked her in so long.

"I'm a little bit thick-headed, my lord, and sometimes I need a lesson repeated before it sinks in."

Brundar chuckled. "I see. Very well." He continued the playful smacking, adding ten more, then switched to rubbing.

His caresses were getting more intimate by the second. "You're very wet, sweetling. Are you aching for me?"

"Yes, sir."

"Hmm." He pushed a finger inside her. "Are your eyes still tightly closed?"

"Yes, sir."

He pulled on the tie holding her apron. "Then turn around." With a quick tug, he took it off, baring her body.

Breasts swollen and nipples aching, Callie waited for Brundar to touch more of her, but he was doing something with her apron. Was he folding it?

When he tied the blindfold he'd fashioned from it over her eyes, she found out.

Didn't he trust her? And why was it so important to him? Was he going to tell her one day?

In the beginning, she'd suspected Brundar had some deformity he didn't want her to see. He'd never gotten fully naked unless she was blindfolded. But since the injury, she'd seen every inch of him, except for his knees that were bandaged, and everything was perfect. Maybe they had been deformed even before the injury?

It didn't make sense though, because he still insisted on the blindfold even though his knees were always covered.

"It's not that I don't trust you. But you might forget in the throes of passion."

It was what it was, though, and at the moment she was more interested in continuing their playacting than solving all of Brundar's mysteries.

For all she knew, he turned into a werewolf when he climaxed. But then he would have felt hairy, which he didn't. The man had very little body hair, none on his chest and only sparse pale blond hair on his arms and legs.

"I understand, sir."

"Good girl." He tugged on her hand, guiding her to straddle him by placing her knees on the bench, then wrapped her in his arms and just held her.

It was such an intimate pose, chest to chest, face to face, even though she couldn't see him. She felt his warm breath on her skin as he whispered in her ear, "You are precious to me."

Callie melted into a puddle. Brundar had called her beautiful, he'd called her sweetling, but not precious, and not like that. It wasn't just a term of endearment, it was his way of telling her he loved her.

Her dark angel had surrendered. The ice around his heart had melted.

"You're precious to me too." She found his lips and kissed him, but he immediately took over the way he always did.

It was fine. She loved his gentle dominance.

Cupping her buttocks with one large hand, Brundar lifted her up and guided his shaft inside her, wedging just the head and waiting for her to adjust to him.

She took over from there, sliding down slowly, enjoying the feeling of his velvety smooth skin, the warmth of him. It felt so different without the barrier between them. Perfect.

The fit was as tight as always, but not uncomfortably so. It felt as if they were made for each other.

When he was fully seated inside her, she didn't move, and neither did he. Being connected like that was so magical that neither of them uttered a sound, not even a moan.

For a few moments, they just held on tight to each other, connected in the most intimate of ways. But eventually, the need to move became overwhelming.

Clasping her bottom in his strong hands, Brundar lifted her up and then lowered her down. Pretty soon, though, he changed tactics. Holding her glued to his chest, stationary, he was thrusting into her as if he weren't injured and had full use of his legs.

There was no way he could lift his buttocks and piston into her with such force without bracing his feet on the tile floor. She was too far gone to object, though, and it seemed that he was too far gone to feel pain.

When his shaft swelled inside her, he latched onto her neck and bit down. Pain exploded where his teeth pierced her skin, but a split second later the pain just wasn't there anymore, and she was climaxing like a woman possessed. On and on her inner walls convulsed around him, milking what seemed like a never-ending geyser of semen.

The last coherent thought Callie had before blacking out was that if she weren't on the pill, Brundar would've most definitely planted a baby in her.

Surprisingly, she felt a pang of sorrow that it was not to be.

RONI

*R*oni glanced through the balcony glass doors at the darkening sky. What was keeping Sylvia?

He'd been waiting impatiently, not counting the minutes, but glancing at his watch every so often. He missed her. Yesterday, she had been studying for a test and couldn't come, and today she was running more than an hour late.

After a day at the lab, he was drained even though he hadn't done much aside from finishing the task William had assigned to him. There had been a few surveillance cameras he'd missed, and he'd added them on to the extensive array he'd already assembled.

Except, it seemed that all that work had been a waste of time because there were no more murders. Unfortunately, the killer hadn't been found, so there was still a chance it wasn't over yet.

Roni had a feeling that the area they had defined wasn't big enough, and he would need to expand their reach. As long as he could play a part in preventing more murders, he didn't mind how hard he had to work, or how tedious the task was.

Lives were at stake.

The pneumonia was still taking a lot out of him. The good news was that Bridget had declared him no longer contagious, and he was looking forward to getting together with Andrew. Meeting Andrew's wife and the baby would also be fun. She'd been an angel, sending him home-cooked meals every day. If it weren't for her, he would've been surviving on those disgusting frozen dinners that he found barely edible.

Roni got up and shuffled to the kitchen for another ginger ale. Sylvia had been harping on him to drink water instead of the fizzy sweet drink loaded with sugar and chemicals, but he didn't like drinking plain water. Besides, the ginger ale helped with the headache and the nausea.

As he was shuffling back to the couch, the door opened, and Sylvia walked in with a huge grin splitting her face.

Turning back, Roni's steps were much livelier. He wrapped his arm around his girl and kissed her cheek. "Where have you been, and what are you so happy about?"

"I have a surprise for you. Come." She took his hand and headed for the door.

"A surprise?" It wasn't his birthday.

"Yeah. You're going to love it."

They entered the elevator, and she pressed the button for one of the underground levels. Maybe she was taking him to watch a movie in the keep's theater? He hadn't seen it yet.

"Can you give me a hint?"

"No. We are almost there."

Where was there? He followed her out of the elevator and down the corridor. The doors on this level had small square windows on top. Some were empty, and some were set up as classrooms. He wondered what was being taught in there.

"Here we are." Sylvia opened one of the doors and walked inside.

It wasn't a classroom, but it wasn't empty either. Big cardboard boxes of varying sizes were stacked in the middle of the room, and several utilitarian chairs were haphazardly scattered throughout. He counted six.

"What is this?"

Sylvia grinned. "Open one of the boxes."

He chose the smallest one from the top of the pile and tore the tape off. There was another box inside, and he pulled it out.

"Drumsticks?"

"Open another one."

Roni could already guess what he would find in the other boxes.

"You got me a drum set?"

She nodded enthusiastically. "The guy that helped me in Guitar Warehouse said that this is the base set and that you can add other things to it. He started asking me all kinds of questions about the kind of music you play, but I didn't know what to tell him. I'll go back and get you whatever else you need."

For once, Roni was speechless. He'd told Sylvia not to do it, but was touched beyond words that she had done it anyway.

Pulling her into his arms, he kissed her. "Thank you. But I have to pay you back. In a couple of weeks, I should be getting my first paycheck, or however money things work here. I don't have a bank account I can use safely, but maybe Andrew can cash them for me."

Sylvia didn't look happy about that. In fact, she appeared offended. "Can you accept it as your birthday present?"

"It's not my birthday, and even if it was I couldn't accept something so expensive."

"What if you buy me something expensive back?"

"Like what?"

"Like a diamond ring. A diamond engagement ring."

For the second time in one evening, Roni was rendered speechless. Was Sylvia proposing?

She punched his chest playfully. "Say something."

"Yes."

"Yes, what?"

"Yes, I'll marry you. Wasn't that a proposal?"

"It was, but for a very long engagement. You're too young to be getting married. You're not ready."

"The hell I'm not. If that's what it takes for you to move in with me, I'm ready today. Your mother can't object to you moving in with your husband, am I right?"

There was hesitation in Sylvia's eyes. "I don't like rushing into things, and my mom is not good with sudden changes. Let's give it some time. Okay?"

Roni nodded, but his jubilant mood had plummeted. He knew exactly what Sylvia was thinking. She wanted to wait and see whether he turned or not, and she wasn't ready to fully commit to their relationship as long as his future wasn't clear.

Not that he could blame her. If he didn't turn, he would grow old and eventually die while Sylvia remained young and healthy and sad. If she loved him, and he was pretty sure she did, the heartache would be unbearable.

Although if the roles were reversed, he would've chosen to be with her even if their time together was finite. If the pain of losing her proved too much to bear, he would've found a way to end his life after she was gone.

"Do you want to start putting the set together? I have no idea what goes where, but you can tell me what to do."

The sad reality was that in his current state Roni was too weak to do it himself and needed her help. Sylvia was strong, was stronger than him even before the pneumonia. Lifting the heavy drums would be nothing for her.

But he didn't want to put his feebleness on display. Not while she was watching. He would get William to help him, or maybe Andrew.

It was about time the guy came to see him, and Roni could guilt him into helping with the assembly.

"I'm too tired, baby. I'll get one of the guys to help me tomorrow."

Sylvia looked disappointed. "You can tell me what to do, and I'll do it by myself while you sit on a chair and supervise."

He shook his head. "And miss out on the fun of assembling it myself? I don't think so."

She pouted. "Fine. Be like that. But once it's up I want to hear you play."

"It's a deal."

29

CALLIE

"*R*eady to go?" Callie asked.

Leaning on his crutches, Brundar nodded.

Yesterday's bareback sex had been epic, but Brundar had paid for it dearly with his knees. In the height of passion, he'd been oblivious to the pain, but once the endorphins and adrenaline levels had subsided, it hit him full force. It had been so bad that he'd even agreed to go back on the painkillers. The man was too stubborn and too macho to take them unless the pain level was intolerable.

He hadn't even argued when she'd called Franco and told him they were not coming in.

"Are you sure? Because if you are still hurting, I can call Franco again and cancel. He was very understanding yesterday."

"I'm good."

"Do you have the painkillers with you?"

He shook his head.

Of course not. Silly man. He would rather suffer than, God forbid, admit he was taking anything for pain.

Callie turned around, snatched the bottle of pills from the counter, and threw it inside her purse.

"Now we can go." She held the door open for Brundar.

"You could've gone yesterday. I didn't need you to stay and watch me sleep."

Brundar falling asleep after taking a hefty dose of the little white pills was the reason she'd stayed. Fearing that he'd overdosed on those pills, Callie wouldn't leave his side. Reading to keep herself awake, she'd checked every few minutes that he was still breathing.

"Yeah, yeah. As if you'd have left me alone at home if the roles were reversed."

"You got me there."

As she opened the passenger door for him, Brundar handed her one of the crutches and got inside, then gave her the other one.

"Thank you," he said when she dropped them in the back seat.

His face appeared as expressionless as always, but by the slight tightening of his jaw muscles, she could tell that he was either irritated or in pain or both. Probably both. Depending on others for his basic needs must be difficult for a man like Brundar.

Easing out into the traffic, Callie cast him a sidelong glance. "Everyone will have a ton of questions for us. What do we tell them?"

"A mugger wouldn't have dragged you with him. We will have to go with a would-be rapist."

"And what happened to him after he shot you?"

"He heard a police siren and ran away."

She shook her head. "They didn't report the incident because they thought we did. The weakest link in this story is why we didn't. Your injuries needed hospitalization, and no one will believe the emergency room personnel didn't call the cops."

"Right. I can claim a criminal record. They would believe it about me."

That was too extreme. Callie was wracking her brain for a better story when an idea struck her.

"Did you talk to Franco or anyone else from the club after the incident?"

"No. You called Franco. Remember?"

"Yes, but I wanted to make sure that you didn't talk with anyone."

"Why?"

She smirked. "Because I only told Franco that you were injured while rescuing me from the lowlife. I said nothing about you getting shot. We can say that you broke your knees while chasing the assailant. He jumped over a wall, and you followed, but your shirt got caught on something, and you fell badly, breaking both knees."

Brundar smiled. "That might work. No one will check what's going on under my knee braces."

"Exactly. In fact, I don't think anyone would've believed that you were shot in both knees and could walk already. I witnessed everything with my own two eyes, and I still find it hard to believe. Your healing is nothing short of miraculous."

Brundar turned to look out the window. "I'm lucky to know Bridget. Without her revolutionary procedure, it wouldn't have been possible."

Callie still had her doubts, but she couldn't argue with the evidence. Brundar was walking less than a week after getting both of his knees shot to pieces. Bridget was a miracle worker.

How the heck had a woman so young achieved so much? She must have been some kind of a prodigy. One of those kids who graduated high school at twelve and got a master's degree at sixteen. She'd seemed pretty normal, though.

"Is Bridget a genius? Did she finish medical school at eighteen or something? How does someone so young become an expert in her field? And not only an expert but an innovator?"

"She is very smart. But I don't think she invented that new procedure."

"I see." That made more sense. Tomorrow, Callie would search the Internet for a new and revolutionary knee reconstruction surgical procedure. Something like that was big news. Someone must've written an article about it in one of the scientific journals.

What was she hoping to find out, though?

That a procedure like that existed?

What if it did not?

Things didn't add up.

Heck, they hadn't been adding up since the beginning. For some reason, Donnie's remark about Brundar's long teeth came to the forefront of her mind. She could've sworn Brundar had bitten her yesterday when they had both climaxed. She had a vague memory of a sharp pain, and what was more, it hadn't been the first time that she'd looked for teeth marks the next day.

But she'd never found any.

It was possible to discount them as phantom bites created by her imagination, except aside from the imagined bites, there were other things. Like Brundar's superhuman hearing, and now his miraculous healing.

He turned to look at her. "So that's the story we are sticking with. I was chasing the would-be rapist and took a bad fall. There was nothing to report because other than hitting you in the face he didn't manage to do anything, and neither of us saw his face. He was wearing a ski mask."

"Sounds good to me."

At the club's parking lot, Callie helped Brundar out of the car, holding the crutches for him, and again he looked irritated by his dependence on her.

Well, tough. That was his reality for the near future, and he'd better get used to it.

"Callie!" Donnie rushed up to them as soon as they rounded the corner, his arms open and ready to envelop her.

"Careful, big guy. I'm bruised everywhere," she forestalled him, holding her palm out.

Donnie slowed down and hugged her with utmost care. "I'm so glad you're okay. You are okay, right?" His eyes roamed her body.

"I am. Thanks to Bru... Brad."

Crap, she'd almost forgotten he went under a different name in the club. Just one more oddity to add to the long list.

Up until now, Donnie hadn't even noticed Brundar standing a few paces behind her. Eyeing the crutches and the braces on Brundar's knees, the bouncer shook his head. "You should have let me come with you, man. What happened to you?"

"A bad fall."

Donnie tilted his head as if trying to figure out what kind of a fall could cause injuries like that. "How far down did you fall?"

"About thirty feet."

Donnie whistled. "You should count yourself lucky for not breaking your back."

"He saved me." Callie diverted Donnie's attention to her. "He chased the scumbag away. I don't want to think what would've happened to me if Brad hadn't shown up on time."

Inside the club, Callie had to repeat the story once to Franco and then again to Miri who wanted more details. At some point, Brundar ducked into the hallway leading down to the basement, leaving her alone to deal with the curious staff.

She was relieved to put on her little apron and get back to work. Lots of makeup combined with the nightclub's dim lighting hid her bruises from the customers, and for the first time in a week, she felt as if things were getting back to normal.

Or as normal as they could get with Brundar in her life.

30

BRUNDAR

*C*alypso was quiet on their way home, either introspective or perhaps tired. Brundar certainly was.

As someone who was used to relying on his body to always function at peak performance, it was difficult for him to accept his new reality. Thank the Fates it was temporary. The crutches were a nuisance, clumsy and chafing at his armpits, but that hadn't been the only problem. His body's rapid healing required him to rest and let it divert energy to where it was needed most. Instead, he'd shuffled through the basement trying to prove, mainly to himself, that his injuries weren't a hindrance to his performance.

No one else expected him to do much. Franco had tried to stick him in the office to go over the books, probably to get him off his feet. Naturally, Brundar had refused, which had been stupid. No one needed a cripple to act as a monitor, but Franco sure as hell needed someone with a head for numbers.

Hell, he could've done it at home.

Yeah, as if he could ever do that. His pride aside, Brundar couldn't stand being apart from Calypso. During the evening, he'd climbed up the stairs twice, a taxing maneuver for someone relying on crutches, just so he could watch her work for a few minutes. It was like taking a deep breath before diving underwater again. It could sustain him only for so long before he needed to surface and take another breath.

"I'll get your crutches," Calypso said as she cut the engine.

He opened the passenger door and swung his legs out. She pulled the crutches from the back seat and handed them to him one at a time.

He hefted himself up, his knees protesting any further pressure. Gritting his teeth, he followed Calypso to the elevator. "You can take the stairs if you want." He knew how much she hated being stuck in the small lift.

"No. I go where you go, big guy. You're not getting rid of me."

He leaned and kissed the top of her head, relieved by her teasing. Her silence in the car had worried him. It wasn't like Calypso to stay so quiet, especially after her first day back at work and most likely plenty of new gossip to share.

"I'm going to grab a snack," she said as he plopped tiredly on the couch. "Do you want something?" she asked a few moments later, whispering for some reason.

Naturally, he'd heard her perfectly well.

"A cup of water, please." He was contemplating taking a couple of pills to numb the throbbing pain so he could sleep.

"Here is your water." She handed him a tall glass.

Her tone was different than usual, and he wondered what this was about. Did she resent waiting on him? Maybe she'd whispered before because her throat hurt. Was she coming down with a cold or flu?

"How are you feeling?" he asked.

"I'm great. It was good to be working again."

Now she sounded like her old self. He must've imagined things before, projecting his less than optimal condition on her. "Could I bother you again? I need the pills. I overdid it tonight."

"Of course." Calypso's eyes immediately softened, and she rushed to bring him the container from her purse. "How many do you need?"

"Three."

She shook them out on her palm and handed them to him.

"Thank you." He popped the pills into his mouth and followed with a long swig of water.

Calypso remained standing, casting him a suspicious look. "How did you hear me from the kitchen? I whispered so low I barely heard myself."

Damnation. This was unexpected and worrisome. She was starting to get suspicious and was testing him.

He shrugged, pretending nonchalance. "I have very good hearing."

She shook her head. "This is not good hearing. This is extraordinary hearing."

"If you say so." He winced, exaggerating the expression to distract her from her line of inquiry.

"I'm sorry. You're in pain, and I'm bothering you with nonsense. You need to shower and get into bed."

He sighed. "Sounds like a plan to me. I'm exhausted."

"Let me help you take off the bandages."

He couldn't wait. Up until tonight, he had showered with waterproof covers over his bandages, but Bridget had called earlier today telling him it was okay to take them off and replace them with the compression knee sleeves she'd left for him. In fact, it had been okay since Tuesday, but she'd forgotten to tell him. He had been supposed to come in for a checkup but had skipped it.

Brundar lifted his butt and pulled down his pants. "I'm all yours."

"I'll get a wet washcloth."

Calypso came back a moment later with a plastic bowl filled with water and a couple of washcloths. "Just in case the bandages are sticking to your skin."

They weren't, but he would let her discover it on her own.

With gentle fingers, Calypso carefully unwrapped the first bandage. Her eyes widened as she bared his knee. "I can't believe it. Look at this. There is barely any sign of the injury. How is it possible?"

Damnation. He hadn't expected it to look so good so fast. "The skin is healed. But the tendons and bones are not. That will take much longer."

"Even so. I was expecting to see scars and stitches, but all that remains are thin white lines." She touched a finger to one of them. "How?"

Brundar let his head drop back on the couch. He was so tired of lying. Maybe he should just thrall Calypso and get it over with. But he'd already thralled her yesterday after biting her, and he was loath to do so again so soon.

"I'm not a doctor. I don't know what kind of magic Bridget performed. You should address all these questions to her. I'm tired. I want to shower and get into bed."

Brundar didn't want to imagine how Bridget was going to retaliate for the hot potato he was dropping at her feet. But he could deal with that tomorrow when he had more energy.

"Do you need my help in the shower?" Calypso looked remorseful.

Brundar had detected notes of both hope and apology in her request, but he needed a few minutes to himself. "I'm fine. Finish your snack. I'll be quick about it. I know you want to shower too."

"Let me finish your other knee first."

"I can do it myself."

"Please?" Her sad eyes pleaded with him from where she was kneeling on the floor.

He couldn't deny her when she looked at him like that. "Fine."

When she was done, Calypso gathered the used bandages and took them to the trash, while he shuffled with the help of his crutches to the bathroom.

Sitting on the bench, Brundar closed his eyes and let the hot water soothe his strained muscles. The nightclub's smells lingered on clothes and skin but mostly the hair, necessitating a shower even if they'd done so before during the day.

He heard her open the bathroom door and a few moments later she entered the shower.

"Do you mind if I join you?" Her eyes looked haunted.

"Come here." He patted the spot next to him on the bench.

She snuggled up to him. "I don't like it when we fight."

He wrapped his arm around her and kissed the top of her head. "We didn't fight. I'm just tired and in pain, and it makes me cranky."

"Would it help if I massaged your scalp?"

No one had ever done that for him. It sounded pleasurable.

"It might."

"I've wanted to wash your hair for so long. It's so beautiful."

31

CALLIE

*B*rundar closed his eyes and surrendered to Callie's massaging fingers.

"Can I use shampoo? It would make the massage feel even better."

"By all means."

He was really enjoying this, which made her feel so much better.

So what if he was a bit strange. Maybe fast healing was a genetic trait his family was keeping a secret. No one wanted to be poked and probed, perhaps even imprisoned and experimented on.

It was a far-fetched scenario, but it was better than believing Brundar was an alien pretending to be human.

Or a vampire.

Provided creatures like that really existed, which was an absurd notion, Brundar with his long canines could have been one. But even if they did exist, he had no problem with sunlight, so that was out. On the other hand, Callie was almost sure he'd bitten her and then made her forget it.

Shawn had accused Brundar of toying with his mind, but then Shawn had been insane.

Callie shook her head. She needed to stay with what made sense and away from crazy ideas. A hereditary genetic trait was a scientific possibility, while the other ones were pure fiction. Perhaps there were other intelligent species in the vast universe and aliens existed somewhere, but they didn't come to visit Earth, and vampires were a myth.

A dollop of shampoo in her palm, she started massaging Brundar's scalp.

"Your hair is so thick and glossy. Women spend a fortune on hair products, professionally done highlights, and Brazilian blowouts to get that look and fail."

Brundar's jaw muscles tightened, and he didn't respond to her compliments. Maybe he didn't like comments about his hair. Which didn't make sense. By growing it out so long, he was practically inviting them.

He was so touchy about so many things that she wasn't sure which topics of conversation were safe anymore. And to think people accused her generation—the millennials—of being too sensitive.

She stopped her massaging. "What's the matter? You don't like me talking about your hair?"

"It's not that. Please continue."

Resuming her kneading, she asked, "Then what? You can't shut me out whenever I ask you a personal question."

He sighed. "As a kid, I was bullied because of my hair. The boys called me a girl."

Kids could sometimes be so cruel. No wonder all her talk about women wanting hair like his reminded him of the taunting. "Was that why you became a fighter? So you could beat up the bullies?"

When he didn't respond, Callie assumed he didn't want to talk about it, but a few moments later he said, "No, only after I was attacked. I vowed to never be weak again. I refused to be a victim."

"Good for you." She kept massaging. "Was your hair as

long then as it is now?" It was wrong to put the blame on the victim, but if he had been bullied and taunted for it, he should've cut it short. It would have saved him so much misery.

"Back then it was only chin length. It was a popular style. It was no different than that of most boys."

Callie frowned. When Brundar was a child, long hair hadn't been in style for boys. But maybe things had been different in the small Scottish village he'd grown up in.

After another moment he continued. "I let it grow out when I was older. It was both a reminder to never let my guard down and a reverse taunt. If I'd been targeted because of supposedly looking feminine, I made myself a more obvious target. But if anyone thought to bully me again, I would teach them a quick and painful lesson. But no one dared."

She rolled her eyes. "Duh, you look lethal. No wonder no one dared to bully you when you were older. But isn't long hair a hindrance to a fighter? Someone can grab you by the hair and drag you. I know how painful it is." The memory of Shawn pulling her by her ponytail and dragging her on the pavement was still fresh in her mind,

Brundar chuckled. "Not to me. No one can ever get close enough to grab it. I'd cut them down first."

Callie nodded even though he couldn't see her. She understood.

"I love your hair. Not for a single moment did I ever think that it made you look feminine. You're the manliest man I've ever met. Bullies will always find something to taunt other people about, and if there is nothing they can latch on to, they'll invent something. And I'm not referring to kids only. Adults can be bullies too. Sometimes those who have nothing they can be proud of put other people down to feel superior."

Brundar covered her hand on his shoulder with his. "True words."

32

KIAN

*T*he house phone rang, once, twice.

Kian ignored it. After the third ring, someone picked up. Either Syssi or Okidu.

If anyone needed him, they knew to call his cellphone. The Guardians didn't use the landline, and no one else had his home number except for his mother and sisters.

Alena never called, and on the rare occasion that Amanda and Sari did, they used his cell number. Which left his mother. But he wasn't expecting a call from her.

It was probably someone in the keep looking for Syssi.

Kian went back to looking over the proposal Shai had summarized for him so he didn't have to sift through pages upon pages of technical and financial stuff that could be boiled down to a few paragraphs.

Shai had been the one to come up with the idea, and it was a life saver, cutting hours off Kian's workday. The problem was, he always found more things he could fill them with. Good for their business, but bad for him and Syssi.

The woman was a saint, tolerating his shitty moods and not complaining about having too little time with him.

The phone line went from blinking red to green, and a

second later Syssi called using the intercom. "It's your mother. She wants to talk to you."

"Thanks."

Fuck. A call from his mother was never good news. Annani didn't call to chitchat. She called to issue orders and demand reports. Not often, thank the merciful Fates.

"Hello, Mother."

"How are you doing, Kian?"

Was he imagining it, or did he detect a note of true concern in her tone? "Busy as usual. I'm in the process of acquiring several new enterprises. Our growth for the last quarter was in the two digits."

"I did not call to inquire about our holdings. I wanted to know how my son was doing."

Great. Someone must've told Annani that he'd been stressed lately. Suspect *numero uno*—Amanda. No one would ever suspect a woman who looked like her to have a yenta personality, but she did.

"I'm doing fine, Mother."

"Fabulous. I want you in a good mood while I am visiting."

"The village is not ready yet." Annani was supposed to come for the grand opening ceremony.

"I know, dear, but I need to come because of Phoenix. That little girl should have been turned already."

A good excuse. But Kian knew it wasn't the reason his mother was coming.

"Shouldn't her parents bring her to you?"

"Indeed they should. But Andrew cannot take another long vacation, and Nathalie refuses to come without her husband."

The door opened quietly, and Syssi walked in. She sat across from his desk and mouthed, "What's going on?"

"Annani is coming for a visit," he mouthed back.

Syssi's eyes brightened, and she did that silent hand clapping to show him she was excited about the news. His wife was probably the only woman in the universe who couldn't wait to spend time with her mother-in-law. Yet another reason to adore her.

"When should we expect you?" he asked Annani.

"The day after tomorrow. I will notify you when I board the plane."

"Very well. I'll send the chopper to pick you up from our landing strip."

"Thank you. I am looking forward to spending time with you and Syssi and Amanda and her mate."

"We are looking forward to it too." Not really, but he was doing his best to sound polite. "Goodbye, Mother."

Ending the call, Kian put his elbows on his desk and dropped his head into his hands. "As if I don't have enough to contend with, the last thing I need is my mother visiting. I don't have time for that."

Syssi waved a dismissive hand. "Don't worry about it. Amanda and I are going to keep her busy. Besides, she will be spending most of her time doting on Phoenix. You know how your mother adores babies."

"That is the reason she gave for coming. Phoenix needs to turn as soon as possible, but her parents are in no hurry." He wagged a finger at her. "I blame your brother for that."

Syssi shrugged. "It's going to be okay. I for one am happy she is coming. Your mom is so much fun."

That was part of the problem. Hosting his mother was like hosting a mischievous teenage girl who needed constant supervision, but who he had no control over whatsoever and had to treat like the celebrity prima donna she was.

Kian raked his fingers through his hair. "Where are we even going to put her? Can she stay at Amanda's again?"

Syssi shook her head. "I don't think she is going to be comfortable with Dalhu there. Or let me rephrase, I don't think Dalhu is going to be comfortable with her there. She still intimidates the hell out of him." She leaned back in her chair and crossed her arms over her chest. "Annani can stay with us. We have plenty of room, for her and her Odus."

"I can send Amanda and Dalhu on a vacation, and she can stay at their place," Kian suggested.

"Really? Is having your mother over so terrible?"

He sighed. "Normally no. But I'm hanging by a thread, and Annani is not easy to deal with."

"Was there a time you weren't stressed? That's your normal."

"I'm not always stressed."

Syssi uncrossed her arms and leaned forward. "Oh, yeah? Give me a recent example."

"Easy. When we make love, and for about half an hour after."

She laughed. "Great. So while your mother is here, all we have to do is have plenty of sex to negate the extra stress her company causes you."

"Aha. But she is going to hear us, and you're still shy about that."

"True." Syssi frowned. "We can't put her in one of the lower level apartments, she will be offended by that, and we can't put her in a hotel for the same reason."

That gave him an idea. "You're right. We can't put her anywhere other than our or Amanda's penthouse without offending her, but we can stay wherever the fuck we want."

"Like the Four Seasons?"

"Sure."

She waggled her brows. "The last time we stayed there, I had dream sex with you. This time we can have the real thing."

He still remembered the scent of her arousal that had permeated the presidential suite. "What exactly did you dream?"

"I'm not going to tell you."

The hell she wasn't. "Tell me!"

Syssi's lips twitched as she pretended to be upset with him. "Tsk, tsk, Kian. We've discussed this before. You're only allowed to boss me around in the bedroom."

"No. I'm allowed to boss you around in any sexual situation. Talking about sex qualifies."

"I could tell you, but I'd rather show you." Syssi winked.

He was out of his chair before the last word had left her mouth. "Come." He reached for her hand.

"Not here, silly boy. At the Four Seasons!"

"Fine. Come with me, and I'll show you *my* dreams."

"You dream about me?"

"Every fucking minute of the day." He pulled her up and wrapped his arms around her. "Let's go."

33

BRUNDAR

*A*n hour of sitting in Franco's ugly office was more than enough for Brundar. He could work on the numbers upstairs while keeping an eye on Calypso. Not in the sense of keeping her safe, the danger was over, but for his own selfish reasons.

He was addicted to her.

Dropping the tablet inside a plastic bag that he'd tied to one of the rungs on his right crutch, he was ready to go. There was no other way for him to carry the damned thing. It was too big for a pocket, and he couldn't stick it under his arm because that was where the crutches went.

If not for Bridget's threat to reset his bones without the benefit of anesthesia, which wasn't an idle one, he would've tossed them aside and walked like a man even if it killed him.

Franco should install a goddamned elevator from the basement to the nightclub. Climbing the stairs with crutches was a circus act Brundar was getting tired of.

In fact, he was getting tired of the whole scene. The basement didn't hold his interest anymore. There was nothing for him down there. The only one he wanted to play with was running around and serving drinks at the surface level, and that was where he wanted to be.

Hence the tablet. Crunching numbers was the one thing that he was still good for.

Brundar shook his head. He'd been transformed from a fighter with a kinky bent to a boring accountant who wanted nothing more than to take his woman home and make love to her.

Yes, make love.

Not have sex, not fuck, not shag, but make love.

Fates, he used to pity Kian for spending his days behind a desk and being so wrapped up in his woman that he could barely function without her.

Was he turning into a version of Kian?

The thing was, it didn't bother him as much as it should. Brundar had discovered that he liked playing with numbers. He was good at making estimates, profit and loss predictions, and calculating returns on investments. And what's more, he found it interesting. For centuries he'd watched Kian conduct business, all along thinking that it was an uninspired, boring job.

He'd been wrong.

Now he understood the rush Kian was getting out of the wheeling and dealing. He was one of the top players in a game only the select few were good at.

Brundar was nowhere near Kian's caliber and would probably never be, but he could play a scaled down game and test his abilities without risking too much.

By the time Brundar reached the top of the stairs, he was winded, and his knees were in agony. Unfortunately, it would be two more hours before he could go home. Calypso's shift didn't end until two in the morning, and she was his ride home.

"Brundar." She ran up to him as he shuffled out of the side

corridor and into the club proper. "Are you in pain? You look pale. I mean paler than usual."

With Calypso, he didn't feel the need to pretend that a tough guy like him didn't need relief from pain. She would've called him on his bullshit right away. "I could use a few of those pills. Did you bring them?"

"Of course. First, let me find you a place to sit, and then I'll go get them."

He nodded, following behind her as she pushed her way in between the many bodies crowding the floor. Friday night was one of the busiest days of the week. The place was packed. Good for business, not so good for Calypso's prospects of finding him a place to sit. Not a single table was vacant. Maybe she could get him a seat at the bar.

Except, Brundar had forgotten that by law a table had to be reserved for people in his situation. The table set aside for the disabled happened to be free.

After Calypso had helped him get settled and run off to get his pills, a couple of girls sauntered over with come-hither smiles plastered on their heavily made-up faces. They were eyeing the two vacant chairs at his table, obviously more interested in the seats and maybe a free drink than in him.

He treated them to one of his more severe stares and pushed with a little thrall, convincing them that sitting next to him was a really bad idea. They kept on walking, searching for their next victim.

Calypso got back and handed him the glass of water, then pulled the pill container out of the pocket of her pants. "If you don't want to be bothered, I can take away these two chairs and add them to another table."

"Good thinking." He dropped four pills into his palm, popped them into his mouth and followed with water.

Regrettably, Calypso couldn't stay long, and Brundar was left all alone at his table with no extra chairs to tempt unwanted company. Pulling out the tablet from the plastic bag, he tried to go over his projections for the month and compare them to what the two clubs actually pulled in. It wasn't a difficult task to perform, but doing so with the loud music playing and people constantly jostling against his chair and his table was proving difficult if not impossible.

Brundar closed his eyes and slipped into the zone. Nothing disturbed him there. Sounds and visuals faded into the background, leaving only one thing to focus on. On the battlefield, it was usually an opponent with a weapon in his hand, but today it was a tablet with numbers to crunch.

Time went by fast or slowly in the zone, depending on which way Brundar needed to stretch it. He lost track of it, shifting from one spreadsheet to another, writing notes, and making estimates for next month. Things were looking good, and with the additional space they were going to add they would look even better.

"Brundar." Calypso's voice reached him from afar.

He closed his eyes again and abandoned his quiet space, his surroundings coming into focus like tunnel vision in reverse. He was expecting a rush of noise, but the music had stopped, the lights were up, and only the staff remained, tidying up and preparing the floor for the cleaning crew.

"Ready to go?" Calypso asked.

"I have been ready for hours."

She frowned. "Why didn't you say so? I would've taken you home."

He took her hand and kissed the back of it. "To leave me there and go back to work? I don't think so."

"Well, I could've asked the boss to let me go early." She winked. "I'm sure he would've okayed it."

34

RONI

"No way. I'm not going to play." Roni took one of the paper bags out of Sylvia's hands. Full of refreshments, including bottles of beer and cans of ginger ale, they were quite heavy. He couldn't carry them all, but he could at least appear as if he was helping.

"You don't have to. But it could be fun. No one expects you to be any good after one hour of practice."

Yesterday, Roni had guilted Andrew into helping him assemble the drum set, meaning Andrew had done all the work while Roni had sat on a chair and gave instructions.

He'd played for as long as he could, but drumming was physically demanding, and after an hour he'd had to quit and go up to his apartment to lie down.

They stepped into the elevator. "I'm rusty as hell. Besides, I don't have the energy."

Sylvia leaned and kissed his cheek. "Then you can just sit and enjoy yourself. I hope." She grimaced. "I've never heard them play. They might be awful."

That was a possibility, but judging by Jackson's taste in music a remote one. "If they get gigs in clubs they can't be too sucky."

"There is no accounting for taste. People listen to heavy metal and love it, while all I hear are screams."

They reached the basement level and exited the lift, heading for what Roni had started calling his music room. By the sound of it, the guys had already started jamming.

"Not bad," Roni said.

Sylvia nodded. "Thank the merciful Fates, I don't hear any screeching screams."

As he opened the door for Sylvia and followed her in, the guys stopped playing.

"Sweet set of drums." The band's drummer pushed up to his feet and walked over. "I'm Gordon." He offered his hand.

"Roni."

The tall, gangly, goth-looking dude leaned his bass guitar against a chair and came over to introduce himself as well. "Vlad." He offered a pale hand with long fingers. His nails were painted black.

"Have you been jamming long?" Roni asked as he shook the guy's hand.

"We've just started." Jackson strummed his guitar. "Want to join us on the drums?"

"Not this time. Today I'm in the audience."

Tessa walked over and gave Roni a hug. "Come and hang out with Sylvia and me. We will be drinking beer and munching on goodies while the guys play."

"Right." He turned to Sylvia who got busy taking things out of the paper bags and arranging them on the table someone had dragged into the room.

"Why didn't you wait for me to help you?" He hated feeling useless.

"Don't worry about it. I've got it. It's not like I'm preparing a gourmet meal here. Pretzels, nuts, fruit, beers, and ginger ale."

"Don't forget the pastries," Tessa said.

Sylvia glanced around the room. "Where are they?"

"I'll get them." Tessa walked over to where the guys had left their guitar cases, and lifted a big pink box from behind them.

"Did you bring any cheese Danishes?" Roni peeked into the box as Tessa started pulling the pastries out and arranging them on paper plates.

She handed him one. "Freshly baked. We ran out, but I remembered how much you liked them and asked Vlad to make more."

Roni turned to the band and lifted the half-eaten Danish. "Thanks, man. I appreciate it. I mean it. No one ever baked anything for me. Not even my mom."

Vlad smiled shyly. "Enjoy."

"I will." He grabbed a can of ginger ale and popped the lid. "I'm in heaven."

The band started playing again, this time with Jackson singing. The guy had a decent voice, and he and his friends played well. Not bad for teenagers, but they needed someone to write better music for them, and lyrics. Still, Roni had to admit that their performance was surprisingly professional.

Taking a seat at the table, he helped himself to another Danish. Sylvia and Tessa were trying to talk over the loud music, but Tessa kept asking her to repeat what she'd said, and eventually, the girls gave up.

The guys played one more song and then decided to take a break, apparently tempted by the food and beers.

"Snake's Venom. Awesome." Jackson helped himself to one. "Where did you get them?"

"In the store. Where else?" Sylvia said.

"They are not easy to find and pricey. We need to split the bill for those."

Sylvia waved a hand. "Forget it. Next time is going to be your treat."

Jackson lifted the beer in a salute. "Deal."

"Who writes your music?" Roni asked.

"Vlad writes the lyrics, and I write the music. Gordon is the ideas man. He comes up with all kinds of weird shit our audiences eat up."

"Would you mind if I wrote something for you guys?"

Jackson lifted one blond brow. "What are you saying, Roni? Do you think our music sucks?"

Fuck. Had he offended them? For a change, he hadn't meant to. "No, of course not. You guys are good. I just want to give it a shot."

Jackson clapped his back. "Don't worry, man. No hurt feelings here. I would love to get new material that I don't need to sweat creating. Besides, you are going to join our band, right? We need you." He wrapped his arm around Roni's shoulders as if they were the best of buddies.

Given that Roni had none, Jackson had no competition for the position. It was his if he wanted it.

With everyone at the table looking at him expectantly, there was only one way to answer that. "Sure. But I'm nowhere near Gordon's level."

Jackson squeezed his shoulder. "You will be. You're a perfectionist and competitive as hell."

With a frown, Roni straightened in his chair. "How do you know that about me? You've known me for what? Two whole hours?"

Jackson shrugged. "Simple. You don't get to be the best in your field unless you have an uncompromising drive and ambition. Whatever you do, you strive to be the best at."

Roni dipped his head. "True. But aside from my obvious genius, which admittedly makes learning new things very easy for me, drumming requires a lot of practice. I have no doubt that eventually, I will get to be as good as Gordon or even better, but it's not going to happen by the time he leaves for college."

His genius remark drew snorts and chuckles from

everyone other than Sylvia, who knew he hadn't meant it as a joke.

He was a damn genius, and he didn't believe in fake modesty.

"Okay, guys." Jackson put down his empty beer bottle. "Now that I have food in my belly, we can go back to jamming." He rose to his feet and offered his hand to Tessa. "Your turn, kitten."

She looked up at him with a puzzled expression on her face. "To do what?"

"Sing, of course."

She shook her head. "Oh, no, no, no. I'm not going to sing in front of people."

Jackson waved a hand at everyone present. "What people? Gordon and Vlad have heard you sing before, and Sylvia and Roni are our friends, soon to become part of the band."

Sneaking a glance at Sylvia and then at Roni, Tessa smiled sheepishly. "One song."

"Awesome. Sylvia is going to sing the next one," Jackson said.

Roni expected his girlfriend to object, same as Tessa, but she surprised him by accepting the challenge.

As the band started playing and Tessa took the microphone, Roni leaned back in his chair and crossed his legs at the ankles.

Tessa had a lovely voice, but weak. Jackson kept adjusting the amplifier connected to the mic, but it didn't help much.

When Tessa was done, he and Sylvia clapped, causing her to blush."

Sylvia didn't need any encouragement to take the mic next. "I don't know any of the songs you guys play. Do you know 'You're Gonna Miss Me when I'm Gone'?

"Sing a few bars and we will improvise," Jackson said.

Wow. Sylvia could sing. He hadn't known that. She had a sweet voice, similar to the original singer of that song. It was clear and strong, and her pitch was perfect. Roni felt his heart swell with pride, and with something else that was new and unexpected.

He liked these people, and they seemed to like him back.

They wanted to hang out with him, not because of his hacking skills, but because they enjoyed his company. These guys wanted him to jam with them, a fun activity people did with friends.

Friends.

For the first time since he was a toddler, Roni had actually made friends.

35

JACKSON

*J*ackson's hands were sweaty on the steering wheel, and he had a feeling that sweat stains were spreading under his armpits.

It was ridiculous. Neither he nor Tessa was a virgin, and he believed that this time she was truly ready. So why the hell was he so nervous?

Apparently, cool Jackson was gone, replaced by an insecure eighteen-year-old. Almost nineteen, he reminded himself.

Tessa didn't look anxious, thank the merciful Fates, but she seemed contemplative. They'd been on the road for over an hour, and she'd barely said a word to him.

"What are you thinking about?"

She shrugged. "This and that. Just random thoughts."

"Care to share them with me?"

Tessa threw him a sidelong glance. "Are you sure? It's mostly girl stuff that will bore you."

"Try me."

"I was thinking about Sharon. She is cool and pretty and smart, but she's never had a boyfriend. She has plenty of hookups, but that doesn't count. I asked her about it, and she said that none of the guys she's been with was a mensch, and most were just meh—boring to talk to and boring in bed. So I was wondering if she was going to like any of the immortals Eva and Bhathian were planning to introduce her to. If she is that picky, she might not like any of them, and there aren't that many to start with. Right?"

Jackson rubbed his jaw. "Frankly, I didn't give it much thought. But yeah, it's possible she won't find what she is looking for."

Tessa nodded. "If she doesn't find an immortal guy she likes and who likes her back, is Kian going to allow these guys to sleep with her and try to induce her transition? And what about telling her the truth? Are they going to do it without her knowledge? If she turns, fine, and if she doesn't, no harm done?"

"I don't know." He chuckled. "I'm very happy I'm not Kian. When I was a kid, I wanted to be just like him—a leader, a successful businessman. But I don't want to be faced with these kinds of decisions."

She was quiet for a few moments. "When I was a kid, all I wanted was a family. A mom and a dad who loved me."

Jackson reached for her hand. "You have a family. Me and Eva and Bhathian, and Nathalie and Andrew and Phoenix, and everyone else in the clan."

"I can't allow myself to think about them that way. Not until after my transition. Except for Eva, of course. She will always be there for me no matter what. Even Kian can't command her to forsake me. He might think he has authority over her, but he doesn't and never will. Eva answers only to Eva and to some extent to Bhathian. That's it."

"What about me? I'll never leave you. You must know that."

She turned her face to the window, looking at the frosted

scenery they were passing on their way to the cabin he'd rented for them in Big Bear.

"If I don't turn, I will not stay with you. I love you too much to cause you that much pain. I know I wouldn't want to see you get old and die, while I stayed young and healthy. I'm a firm believer in not doing to others what I don't want done to me."

Jackson shook his head. They were on their way to what he considered an equivalent of a honeymoon, and Tessa was talking about leaving him.

"Then I'm not like you. Because I would rather be with you for as long as I can than not at all."

"What if the roles were reversed and you were the human and I the immortal?"

He grinned. "Then I would've been doubly happy because I would have had a forever hot woman by my side. What guy doesn't want that?"

Tessa crossed her arms over her chest. "If Eva's ex didn't suffer from dementia, you could've asked him. He had a gorgeous, young-looking wife, and he still cheated on her with others."

"Idiot."

"Yeah. I agree."

"Finally we agree on something. I didn't plan this romantic getaway so we can contemplate every catastrophic scenario imaginable." He cast her a sidelong glance. "I'm a firm believer in the glass half full as opposed to half empty."

"You're right. Let's talk about something else. Where are you taking me?"

"To a magical place."

"Seriously. I know it's up in the mountains because you told me to pack a sweater and we've been climbing for the past forty-five minutes."

If Tessa were a native Californian, she would have known

where he was taking her, so there was no harm in telling her the destination. The cabin he'd rented, though, he was going to keep a surprise. He wanted to see her face as she entered.

Jackson had paid for the honeymoon package, which included the fanciest cabin in the resort, fresh flowers, a bottle of champagne, and a fruit basket. In addition, he'd asked for candles to be lit before their arrival but had been refused. Apparently, candles were considered a fire hazard.

It put a little dent in his plans, but he had it covered. There was a bunch of assorted candles in his travel bag, three bottles of wine, and enough Godiva chocolates to land Tessa in a hospital. Naturally, he was going to portion those out so she wouldn't overdose. The girl had no self-control when faced with those sweet treats.

"We are going to Big Bear. I rented us a cabin. It's summer, so there will be no snow, but the place is beautiful all year round."

Tessa frowned. "That sounds expensive. I hope you didn't spend too much on the cabin."

Given the state of his finances, it had cost a fortune, but he and Tessa were going to have their first time together only once. He needed to get it right because there were no re-dos on that.

"No, not too much." Not a lie. Nothing was too much to make this day and night special.

"How did you manage to take a day off tomorrow?"

"Our wayward waitress came back."

"Oh, yeah? Where was she?"

"Got another job. They promised her better pay but ended up paying her less. So she is back."

"And you took her back? She is unreliable."

"True, but I know she is not going to disappear at least until she gets her paycheck, which is in two weeks. She needs the money."

"What if she doesn't show up tomorrow? What are Vlad and Gordon going to do?"

Jackson shook his head. "Glass half full, kitten. I have to stick with that."

Twenty minutes or so later, they arrived at the resort.

"Stay here. I'll get us checked in."

"Okay."

It was good she had no problem staying in the car. He didn't want Tessa to come with him in case the clerk at the reception started blabbing about the honeymoon suite and spoiled his surprise. After checking them in, Jackson made reservations for dinner in one of the restaurants the guy at reception had suggested, then headed back to the car.

"Our cabin is a short drive from here," he told Tessa.

Even from the outside, it looked bigger and fancier than all the other cabins they had passed on the way.

Dropping their bags on the front porch, Jackson pulled the key out of his pocket and unlocked the door but opened it only a tiny crack.

"Close your eyes," he told Tessa.

She smiled. "Okay."

Lifting her into his arms, he pushed the door open with his foot. "You can open your eyes now."

"Jackson, it's beautiful." Tessa turned her head this way and that, taking in the ultra luxurious cabin. "This must have cost a bundle. And you said you didn't pay much for it." She cast him an accusing glance.

"You asked me if I paid *too much*, and I said no because nothing is too much to make this day special for you. For us." He kissed her tenderly.

Eying the huge bed, Tessa worried her lower lip. "What now? Is there a protocol for how this should be done?"

"Item number one on the agenda is to feed the bride so she'll have the energy for a long night of great sex."

He turned her in his arms, so her chest was pressed against his and kissed her again.

After letting him cuddle and kiss her until he had his fill, Tessa shimmied down his body. When her feet touched the floor, she tugged her shirt down. "I bet you made reservations."

"Of course. I leave nothing to chance."

TESSA

*D*inner ended up being a drawn-out affair.

Tessa had ordered a glass of wine, and then another one, sipping on them as slowly as she could. It wasn't that she'd changed her mind, or felt that she wasn't ready after all.

She felt pressured. For lack of a better term, Tessa was suffering from what she suspected was the equivalent of performance anxiety.

What Jackson hadn't realized was that the elaborate setup was more of a hindrance than an aphrodisiac. Things would have been simpler if they had done it in his room atop the café. There was no pressure there. They would have started with kissing and fondling, and one thing would have led to another, and things would have progressed naturally to where they were supposed to.

But Jackson wanted to make it special, and she had no heart to tell him that all that preparation was making her anxious.

"Are you ready to go, kitten?" he asked when the last drop of wine in her glass was gone.

No more stalling. "Yes." She rose to her feet, or rather to

her six-inch platform shoes. Several guys glanced her way, but the new Tessa was able to interpret their appreciative looks as a compliment and not a threat.

Tessa expelled a breath. She could do it. She wasn't a scared little girl anymore. She was a confident young woman who could kick ass when necessary, and who was secure in her own sexuality. Not only that, she was going to make love to an amazing guy who loved her to pieces, and whom she loved back just as much.

On the front porch of the cabin, Jackson opened the door and lifted her in his arms again, then carried her over the threshold. She wrapped her arms around his neck and snuggled closer. For a slim guy, he was always warm—her own personal blanket for whenever she got cold, which was often.

"Where do you want to go, bed or bath?"

"Bath, definitely. I bet they have a jacuzzi in there."

"They do. A two-person whirlpool spa."

Oh, goodie. Jackson was going to get in the tub with her. They would start with a little fondling and continue to bed.

Jackson set her down on the counter, then turned around to start the water for their tub.

Her legs dangling over the edge and her arms propped on the marble countertop, Tessa felt like a little girl again. A naughty girl who was planning on doing naughty things with her hot fiancé all night long.

She was getting all hot and bothered just looking at Jackson as he crouched next to the tub. With his broad back, his powerful thighs, and the tight ass that was a work of art, he was a man any woman would've loved to call her own.

He was also three years Tessa's junior.

She should be the one babying him, and not the other way around. The thing was, she loved how he always took care of her.

Age was irrelevant.

Their personalities dictated the roles they assumed in

their relationship. Jackson was the caretaker, and she was the one being taken care of, and they both enjoyed the roles they played.

So what was the harm in that?

She would do anything for him, and if Jackson ever needed her to take care of him, she would. But in their day to day life their default modes suited them perfectly well.

Satisfied with the temperature of the water, Jackson straightened up and turned to her. "Is my kitten waiting for me to undress her?"

"Yes." She treated him to a bright smile, letting him know she liked the direction this was going.

"My pleasure."

He started with her shoes, the very tall ones he'd bought for her, removing one at the time and then massaging her toes and her arches until she purred like a real cat.

Next, Jackson tackled the buttons of her white, silk blouse, opening each of the tiny fake pearls with nimble fingers. When the last one was done, he parted the two halves of the shirt and slid the sleeves down her arms, letting it fall on the counter behind her.

"Very nice." He trailed his fingers over the top of her breasts, leaving goose bumps in the wake of his feather-light touch.

"A new bra?"

"Yeah." Tessa cupped the undersides of her bra-encased small breasts. "The latest in bridal lingerie. Adds two cup sizes." It was also embroidered with tiny fake diamonds on the sides. Apparently, Jackson hadn't been the only one who thought of this as their honeymoon. Tessa had gotten the bra because she needed a white one under the sheer fabric of her new blouse, but there were many others she could've chosen, and yet she'd been drawn to the bridal model.

Jackson's eyes started glowing. "Did you get the matching panties?"

She waggled her brows. "You'll have to find out."

Wrapping an arm around her waist, he lifted her a couple of inches off the counter and pulled her tight stretchy pants off with his other hand. His eyes zeroed in on the tiny lace triangle covering her mound. "Very nice indeed." He trailed a finger over her cleft. The lace panties were useless as far as absorbing any moisture, and the evidence of her arousal had already seeped through.

Jackson lifted his wet finger to his mouth and licked it clean. "There is no better taste in the world." His speech was getting slurred.

His fangs were such a turn-on.

But they were nowhere near their full length yet. She knew exactly how to get them there. "There is a surprise for you in the back."

"Show me."

Oh, she was going to have fun with that. Sometimes, being small was an advantage, because a tall woman could not have done what Tessa had in mind. The ceiling was too low for that.

Bracing on her hands, she lifted herself and pulled her legs up. When her feet were on the counter, she pushed up and turned around, leaning against the mirror and pushing her ass out.

The panties were thong style, tied with a little bow at the back. All Jackson had to do was tug on that bow, and they would fall off.

After all, it was a bridal set.

Jackson gasped. "Dear Fates. I have to take a picture of that."

What the hell? That wasn't what she'd expected. "Don't you dare! I don't want pictures of my butt all over the Internet."

"I'll erase it as soon as I show it to you. I bet you have no idea how hot you look."

Naturally, she'd checked herself in the mirror when she'd put them on, but not from the angle Jackson was seeing now. "Okay. Just one."

He pulled out his phone and snapped three in quick succession, then handed her the phone. "You can erase them yourself when you're done."

Wow, that was one hell of a view. Slightly lewd, since the thong didn't cover much, but sexy as hell.

Damn, she was turning herself on.

Tessa erased the pictures, crouched down on the counter, and reached behind her to hand Jackson his phone back.

"Stay like that," he hissed, cupping her butt cheeks in his large hands.

She looked at him over her shoulder. "Are you going to pull on the bow?"

He answered with a growl, catching the little white bow between his front teeth, which were now framed by his huge fangs, and pulled. The thong fell off, leaving her naked save for the bra.

"I'm going to eat you up like that." Holding her in place, Jackson dipped his head, extended his tongue, and treated her to a long lick. "Yum. So tasty."

Panting, Tessa leaned her head against the mirror and surrendered to pleasure.

37

JACKSON

*T*essa was trembling with the aftershocks of her orgasm as Jackson lifted her off the counter and hugged her to him, careful not to squash her. But it was hard not to tighten his arms around her when he was overflowing with emotions.

Every time he brought her to a climax felt like a triumph, hers as well as his. Especially one that had left her boneless like she was now.

"Ready for your bath, kitten?"

She opened her bliss-glazed eyes and cupped his cheek. "Could you take off my bra first?"

He bent to plant a soft kiss on her lips. With his fangs at full length, he needed to be extra careful not to nick her. "Of course."

Holding her with one arm, he snapped the bra open with his other and tossed it on the counter next to those sexy panties he was going to keep as a souvenir.

"I'll dip your tush first. Tell me if the temperature is okay." He lowered her gently into the water.

"It's good."

Jackson lowered Tessa all the way until she was sprawled

comfortably in the bathtub, then shucked his clothes and joined her. Slipping in behind her instead of taking the spot across from her as the tub's design suggested, he hugged her close and nuzzled her neck. His cock was hard enough to hammer nails with, but he didn't want to rush her. It wouldn't be the first time he'd suffered a woodie and the way it was nestled between her ass cheeks it was getting even harder.

Tessa rested her head on his chest and sighed. "You're so good to me."

"And you are to me."

She chuckled. "Not really. You just treated me to an orgasm that left me boneless, while you're still sporting a boner."

"I'm a patient man."

"Yes, you are. And a wonderful one." She turned in his arms, pressing her breasts against his chest. "How about we get out of here and put that king-sized bed to good, rigorous use?"

He kissed her cute little nose. "You can barely move. I think you need to rest a little."

"Not necessarily. It's not as if I'm going to do much work out there. My only job is to moan loudly as you pound into me."

The image she'd just painted in his mind had his cock twitch and release a bead of moisture. Tessa was definitely over her aversion to sex and anything that had to do with it.

A few weeks ago he would've never believed she could talk like that.

"Is that what you want? Just a pounding?"

"Is there anything else?"

There was still so much he could teach her. "Plenty. Though eventually it all leads to that."

Even through the water, he could smell the flare in her desire that his words brought about.

Her eyes hooded, she trailed a finger down his chest. "I want everything. But most of all I'm looking forward to the pounding."

Jackson didn't need any more prodding. Lifting Tessa with him, he stepped out of the tub and grabbed a towel.

"I love how strong you are." She had her arms wrapped around his neck.

He put the towel on the counter, then set Tessa on top of the folded towel, and grabbed another, wrapping it quickly around her.

His girl got chilled easily. He couldn't allow that to happen.

Once he had Tessa cocooned in two towels with only her head peeking out, Jackson pulled one for himself.

"I can't move my arms," she complained.

"But you're warm. I'll unwrap you when you're under the blanket."

"Can we light the fire?"

Done toweling himself dry, Jackson dropped his bath sheet on the floor and lifted Tessa up together with her towel cocoon. "Good idea. It will make the room all warm and cozy for my girl who doesn't like to be cold."

Stretching her neck up, she kissed the underside of his jaw. "Did I tell you how much I love you?"

"Once or twice. But I can never get enough." He put her down on one side of the bed, lifting the thick, down-filled comforter with the other. "Okay, kitten, on three." He helped her out of the towels and under the blanket.

"It's cold. Can you get in and warm me up?"

"Don't you want me to start the fire first?"

"Later."

He was fine with that. Getting under the blanket with a naked Tessa wasn't a hard sell.

"Come here, baby." He wrapped himself around her small

body. She was so tiny. At six feet two inches, he was a tall guy. Were they going to fit?

He would've been really worried if Tessa were a virgin.

"Jackson?"

"Yeah?"

"I'm not on any contraceptives. Are we going to use a condom?"

"No. I told you what Bridget said. The bite has to come together with intercourse."

"I thought she meant the act."

"I have to get my seed inside you at the same time as my venom."

"What if I get pregnant?"

"Very unlikely. Immortals don't procreate much."

"I'm still a mortal."

"But I'm not. And I haven't gotten anyone pregnant yet."

"You did it without condoms?"

He shrugged. "I can't get or transmit diseases. All I had to do was push a little thrall to let them think I had protection when I didn't, and no one got pregnant."

"That's because all those girls are on the pill or something else."

It was going to kill him, but if she wanted to get contraceptives first, he was okay with going home without consummating their union. They had managed up until now, they would manage a few more days.

"Do you want to get pills first? We don't have to do it tonight. What's one more week, right?"

"No way in hell. If you're willing to chance it, then I am too."

Fates, what a relief. "I am. And if by some miracle I put a baby in you, I will not mind it at all."

"Me neither," Tessa whispered into his chest.

38

TESSA

a baby.

Images of her and Jackson with their baby popped behind Tessa's closed eyelids, and there was nothing but joy in them. She would finally have a family of her own. Not an adopted family, not a foster family, but totally hers.

It would be wonderful.

That didn't mean she would be devastated if she didn't conceive on their first try. They had plenty of time, and Tessa wanted to transition first.

Nathalie and Andrew had had a hell of a time worrying about the baby because Nathalie had gotten pregnant as a human. On the other hand, conception was much more difficult for immortals. Tessa's chances would drop significantly after her transition.

She kissed Jackson's chest. "Whatever happens, happens. Your Fates are going to decide."

He cupped her breast and thumbed the nipple. "I don't trust them. They do as they please, and our prayers fall on deaf ears, but there isn't much I can do about it other than helping them along with lots and lots of sex, that is." He waggled his brows.

She could live with that. "Starting tonight."

"Yes." His eyes blazed in the dark room. "Are you all warmed up?" He started pulling the blanket down, exposing her breasts.

"I am, but my nipples are getting cold."

"Not for long."

With a gentle push, Jackson turned her on her back, and covered her body with his. Bracing on his forearms, he looked into her eyes and waited.

It took her a moment to realize what he was waiting for.

He was on top of her, his big body pressing hers into the mattress, a position that used to freak her out because she couldn't stand being trapped under a man's body. Except, the fear was so completely gone that she'd forgotten she'd ever had a problem with that. All she felt was love, acceptance, and simmering arousal.

Tessa smiled and wrapped her arms around Jackson's neck, pulling him even closer, so his entire weight was pressing into her. He wasn't too heavy, he was just perfect, feeling wonderful on top of her. She could stay like this forever. "Kiss me," she breathed.

He took her lips gently, his tongue flicking over them in a playful request for entry, then getting bolder when she granted it. His kisses were still gentle as he moved to her neck, then her collarbone, and then slid down her body to take one aching nipple into his hot mouth while his fingers teased the other.

How the hell was he doing it? Being so patient with her and holding back the inferno she was seeing in his blazing eyes?

His erection hadn't eased since he'd brought her to a shattering climax in the bathroom. Jackson was no doubt desperate to get inside her, but he was taking the time to give her slow and sweet, showing her love with every touch, every caress.

Threading her fingers through his silky blond hair, she whispered, "I love you."

His mouth left her nipple with a plop. "I know, kitten. I love you too."

"I'm ready," she said.

He shook his head. "I'll be the judge of that."

Even if she wasn't before, she was now. Bossy Jackson was sexy as hell, especially since his bossiness was always about ensuring her pleasure.

He was such a giver.

Resuming his suckling on her other nipple, he pushed a hand down to her center, first just cupping it possessively, then trailing a finger down her drenched folds.

She groaned as he pushed a finger inside her, the muscles in her sheath clamping around it. He pulled it out, dragging the moisture up to her throbbing bundle of nerve endings, then circling it without actually touching. A moment later, he came back with two fingers, pumping a few times, and then pulling out to smear more juices before resuming the maddeningly slow circling.

Waiting for his invasion, she was on the verge of climax, panting breathlessly. But instead of his shaft, he used three fingers to stretch her wide.

Tessa knew he was doing what he thought was best to prepare her, but fingers weren't what she needed.

"I want you inside me when I come."

As he lifted his head from her breast and looked up at her, Jackson's conflicting emotions were all over his face. There was lust, and need, and love, but also fear. He didn't want to hurt her, to trigger a panic attack, and she didn't know how to reassure him that it wasn't going to happen.

Cupping his cheeks, she held his gaze as she gave it her best. "Right now, there is nothing in the world I want more than for you to fill me so completely that I wouldn't know where you end and I begin. Make us one, Jackson, I don't want to wait another second."

She watched as the last of his fears dissipated from his eyes, and all that was left was love and lust.

That was how she wanted him to look at her for the rest of their lives. No longer as the broken doll who had to be handled with care, but a woman who loved him and lusted after him.

A true partner, not a fix-up project.

Jackson fisted his shaft and guided it to her entrance, but he didn't immediately push in, as she'd expected. Rubbing the velvety smooth hard length over her slit, he coated it in her juices, teasing her for a few moments longer before pushing in with just the very tip.

There was no panic, just an intense craving for more.

His eyes were locked on her face as he pushed another inch in.

It was a tight fit, but delightfully so. Her own eyes hooded with desire, she let out a moan that was a mix of pleasure and relief.

Finally, Jackson was inside her, and it felt perfect.

Encouraged by her moan, he pushed a little deeper and stopped again.

Was she half full or half empty?

Tessa lifted her butt off the mattress, impaling herself on another couple of inches before he stopped her with a hand on her chest, pushing her back down. "Patience, kitten."

"I'm all out." She clutched at his shoulders, letting him feel her short nails.

That broke the last of Jackson's resistance, and he surged all the way in, filling her completely.

For long moments, they just clung to each other, savoring the unbelievable feeling of connection, of oneness. It was more than desire, more than love, it was magical.

"I love you so much," Jackson breathed.

He was so tall that lying down they couldn't be face to face unless he folded himself. As it was, her face was pressed against his pecs. Tessa put her lips on them, kissing, licking, nipping, she couldn't get enough of him.

Bracing on his forearms, he lifted his torso and looked down at where they were joined. Moving with shallow thrusts, he watched himself going in and out of her, his expression one of awe.

His blue eyes shining with inner light and his fangs long and pointy, Jackson would've looked terrifying to anyone but her.

To Tessa, he was just breathtakingly beautiful. There was nothing about him that she feared. She loved everything, accepted everything, and would have not changed a single thing about him.

There was only one of him in the world, and he was hers.

As Tessa spread her legs wider, taking more of him inside, Jackson lifted his head and dipped it again to kiss her, the force and tempo of his thrusts increasing.

His control was admirable.

Still holding back, he was increasing the ferocity in small increments instead of going all out, making sure not to overwhelm her. His reserve was sweet and considerate, but at the same time, it implied that he still saw her as a broken doll.

Tessa felt a tinge of disappointment, but then pushed it away. It might have had nothing to do with her past. After all, she was still a fragile human, while he was a super strong immortal who could easily break her if he weren't careful.

She bucked into him, meeting every thrust with one of her own and spurring him on.

He threw her a wicked grin before adding a slight spin to his forward thrusts that had him rubbing against an ultra-sensitive spot inside her.

"Oh, my, God, oh, oh!" she exclaimed as her climax started building up momentum at a ferocious pace. Reaching the point of no return, she let it wash over her in wave after wave of electrical currents that were shocking in their intensity.

As her inner walls clamped around his shaft, Jackson emitted a feral snarl, and his restraint snapped. His hard pounding wringing another orgasm out of her, he erupted inside her, pouring his essence into her for long moments until she was overflowing with it.

But that wasn't the end of it. Just when she thought he couldn't have any more in him, Jackson cupped her head, tilted it sideways, and with a hiss struck her throat.

A split second of pain, and then unimaginable bliss.

39

KIAN

Up on the roof of his keep, Kian awaited his mother's arrival with Syssi at his side.

He was grateful. Syssi could've easily wriggled out of having to welcome his mother, but she hadn't, taking the day off and in doing so forcing Amanda to do the same.

After all, the daughter could do no less than the daughter-in-law.

His sister, however, was late as usual. Not much of a welcoming committee if she arrived after Annani had landed.

"Are you cold?" Kian glanced down at Syssi who huddled close to him.

She wrapped her arms around his middle and pressed her cheek to his chest. "A little. But mostly I'm tired. Someone didn't let me sleep much last night."

He smirked. "Guilty as charged." In preparation for his mother's impending visit, Kian had been in desperate need of lowering his stress levels a notch, and there was nothing that could do it better and faster than a night of wild sex with his wife. "Do you want to go back inside? I'll tell Annani that you are waiting to welcome her in the penthouse. You could lie down for a few minutes. Fates know you will not get a chance once she is here."

His mother was a very demanding lady and an attention-hogger. He was so glad he had Syssi to take some of the burden of dealing with her off his shoulders.

Annani would've driven him crazy. She still might.

"I think I hear the chopper," Syssi said.

"I'll call Amanda and tell her to hurry up."

"Tell her to bring me a jacket."

He nodded and speed-dialed his sister. "The chopper is landing. You better hurry up. And bring Syssi a jacket, she is cold."

"I'll be right there."

Kian ended the call and put the phone back in his pocket.

A few moments later, Amanda joined them on the roof and handed Syssi a leather coat.

"What is it?" Syssi put it on. The coat was black, shiny, and long, reaching down to her calves. "I feel like I'm in *The Matrix* movie and should have machine guns under here."

Amanda smirked. "Are you warm?"

"Yes, thank you."

"I figured you were cold all over and this is the only long coat I own."

Kian lifted a brow. "I find that hard to believe."

Amanda crossed her arms over her chest. "I donated the rest to charity."

That explained it. "What happened? Long coats been out of fashion for the last couple of days?"

"The past year. I don't keep anything for longer than that."

Well, at least she was donating all of it to charity. It was probably selling well in second-hand stores specializing in fine clothing and bringing in good revenue to whatever charity Amanda had chosen.

"Here it is." Syssi pointed to the black dot getting larger as it got closer.

Kian took in a long breath and prayed for patience.

When the chopper landed, Kri exited first, then offered her hand to Annani to help her down.

Nimble as ever, his mother took Kri's hand, but then jumped down in a flurry of silk as the bottom of her midnight blue dress was caught in the wind created by the chopper's slowing blades.

Syssi leaned closer. "No matter how many times I see her, I can't help my reaction to her beauty. It's literally breathtaking."

"She is a goddess," Kian said. No further comment was needed. Her kind had been perfect in every way. Physically, at least. According to Annani, all the gods had been incredibly beautiful, though not all of them had been sane, or kind.

"That makes her even more awe-inspiring. It's easier to think of her as just an incredibly beautiful woman."

"Come on, we need to meet her halfway, or she'll be offended." With his hand on the small of her back, he propelled Syssi toward Annani.

As they reached her, Syssi bowed her head. "Clan Mother, it's an honor to receive you."

"Oh, none of that, child. Come here." She opened her arms, and Syssi walked into the embrace. "To you, I am just Annani." She kissed Syssi on the cheek and then on the other one. "If you keep up that Clan Mother nonsense, I will start calling you she who is my son's mate."

Syssi laughed, which had been Annani's goal.

His mother let go of her daughter-in-law to embrace Amanda next. "You look lovely as ever, my sweet little Mindi."

"You too, Ninni." *Little Mindi* had to bend considerably to align herself with their petite mother.

When his turn came around, Kian knelt in front of the goddess, in part to save them both from body acrobatics, and in part because it pleased her. The more pleased Annani was, the less likely she was to pester him.

"Welcome, Mother. Thank you for coming to spend time with Phoenix. We will all worry less once this baby transitions."

Annani smiled and cupped his cheeks, then kissed his forehead. "She is not the only reason I am here. I want to spend time with the rest of my family as well."

He rose to his feet, towering over her physically, and yet feeling dwarfed by her power. "Let's get you settled. This time, you're staying with Syssi and me."

"Thank you. I am going to have the best time."

Annani threaded one arm through Syssi's and the other through Amanda's, and the three walked into the vestibule. Behind them, Annani's two Odus followed, each carrying two large pieces of luggage.

That was a worrisome sight.

How long was she planning on staying that she'd brought so much clothing with her?

Kian raked his fingers through his hair and sighed, then joined the procession back to his and Syssi's penthouse.

Okidu had a welcome feast prepared for the immediate family, which besides Kian and Syssi, included Amanda and Dalhu, Andrew and Nathalie and their little daughter.

Thank the merciful Fates for that cute baby.

As soon as Annani saw Phoenix, she squealed with happiness and forgot about everyone and everything.

"Who is this beautiful little girl?" She took her from Andrew's arms.

Phoenix regarded Annani with curious eyes, then reached for her red hair, clutched a handful, and pulled.

Nathalie jumped up to help the goddess, but Annani would have none of that. "I am used to the little ones pulling on my hair. The color fascinates them."

Annani refused to give the baby back, eating dinner with

one hand while holding Phoenix with the other. Andrew and Nathalie looked nervous. As small and as charming as Annani was, she was also intimidating.

But the baby seemed unfazed by the powerful vibe emanating from the woman holding her. Kian regarded it as a good sign. That little girl would grow up into a strong woman who wouldn't be easy to intimidate.

When they were done, Nathalie cleared her throat. "May I ask you a question, Clan Mother?"

"Of course."

"How long does Phoenix need to spend in your presence to turn?"

Annani smiled at the baby and offered her a finger to chew on. "Every child is different. For some, it takes a few days, for others, weeks."

Everyone at the table accepted her statement at face value. Only Kian knew the truth his mother and older sister were hiding. It wasn't the goddess's magnificent presence that turned the little girls, it was her blood. The same blood that had saved Syssi's life during her transition.

With Andrew and Nathalie constantly hovering over their daughter, the trick would be to get the child alone with Annani long enough for her to administer the tiny transfusion.

40

ANANDUR

*A*nandur put the case of Snake's Venom on the conference table and started pulling out the beers he'd chilled overnight in preparation for Uisdean and Niall's welcome party. It wasn't every day that two new Guardians, or rather old ones, came back to fortify the force.

The seven would become nine.

"Are we having a party?" Kian said as he walked in.

"Yes, we are. I'm doing my part in making Uisdean and Niall feel at home."

Kian clapped his back. "Good. Then you won't mind being in charge of their training."

Great. As the saying went, no good deed went unpunished.

"I'm already doing double shift rotations. How am I supposed to find time to train them?"

"Being in charge doesn't mean you need to do everything yourself. It means you test them, determine what they need to work on, and then make a schedule. These two are experienced fighters, they don't need babysitting while running on the treadmill or practicing in the shooting range."

"What about hand to hand?"

Kian lifted a brow. "Do you want to assign that part to someone else?"

"No. I'll do it."

"That's what I thought."

As the champion of that form of fighting, Anandur considered it his duty to refresh these old timers' skills. Besides, they needed a reminder who was boss lest they'd forgotten.

"Good evening, gentlemen." Arwel walked into the conference room carrying four bottles of Chivas, and put them on the table next to the beers.

Kian shook his head. "You really want to get everyone drunk, don't you?"

Arwel grinned. "I'm aiming for joyous. That's not enough booze to get nine Guardians and one Regent drunk."

"Too bad," Kri said as she put a covered tray on the table. "I was hoping everyone would be too drunk to care that I burned the pizza pockets."

It took a special talent to burn ready-made snacks, but then Kri had never pretended to know her way around the kitchen. He'd been hoping Michael would do it, but apparently the kid had been busy.

Anandur lifted the lid and took one out, then popped it into his mouth. It was a little burned and crusty but still edible. "It's good. Don't worry about it."

Looking at the burned pockets with disdain, Kri shook her head. "I hope Niall and Uisdean are as easy to please as you are."

"We've eaten worse." Anandur grimaced.

"When are they going to get here?" Kri asked.

Kian glanced at his watch. "Niall called over an hour ago to let me know they had landed. Luggage, customs, and immigration should take an hour or so, and then they still have to battle the traffic."

Anandur frowned. Kian's time was too valuable to waste waiting for the two Guardians to arrive. "You're early."

"Yeah. A good excuse to leave the other welcoming party."

Aha, Kian was hiding from his mother. "I assume her Highness's visit is to remain confidential?"

"I prefer it this way. Thankfully there are no weddings for her to preside over so I can sleep at night without worrying about too many people knowing she is here. We can't provide adequate protection for her. It maddens me to be in this situation. I wish we had an army of Guardians."

"Who would be scratching their balls with nothing to do."

"True, but how is it different from any army during peacetime? The USA is not sending all of its soldiers into early retirement because there is no war to fight at the moment. They train."

Anandur scratched his beard. "Yeah. It's even true for the Doomers. They maintain a huge force, but they haven't participated actively in any of the recent wars. They send a few units here and there, but most of the force stays home."

"Exactly. But we can't manage to build up a force despite all of our efforts. I had to promise the moon to get two additional Guardians."

"What did you offer them?"

Kian's lips twisted into a grimace. "A huge recruitment bonus and a month's paid vacation a year."

Anandur whistled. "Are the rest of us getting the same deal?"

"Do I have any other choice?"

Kian would have a mutiny on his hands if he didn't treat them all equally. But if each took a month off, they would actually have fewer Guardians on duty at each given time than without the two new ones, and with the two weeks' vacation they were getting currently.

"How does that math work for you?"

"It doesn't. But I hope more Guardians will take the bait."

Kian grabbed a beer, popped the cap, and taking a long swig, he then walked over to his desk and booted up his computer.

Bhathian and Yamanu joined them a few minutes later, the first one with the box of pastries he'd picked up from Jackson, the second with a huge bag of trail mix. Not a bad spread for an impromptu party Anandur had decided on a couple of hours ago.

Onegus arrived last and took a seat across from Kian's desk. "How is our esteemed Clan Mother doing?" he asked.

Kian glanced up. "Harping on at me to take a vacation."

Onegus inclined his head. "Wise as always."

"Oh, yeah? Do you want to take over for me while I'm gone?"

"I can give it a try."

Kian dismissed him with a wave of his hand. "Right."

Anandur walked over, leaned his butt against the desk and crossed his arms over his chest. "I wouldn't mind a short visit to our resort in Hawaii and to say hi to Lana in person. We can depart Thursday morning and return Sunday night. Just a long weekend."

Kian drummed his fingers on the desk. "I like your idea. I can do a tour of the property, and if needed I could commandeer an office and work from there. Annani will be happy I'm vacationing, while I can still put in the work."

Anandur offered a silent prayer of thanks to the Fates. With Kian away from the keep, he wouldn't have to worry about the boss discovering that Brundar was spending his recovery time in his human girlfriend's apartment.

Besides, a trip to Hawaii, even as Kian's bodyguard, was still a trip to Hawaii. He rubbed his hands. "I can't wait. Are we going surfing?"

"You can surf. Syssi and I will watch while sipping tropical drinks on the beach."

"Sounds good."

Kian frowned. "But if I take you with me, who is going to be in charge of Uisdean and Niall's training?"

Onegus lifted a finger. "I'll do it. Until Anandur comes back, that is. The important thing here is to make the Clan Mother happy. Am I right?"

Kian smirked. "Yes, you are. And it's also a perfect opportunity to convince her that I don't need more than one bodyguard. I'll make it a condition for taking the fucking vacation. I can't take two Guardians away from the keep, especially not during her visit."

Onegus grinned. "Every cloud has a silver lining, eh?"

Anandur clapped the chief Guardian's back. "I hope there are no clouds where we're going."

41

CALLIE

Life is good, Callie thought as she cracked another egg into the bowl. With the absence of the constant fear, she finally felt free. Brundar's guy had hacked into the university's computers again and changed her name back to Calypso, and Meyers instead of Davidson.

She'd also applied for a new driver's license under her maiden name.

It bothered her that there was no mention in the news about Shawn's *suicide.* Not only because she couldn't call her father and her best friend to let them know she was no longer in danger, but because it was awful if Shawn's body was still rotting in that house.

"Brundar, can you call Andrew again and ask him if there is any news about Shawn?"

"I don't want to call him at work. I'll do it when I know he is home." He walked over to her and wrapped himself around her back. "What are you making?"

"A mushroom omelet." She looked at him over her shoulder. "Where are your crutches?"

"I don't need them anymore."

Callie put the spatula down and turned around in his arms. "Did you ask Bridget if it's okay?"

"Yes."

"And?"

"She approved."

"That's a cause for celebration." Callie threw her arms around Brundar's neck and kissed him long and hard.

"Your omelet is burning," he said when she let go of his mouth.

"Oh, crap." Callie grabbed the pan by the handle and moved it away from the burner. "I'll make a new one."

Brundar reached behind her and took the pan. "I'll eat it."

"No way. I'm making a new one."

She tried to take it away from him, but he lifted the pan up so she couldn't reach.

"I'll eat this one and the new one you make."

The guy would eat anything. Except for seafood, that was. "Fine."

Brundar took out a plate and dropped the slightly charred omelet onto it, then returned the pan to the stove.

Leaning against the counter, he folded the omelet in half and ate it as if it was a taco.

"You must be hungry."

He finished chewing the last bite and wiped his hands and mouth with a paper towel. "I need to feed this body to heal."

Callie still couldn't wrap her head around his miraculous recovery. She'd searched the Internet for revolutionary knee reconstructive surgery techniques, and had even found a few articles, but none promised new knees in two weeks.

Maybe Bridget had used something experimental that was not approved for publication yet. Whatever it was, a new procedure or marvelous genetics, Callie was grateful for it. Brundar's knees had healed, and he was walking without crutches.

"Let's invite your family over to celebrate. Syssi, Amanda,

Bridget, and Anandur." She cracked several more eggs into the mixing bowl.

Brundar groaned. "Why? I'd rather celebrate just with you."

"I know. But you need to be more social. We are talking close family, not a bunch of strangers."

"I don't know if Syssi would want to come without Kian, but we can't invite him because he doesn't know I'm staying here, and we want to keep it that way. Amanda may want to come with her mate, though."

Again with the mate thing. Must be Scottish slang for significant other. The same as it was slang for friend or buddy for the English and the Australians.

"Then let's invite him too." Callie poured the mixture into the pan.

"On second thought, scratch that. He is not comfortable with new people."

She snorted. "Must be hell for him to live with an extrovert like Amanda. What does he do when she invites people over, hide in the bedroom?"

Brundar shrugged. "I don't know. She never invited me."

Callie felt offended on Brundar's behalf. How come he'd never been invited to his cousin's place?

"Is there a reason for that? Did you have a falling out?" She folded the omelet over the mushroom and onions mixture and transferred it to a plate.

"No. I don't think she invites people over that often. And we are not close."

"Here you go." She handed Brundar the second plate. "Close enough for her to come visit you when you got injured."

Brundar snorted. "That's because she is nosy and wanted to check you out."

Callie poured the rest of the mixture into a pan for another omelet. "I hope I passed."

"With flying colors."

She glanced at him over her shoulder. "How do you know, did she say something to you?"

"No, but the way all four of you were chatting away and then hugging and kissing, it looked like you were old friends."

It was true. Callie wasn't socially awkward and befriended people easily, but not as easily as she had those three. For some reason, she'd felt comfortable with these women almost like she did with Dawn, whom she'd known for years.

"That's another reason to invite them over." She put the omelet on a plate and joined Brundar at the counter.

"I see that I can't talk you out of this."

"Nope."

"It will have to be today, though. Anandur has rotation tomorrow, and the day after that he is off to vacation with Syssi and Kian. Theirs, not his. He is going as the bodyguard."

If Brundar thought to dissuade her from inviting his family for dinner by not giving her enough time to prepare, he had another thing coming. "Make the calls and tell me who is coming and who is not. I can have everything ready by five."

Brundar cocked a brow. "And what about work?"

She leaned and kissed his cheek, then whispered in his ear, "Don't tell anyone, but I'm sleeping with the boss. I can take a day off whenever I want."

That got a chuckle out of him. "What do I tell Franco when he asks why you are not coming in tonight?"

Callie pretended to think it over. "You can tell him that you're giving your girlfriend the night off."

42

BRUNDAR

"It's a shame Syssi and Amanda couldn't come." Calypso cut an avocado in half and scooped the flesh out with a spoon.

"Syssi is packing for their trip to Hawaii, and Amanda didn't want to leave Dalhu alone at home."

Calypso reached for the next avocado. "She could've come with him. Is he as scary as Kian?"

Brundar chuckled. "That depends on what you find scary. Dalhu is even bigger than Anandur, and he lacks my brother's sunny disposition."

Callie started mashing the avocado flesh she'd scooped out with a fork. "Amanda is tall. I figured her guy would be tall too. Is that why she doesn't want him to come? She thinks he'll intimidate me?"

"No."

"Then why?"

"As I told you, Kian doesn't know that I'm not staying at the keep. Amanda and Syssi are okay with keeping my secret. They think of it as a game. The thing is, if Kian finds out, he will have no choice but to forgive them because one is his wife and the other his sister. Dalhu is not in the same position."

"I see. So Amanda prefers not to get him involved."

"That's right."

Crouching down, she disappeared behind the counter to reach into one of the bottom cabinets, then reappeared with a large cutting board in hand. "To tell you the truth, I'm relieved. I didn't have time to prepare anything elaborate, and I would've felt bad about serving fajitas to Syssi and Amanda. Especially Amanda. She seems so fancy. Next time, when I have a few days to plan, I can really wow them with my culinary skills."

There wasn't going to be a next time.

In a few days, he would be back at work and have a talk with the few people who knew about Calypso.

He would keep her for as long as he could, but he knew better than to delude himself that it would last more than a few weeks, or maybe a few months if he were incredibly lucky.

The less talk there was about Calypso, the longer his time with her could be. Amanda and Syssi and Bridget needed to pretend that they had never met her. Perhaps he should thrall her to forget them. Her memory of Anandur coming to their rescue was too traumatic to suppress, but he trusted Anandur to keep his mouth shut and act as if he knew nothing if asked.

Amanda was pretty good at that too. But if confronted, Bridget and Syssi would spill the beans.

"I'll set the table," he offered.

Calypso lifted a brow. "Do you know how?"

"I think I can manage." He might have had zero skill in the kitchen, but he could manage a tablecloth and four place settings.

An hour later, Brundar welcomed their two guests and showed them to the table.

"It smells good," Anandur said, clapping Brundar on the back, then headed to the kitchen to pull Calypso into a brotherly hug, which was how Brundar forced himself to think about it to stop the growl building up in his chest from coming out of his mouth.

"Hello, Brundar." Bridget entered. "Hi, Callie." She waved at Calypso then turned back to him. "I see you're moving around without the crutches. Any pain?"

"Only when I bend my knees."

Bridget nodded. "Let me take a look."

Sitting on the couch, he lifted a leg and propped it on the coffee table. Bridget took hold of his ankle with one hand and put the other one on his thigh, a little above his knee.

"I'm going to bend your leg, and you need to tell me when it starts to hurt." She eyed him with a stern expression on her face. "And don't try to be macho about it and pretend like you don't feel any pain. I need to know exactly when it becomes uncomfortable."

After checking both knees, Bridget lowered his feet to the floor. "You're doing very well. I want you to exercise bending your legs a few times every hour. This will speed up your recovery." She leaned closer and whispered, "If you were a human, I would have said to do it once a day, but at the rate you're healing, it needs to be done every hour."

Brundar cast a sidelong glance at Calypso. Her frown indicated that she'd seen Bridget whisper in his ear, and she didn't like it one bit.

Damnation. Later, she would put him through one hell of an interrogation. In fact, once the dinner was done, she would probably have a long list of things to ask him about. Bridget and Anandur would have to be very careful with what they said around her.

"Just don't say anything you're not supposed to," he whispered to Bridget. "Calypso is very bright. There isn't much that escapes her notice."

Bridget nodded, then crossed her arms over her chest. "I'm your doctor, Brundar," she said loud enough for Calypso to hear. "Whatever you choose to share with others is your prerogative. My job is to keep your health issues confidential." She winked at him.

A good coverup, but he expected many more would be needed before this get-together was over.

"Dinner is served. To the table, everyone," Calypso called out.

Anandur took a seat and rubbed his hands. "I hope you made enough to feed this." He waved over his middle.

"Don't worry. I made enough to satisfy even your and Brundar's appetites."

"Is that a challenge?"

Calypso laughed. "I think Bridget and I should load our plates first. Otherwise you boys are not going to leave us anything to eat."

As dinner progressed, Brundar enjoyed watching Calypso chatting with Anandur and Bridget and laughing at Anandur's jokes. Admittedly, spending time with his family wasn't as bad as he'd expected. His contribution to the conversation was limited to a few nods and grunts, but Calypso was so animated and happy that nothing more was needed to keep the lively atmosphere going.

Unfortunately, as pleasant as this evening was, it would probably be the last. Brundar would eventually have to choose between his family and Calypso.

Coexistence was impossible.

He knew better than most that humans and immortals didn't mix. The two could coexist only if the immortals kept to themselves and didn't befriend humans. Romantic entanglements were not the only kind of human and immortal interactions that were fraught with danger.

Brundar had once thought he could be friends with a

human. The results had been disastrous not only for him but for his clan as well.

Knowing that as soon as the villagers discovered the bodies, they would come after their number one suspect—their strange neighbors—his family had had to pack up and run.

Back then, the clan had been much smaller, poorer, and scattered throughout the countryside. Escaping in the middle of the night, they had left behind everything they had worked so hard for, with only the clothes on their backs and the few provisions they could amass on such short notice.

After that incident, Annani had gathered the clan, announcing that they were all going to live together in one defensible location, far away from the humans.

It had taken them decades of back-breaking work and all of their combined resources to build their Scottish fortress. The Scottish Highlands were freezing cold in the winter, and living in temporary shelters while every able-bodied male and female worked on building the fortress had been miserable.

Even the food had been scarce.

One stupid mistake had cost the clan decades of misery. How they had managed to forget and forgive Brundar was beyond him. Other than Anandur, none of them knew what had been done to him. All Anandur had said was that his little brother had been attacked and Anandur had killed his assailants. The violation Brundar had suffered remained a secret he and Anandur were going to take with them to their eventual graves.

43

CALLIE

"*I* had fun," Callie said after Anandur and Bridget had left.

Brundar nodded.

He hadn't said much throughout dinner, but while he'd looked as if he was enjoying himself at the start of the evening, a gloom had settled over him toward the end.

Maybe he was in pain.

The guy had pushed himself too hard on his first day of walking without crutches. He should've taken it easy as Bridget had told him to.

Typical man. Less than two weeks after having his knees blown to pieces, he couldn't wait to prove that he was back to his old self.

Freaking Doctor Bridget was a miracle worker. Or a witch.

Brundar and his family were all a bit strange, but as far as she could trust her judgment, they were good people. So what if sometimes it had seemed as if there were two separate conversations going on at the table, one of which she hadn't been privy to. All families had secrets, some more than others.

Brundar came up behind her and wrapped his arms around her. "Andrew texted me while we were having dinner, but I didn't want to spoil the mood."

Callie stilled. "Shawn's body has been found?"

"Yes. Apparently, he was found a week ago. But because it was a clear case of suicide, it didn't make it to the news."

"How did Andrew find out?"

"He checked the morgue records."

"I see," she whispered. "I feel sorry for Shawn's family. I don't think they knew he was insane."

"You should call your father."

"Yeah, I should." Shawn's parents had probably contacted Donald looking for her. Hopefully, he hadn't told them anything.

Callie left the dirty dishes in the sink and dried her hands with a paper towel. "I'll finish these later."

"I'll do it. Make the call."

"Thanks."

Callie walked to the bedroom on shaky legs and retrieved her phone from her purse. Sitting on the bed, she wondered what exactly she was supposed to say. With Shawn's suicide not making it into the news, how was she supposed to know that he was dead?

Should she pretend she was calling to let them know she was okay and wait for her dad to break the news to her?

That was probably the only way.

Her dad, who'd always been happy to let Iris get the phone, answered on the first ring as if he was sitting and waiting for her call. "Hello?"

"Hi, Daddy."

He released a breath with an audible whoosh. "Callie, thank God you called. I've been so worried."

"I'm fine. Sorry I didn't call before."

"That's okay. You had a good reason. Did you hear about Shawn?"

Callie hated to lie to her father, but there was no other way. "No, is it anything that I need to worry about?"

"Not anymore. He committed suicide."

"Oh, my God."

"Good riddance, that's what I have to say."

Amen to that. "Did he leave a note?"

"No, but they found the divorce papers on the floor, right under where he hung himself."

Callie sighed. "I feel so sorry for his parents."

"Don't. They had some choice words to say about you."

"I hope you didn't tell them what I've told you."

"I'm not a heartless bastard. They were out of their minds with grief. I wasn't going to tarnish the memory of their son. I just told them the regular crap about fifty percent of marriages ending in divorce. I also said that you were devastated by it, and that was why you left on a long trip to meditate over the breakup, leaving your phone behind."

"Thank you. I appreciate it. I don't think I could've gone to the funeral."

"I understand. So now that the coast is clear, when are we going to see you?"

"I'll come when the baby is born. I just started a new job, and I don't want to ask for time off right away."

"Sweetheart, your baby brother was born three weeks ago."

Callie gasped. It was as if ever since she'd fled Shawn, she'd existed in some parallel universe, imagining that the life she'd left behind remained frozen in the same time frame she'd last remembered.

"Oh, my God! How is he? How is Iris?"

"They are both fine. Justin was born a healthy seven pounds and seven ounces." Her dad sounded proud. And happy.

She hadn't heard that upbeat tone in his voice for as long as she could remember.

"Justin. I like it. I wish I could hop on a plane and come see him right away. You need to warn him that his big sister is coming to kiss him all over."

Her dad chuckled. "Don't do anything rash just because you're excited about the baby, and don't jeopardize your new job to come see him. Right now he doesn't do much besides sleeping, eating, and pooping. Come when the time is right for you."

"I'll see what I can do. I'll talk to my boss."

"Don't if you think it will upset him. Or is it a her? And what kind of job is it?"

"I serve drinks at a nightclub that is owned by two very nice guys." Callie rolled her eyes as she waited for her father to disapprove of her new job.

"Do you like it there? Are the tips good?"

"Excellent. And I like the people I work with. We are like one big happy family."

"I'm glad. What about school?"

"I start in the fall."

"I'm so happy to hear that." Her father sighed. "I feel like the rainbow has finally come out after years upon years of nothing but dark clouds."

Callie felt tears well in the corners of her eyes. "Kiss Iris and Justin for me."

"I will. Take care of yourself."

Ending the call, Callie flopped down on the bed and closed her eyes for a moment, opening them when she heard Brundar enter the room.

"Here, take this," he said, handing her a tall glass.

She sat back up. "What's in it?"

"Your favorite cocktail. I think a toast is in order." He lifted his own glass.

A drink was exactly what she needed. "What are we toasting?"

"New beginnings."

44

BRUNDAR

"To new beginnings." Calypso clinked Brundar's glass and took a long sip. "You made it exactly how I like it. Thank you."

He nodded. "Congratulations on your new brother."

"Thanks. I would've asked you how you knew, but I'm not going to, Mr. Bat Ears."

Her scent was a mixture of happiness and anxiety. The happiness was because of the baby, but why the anxiety?

"How are you feeling, Calypso, everything okay?"

"Happy, relieved, excited about the future but also sad." She touched a hand to her stomach. "I feel uncomfortable here. I know it's because of Shawn and his death and his funeral and his poor parents, and I also know that what happened wasn't my fault, but I still feel guilty. So horribly guilty. If he'd never met me, he wouldn't be dead now."

"True. He would've most likely been tormenting some other woman. Someone who didn't have friends like my brother and me to rescue her. With no one to stop him, he would have had a lot of years to make someone else's life a living hell."

Calypso's hand moved from her stomach to her heart.

"When you put it like that, it almost sounds as if I should feel lucky and not guilty. Maybe I was put in Shawn's path and then yours for a reason. Maybe Fate maneuvered us into place so we could take him out and save his next victim."

The bitter undertone had dissipated from her scent, leaving behind only the familiar scents of sweetness and sunshine that Brundar associated with Calypso.

"Feeling better?" he asked even though he knew the answer.

"Much. What about you? You seemed a little down toward the end of dinner. Are you in pain? Are your knees bothering you?"

Brundar took the glass from her hand and put it on the nightstand. "Let's celebrate life the way it should be celebrated." Pushing her back on the bed, he pulled down her sexy black dress. Underneath, Calypso had her beautiful breasts bound in that torture device he'd told her not to wear.

"Tsk, tsk. You disobeyed me." He reached around her back and unclasped the bra. "I told you I never want to see you wearing this painful contraption again." He tossed it behind him.

Calypso's scent became musky with her nascent arousal. "I couldn't entertain your brother and Bridget braless, and this is the only strapless one I have. Nothing else works with this dress."

"Then it's time you went shopping, sweetling."

"Yes, sir." She saluted.

He gently massaged the bra's angry red compression lines. "Marring your perfect skin like this is a punishable offense."

Calypso's arousal intensified. "Are you going to spank me?" She sounded breathy and excited.

"I could take you over my knee at last. But I have other ideas." He glanced at the melting ice cubes in the glass on the nightstand. But first things first, he needed to blindfold her before his own arousal pushed his alienness to the surface.

In one swift move, he divested her of her panties and lifted Calypso up to reposition her in the center of the bed.

"You shouldn't lift heavy things. It's too much strain on your knees."

"I didn't lift anything heavy." He pulled the silk scarf from the drawer.

Calypso lifted her head without him having to ask her to, holding it up until he was done tying the blindfold over her eyes.

"I love it and hate it at the same time." She dropped her head on the pillow. "I love how every sensation is amplified by the lack of sight, but I hate not seeing you. I've never seen you truly aroused."

"It's not a pretty sight. I drool," he said to make her laugh, which was so unlike him. Brundar didn't know what had possessed him to do it.

But it worked. Calypso giggled. "No way. I know you don't."

He pulled out the stockings and tied them to the four corners of the bed. "I do. I can't help it. You're so drool-worthy. Whenever I see you naked, my tongue lolls out like a dog's. A visual not at all conducive to your arousal." He secured her left wrist with the stocking, then moved to the right.

She cooperated beautifully, stretching her arms and legs, spread-eagled for him. "Do you really? Because I can't hear you panting."

Brundar leaned over her and kissed her lips. "You're going to hear me panting very soon." He nipped those perfect puffy pillows. "When I'm buried deep inside you."

Calypso was stunning all over, but her lips were his favorite. No, that wasn't true, her green eyes were, especially when they were smiling. But the lips were a very close second.

Her perky nipples were third.

Dipping his head, he took one into his mouth, sucking it in and licking round and round, then repeated the same on her other side while reaching for the ice cubes.

He pulled one out and touched it to the nipple he'd just finished warming up with his mouth.

Calypso hissed and arched her back. "That's cold. You're mean."

He moved the ice cube to her other breast and took the chilled nipple into his mouth. Going back and forth, Brundar fell into a predictable rhythm, letting Calypso learn the sequence and relax into the contrasting sensations.

When the ice cube melted, he pulled another one out of the glass and slowly trailed it down her belly until he reached the juncture of her thighs. Calypso hissed again, but then sighed with pleasure as his tongue replaced the ice.

"Oh, that's much better."

He replaced his hot tongue with the cold ice, then his tongue again, lapping up the melted water together with her juices, then chilling her again until the ice cube was no more.

Calypso might have hissed and whined, but the powerful scent of her arousal betrayed the pleasure she derived from the torment.

"You like this, sweetling, don't you?" He pushed a finger into her wet heat.

She shook her head, then quickly nodded when he removed his finger. "Don't stop, please."

He chuckled, returning with two and curling them up to touch that sensitive spot that had her arching off the bed as far as her restraints allowed her.

"Beautiful," he whispered as he took his clothes off. "I can never get enough of looking at you." He covered her with his body, his heavy length wedged between her thighs.

Calypso panted, her hips swiveling under him, urging him on. "Don't tease me, Brundar. I need you inside me."

Turned on by her frantic gyrations, he cupped her cheeks and kissed her long and deep. "Poor, baby, I think I've teased you enough." He surged into her.

"Yes." She threw her head back, her arms straining against her bonds which aroused her and frustrated her at the same time.

Brundar knew Calypso wanted to touch him, and the truth was that he wanted that too. He craved her arms around him, her fingers digging into his back and holding him tight, and her nails leaving small moon-shaped gouges on his skin.

It was too late to do anything about it now. Sheathed inside her wet heat, he could do nothing other than move, faster, harder, until he was pounding into her without holding back, mindlessly driven by a primitive urge to claim, to possess, to plant his seed inside her.

As Calypso shouted her climax, Brundar kept going, wringing another one from her. When his own erupted, his guttural groan sounding more animal than human, he clamped his fangs on her neck and bit down.

Calypso climaxed again.

45

TESSA

"*L*adies, can I have your attention please." Karen clapped her hands. "Please form a circle around me."

She waited until everyone was in position. "Today, you are going to practice on each other. I'm going to pair you up according to skill, not size. Because what is my motto?" She put a cupped hand to her ear.

"Size doesn't matter!" they all responded—some mumbling in obvious disagreement, and some, like Tessa, shouting it out with conviction.

"That's right," Karen said. "Skill compensates for size." She smirked. "And not only in a fight, eh?"

Again, the responses were mixed.

Karen waved a hand. "Those who disagree haven't experienced real skill yet. When you do, you'll come back here and tell me, Karen, you were right."

Tessa hid her smile. Being small had caused many of her insecurities, but thanks to Jackson and Karen she'd gotten over them. Karen had taught her that she could be a good fighter despite her size, and Jackson found her sexy and desirable even though she was small all over.

And as to what Karen had hinted at not too subtly,

Jackson was the whole package. He was both big and skilled. The perfect lover. They had made love three times in the cabin, and two times last night, and each time she'd climaxed, sometimes more than once.

Five sessions of lovemaking, seven or eight orgasms, but only two bites.

Apparently, once a day was the limit on venom bites as far as Jackson was concerned. Though she couldn't understand why. He didn't need to thrall her after biting her, and she wasn't aware that the venom on its own could cause any damage.

It was supposed to be a miraculous elixir, delivering fast healing, euphoria, and a string of orgasms.

She'd wanted to ask Jackson if it was a physical limitation but then decided not to. After the wonderful weekend he'd treated her to, the last thing she wanted was to accidentally hurt his feelings.

Still, she couldn't help wondering if more venom bites would have resulted in a faster transition. Two were probably not enough to trigger it, so there was no reason to worry yet, but Tessa couldn't help but feel the tension mounting.

It's only Tuesday, she reminded herself. *Give it at least a week.*

"Tessa, you are with Megan." Karen pulled on both Tessa's and Megan's hands, leading them to where the other pairs were waiting.

When everyone had a partner, Karen waved her hands wide. "Okay, girls, let's spread out. Let's start with the mugger move."

After half an hour, Tessa was sweating buckets, but Megan was in no better shape. In fact, she was panting so hard Tessa was afraid the woman might pass out.

"Let's take a break. I need a drink of water," she said, more for Megan's benefit than her own.

Megan glanced at Karen for approval. The instructor nodded and clapped her hands. "Good work, ladies. Take a five-minute break to hydrate."

The class was divided into two camps. One comprised of those who were serious about self-defense, women who had worked their asses off for the past thirty minutes and looked no better than Tessa and Megan. The other camp, the one Sharon belonged to, joined the class to get in shape or just to hang out with friends, and had barely broken a sweat.

Megan filled two paper cups with water from the cooler and handed one to Tessa. "I thought it would be easy to go up against you. But you're proof that Karen is right and skill trumps size." The woman was in her mid-thirties, heavier than Tessa by at least twenty pounds and half a head taller.

But then Tessa had youth and energy on her side.

Not that she felt very energetic at the moment. Her head was spinning, and she was a little nauseous. Blaming dehydration, Tessa gulped down the water, then refilled the cup and downed it too.

It didn't help. "I need to sit down for a moment." She barely made it to the chairs lined up against one side of the room.

Karen rushed to her. "Feeling dizzy?"

"Yes."

"Put your head down." She pressed on Tessa's back until her head was between her spread knees. "Breathe in, and out, slowly, don't force it. In and out."

Sharon crouched in front of her. "Do you want another cup of water? Do you have a headache? Because I have some Motrin in my purse."

Tessa shook her head, which worsened the dizziness. "I'm fine. Just give me a moment to catch my breath."

"Does she look pale, or am I imagining it?" Sharon asked Karen.

"Don't fuss so much. The girl pushed herself too hard,

that's all." The instructor turned her back to Tessa, blocking her from the others' view. "Back to work, ladies. Megan, you're with me."

Thank God for Karen's no-nonsense attitude. A few moments without anyone hovering over her would be golden.

Trying to contain the nausea, Tessa closed her eyes and continued the careful breathing. For a few minutes, it seemed like it was helping, but then a violent twist in her stomach stole her breath and pushed everything out in a geyser of mostly water.

A moment later she blacked out.

"Oh, my God. I'm calling an ambulance." Tessa heard Sharon as if she was talking through a tunnel.

"Calm yourself down, Sharon. It's just puke. My commandos puked all the time after I made them run on the sand for hours. The poor guys couldn't keep up with me, but they sure as hell tried. That's how endurance is built."

As consciousness returned, Tessa found herself lying on the floor with a towel folded under her head. Someone must have cleaned up the vomit, but the smell lingered, bringing the nausea back.

Tessa's stomach contracted again, and she lifted her torso, turning her head sideways, ready to hurl on the floor, when Karen stuck a wad of paper towels under her.

"Just let it all out, girl." Karen held her head up and pushed her hair out of the way. "You'll feel better."

A little stinky liquid was all that she managed to purge.

"Is she pregnant?" Tessa heard one of the women ask.

She couldn't be. Even if she were, she wouldn't be puking a day or two after conceiving. It was either a virus or something she ate.

"I'm calling Eva," Sharon said.

Tessa was too weak to protest. Besides, it might be a good

idea for Bhathian to come pick her up. At the moment, walking to the car seemed like mission impossible.

Someone came with a wet towel and gently wiped her face.

"Thank you," she managed feebly, struggling to stay awake.

One by one the women left, with only Karen and Sharon remaining by her side.

"Eva and Bhathian are coming to take you to a doctor," Sharon said.

Tessa knew better than to shake her head. Instead, she lifted her hand. "I want to go home. It's just a stomach flu."

"The doctor will decide that."

"I stink."

"I'm sure you won't be the first stinky patient or the last one the doctor sees."

Ugh, she was too weak to argue, and the temptation to close her eyes and drift away was too powerful to ignore.

She must've dozed off, or maybe she'd blacked out again, because the next time Tessa opened her eyes, she was being carried by a pair of powerful arms. "Bhathian?"

"I'm here, and so is Eva."

"You're going to be fine, sweetheart." Eva took her hand.

"I want to go home," she said as Bhathian laid her down on the back seat of his car.

Eva slid in and lifted Tessa's head to rest on her lap. "We are taking you to see Bridget."

"Why? It's just flu."

"It might be, but I want Bridget to take a look at you. Bhathian called Jackson, and he is going to meet us at the clinic."

"Do you think it can be the transition?"

"I don't know, sweetheart. That's up to Bridget to decide. Now enough talking. Rest."

If she weren't feeling so shitty, Tessa would've smiled.

Even at twenty-one she still liked it when Eva treated her like a child.

Being cared for was precious, reassuring. It proved that Tessa wasn't alone, and if Eva had a say in it, she never would be.

JACKSON

"*I*'m leaving." Jackson threw his apron on the counter. "Close up for me."

Vlad cast him a worried glance. "What happened?"

"Tessa is not feeling well. Eva and Bhathian are taking her to Bridget."

Vlad's pale face turned even paler. "Is it, you know, the transition?"

"I don't know." Jackson grabbed his keys and opened the back door. "You'll have to deal with whatever happens in here. I'm not leaving Tessa's side even if the place is on fire. Not until she is well again, that is."

"Don't worry about a thing. Gordon and I will manage. Let us know how Tessa is doing."

Jackson nodded. "Thanks."

It was probably flu. Vomiting wasn't one of the typical symptoms of transition. Bridget had told him about fever and chills, and about passing out, but nothing about an upset stomach and puking.

He stopped at Eva's house to collect the overnight bag Sharon had packed for Tessa, deflected questions about where Bhathian and Eva had taken her, and rushed back to his car.

Twenty minutes later he knocked on the clinic's door and walked in.

"Hi, Jackson. She is over there." Bridget pointed.

"How is she?"

"Waiting for you impatiently. I told her that she can't take a shower without assistance, and she doesn't want anyone's help but yours."

"I meant healthwise."

Bridget shrugged. "I don't think it's anything serious. She has no fever and her blood pressure is stable."

Jackson let out a relieved breath. "So it's not the transition."

"I didn't say that. It might be."

"But you said it usually comes with a fever."

"We have a very small group of transitioned Dormants, and each case was different."

Great. If the clan's doctor didn't have answers, who did?

"I'll go check on Tessa."

The door to her room was ajar, and he knocked on it while pushing it open.

Tessa's eyes brightened. "Jackson, you're here. Did you bring me a change of clothes?"

"Hello, Jackson." Eva got up from the chair she'd been sitting on and gave him a quick hug.

"Hi." He barely spared Eva a half smile.

His entire focus was on Tessa. She looked pale, and the dark circles under her eyes were more pronounced than usual, but she was sitting in bed and smiling at him.

"And here I thought you were happy to see me." He walked over and leaned to kiss her.

She stopped him with a hand to his chest. "I stink of puke. Help me into the shower, will you?"

"Of course." He dropped the overnight bag on the floor.

"I'll leave you two alone and go find Bhathian." Eva made a hasty exit.

Tessa swung her legs over the side of the bed, but Jackson had no intention of letting her walk to the bathroom and scooped her into his arms.

She looked away. "Close your nose. I don't want you to smell me."

"Don't be silly. It's not like I never puked myself. Did I tell you about how Vlad and Gordon and I got drunk at Syssi and Kian's wedding?" He marched into the utilitarian bathroom adjacent to the room and lowered Tessa to the stool inside the open shower.

"I remember you telling me something about it."

Jackson pulled Tessa's exercise shirt over her head. "We stole several bottles of whiskey and hid in one of the underground classrooms." He crouched in front of her and pulled her leggings down. "We missed the whole party while getting shit-faced in there."

Tessa unclasped her bra and threw it on the floor outside the shower.

Jackson helped her get her panties off. "We thought we were so tough and grown up, forcing that vile stuff down our throats to prove we were so cool."

"You don't like whiskey?" she asked.

"I hate it." Jackson kicked off his shoes and removed his socks, then grabbed the handheld and turned the water on.

"You are going to get wet. Take off your clothes."

Good point. "Here, hold this." He handed her the shower head, got rid of his clothes, and got back into the shower with her.

"Damn, I forgot to bring the bag in here. Sharon packed your shampoo and conditioner. I'll be right back." He grabbed a towel, wrapped it around his hips and ducked back into the room.

"That's a good look for you." Bhathian chuckled. "You rock the Egyptian."

Jackson pointed a finger at him. "You didn't see a thing."

"Right. How is Tessa?"

"She seems fine. Just weak."

"Take care of her."

"I'll do my best." Jackson lifted the overnight bag and returned to the bathroom.

Tessa was holding the handheld over her head, letting the water drench her chin-length hair.

Rummaging through the bag, he pulled out her shampoo and conditioner.

"Are you going to wash my hair?"

"Do you want me to?"

She nodded.

Jackson wondered why he'd never thought of doing so before. Taking care of Tessa filled him with a sense of satisfaction, of purpose, he was meant to do that.

Squirting a dollop into his hand, he stood behind her and gently massaged the shampoo into her hair.

Tessa leaned back against him and sighed. "This feels heavenly."

"Tilt your head back, kitten." He took hold of the handheld and rinsed the shampoo out of her hair, then repeated the process before applying conditioner.

Her eyes closed, Tessa sat limply on the stool, letting him soap her and rinse her. By the time he was done, she was almost asleep.

"Hang in there for a few moments longer." Jackson was thankful for his long arms allowing him to reach for the towel without moving away from Tessa. He had a feeling she would fall over the moment he let go.

With the big towel wrapped around her, he lifted her up and carried her to the bed. While they had been in the bathroom, someone had replaced the sheets with fresh ones. He laid Tessa on top of them, then went back for another towel and her overnight bag.

Jackson found a long sleep shirt in the bag and pulled it over Tessa's head, then fitted her limp arms through the sleeves. By the time he tucked the blanket around her, she was fast asleep.

With only his pants back on, he sat on the chair Eva had vacated and watched Tessa sleep. She was so small, so fragile. She seemed bigger when awake. But that was okay. He was there to guard and protect his treasure—small but priceless.

KIAN

"I will have another cup of coffee, Okidu," Annani said.

"Of course, Clan Mother." He bowed, then lifted the thermal carafe to refill her cup.

Kian cut another piece of waffle, piled it with strawberries, and popped it in his mouth. He hadn't seen his mother the entire day yesterday, working in his basement office until late at night.

He was trying to spend as little time around her as possible, but that hadn't been the reason for his late-night session in the basement. With the noise levels in his penthouse, working from his home office had been impossible.

Since Annani's visit was kept on a need to know basis, Nathalie had to bring Phoenix to her instead of the goddess going over to Andrew's apartment. Only the penthouse level was fully restricted to its occupants. Even the Guardian floor wasn't forbidden to other clan members. Which meant that his home had been invaded by a baby and her array of baby toys. The question was whether Annani had managed to get Phoenix alone for long enough to administer the transfusion.

The goddess wasn't going home until that mission was accomplished.

Later, when he'd been sure the coast was clear and was about to head home, Kian had gotten a call from Bhathian about Tessa and had gone to pay her a visit. The girl had been asleep, but Jackson had looked so distraught that Kian had stayed with him for an hour or so.

By the time he'd gotten back home, Annani had retired to the guest room.

"How did it go yesterday? Did you have fun with the baby?" he asked.

Annani smiled, her intense eyes growing soft. "She is such a sweet little darling. I got to hold her and play with her for hours. Poor Nathalie hovered like a mother hen, worried I would somehow hurt her daughter as if I had not handled countless generations of babies before her."

Translation, Nathalie hadn't left the baby alone with Annani for a moment. "It will pass. She'll see that you're capable and that Phoenix is happy in your arms." He turned to Syssi. "Maybe you could suggest an adults-only outing to Nathalie."

Syssi put her coffee cup down. "I don't think Nathalie will agree to leave Phoenix with Annani. Not yet." She glanced at the frowning goddess. "It's not that she doesn't trust you. Phoenix doesn't know you well, and she might get scared if her mother leaves her with you. You're still a stranger to her."

"Maybe in a day or two?" Kian pushed.

Syssi threw him a puzzled look. "Why is it important?"

"For the child to bond with me, I need some alone time with her," Annani said.

It had sounded so well rehearsed, that it was probably what she said to all the new mothers.

"I'll test the waters later today. Maybe I'll suggest visiting Amanda. Nathalie won't mind if it's only a short visit across the vestibule."

"It is a splendid idea," Annani agreed.

Nathalie's reluctance to leave the baby with Annani could be the excuse he needed to cancel the vacation his mother was forcing him to take. "I think Syssi and I need to stay. Nathalie will not feel comfortable alone with you."

Unfortunately, Annani was too smart and too stubborn to fall for that. "Nonsense. She will get used to me, and if need be, I will summon Amanda."

It was a long shot, but Kian had another ace up his sleeve. "I can't leave anyway. Tessa, a young woman we believe is a Dormant, is down at Bridget's clinic, and we don't know if she is transitioning or just sick. I have to stay until we know she is okay. The vacation will have to be postponed."

Annani pinned him with a hard stare. "There is nothing you can do for the girl, Kian. You are not a doctor, and Bridget does not need your assistance taking care of her, so it does not matter if you are here or on vacation when you receive updates about her condition."

Fuck. His mother was the most stubborn, difficult woman on the face of the earth. Hell, probably in the entire known universe.

He crossed his arms over his chest. "I'll be too worried to enjoy my vacation."

Annani looked down her nose at him. "You have nothing to worry about while I am here. I will give the girl my blessing to ensure her safe transition."

Checkmate. Kian had lost, but he was going to try one last thing. Annani didn't like leaving her sanctuary for too long. "Will you stay until we are back?"

She nodded. "Yes. How long are you going to be gone?"

"We are coming back Sunday night," Syssi said.

Annani's lips compressed into a thin line. "I thought I told you the vacation should be a week long at the minimum."

"You did. And I said I can't be gone for so long. This is a

compromise." Annani was big on compromising. She would have a hard time arguing that.

For a moment, she just glared at him, then a beautiful smile bloomed on her face, scaring him way more than her glare. "That means you will have to take another vacation soon."

As long as it wasn't now, he was good. "We will discuss it when the time comes."

"You can be sure of that, my son." She took one last sip of her coffee and put her cup down. "I am going out on the terrace to soak up some sun. Call me when Nathalie gets here."

Kian pushed to his feet in deference to his mother and remained standing until her Odu closed the door behind her.

Syssi poured herself another cup from the carafe. "Why are you fighting this vacation so hard? It's only a few days, and we are going to have fun. Hawaii, sandy beaches, me in a bikini..." She waggled her brows.

Kian growled. "Only on our private beach, unless you want to leave a trail of mutilated males in your wake."

Her eyes widened. "We have a private beach?"

"We are not staying at the hotel. I purchased a house with a stretch of beach inaccessible from either side. So yeah, it's private."

"I can't believe it. Did you buy it just for our vacation?"

"No. I got it even before we bought the property for the hotel."

She let out a breath. "Good, because talk about extravagant gestures. Are we taking anyone other than Anandur with us?"

"The pilot, but he is going to stay at the hotel."

"Is the house big?"

"Pretty big. Why?"

She shrugged. "To tell you the truth, I was looking

forward to staying at the hotel and getting some human interaction."

Kian raked his fingers through his hair. "I don't like being surrounded by humans. We can go out to restaurants and visit the sights and do all the tourist things people do when they vacation in Hawaii. But I need a place where I can relax and be myself."

Syssi got up and sat on his lap. "Be honest." She smirked. "You don't want to stay in the hotel because you don't want the other guests to hear my moans of ecstasy."

He cupped her head, holding her still as he took her lips. As always, she melted into him, her hands going under his shirt to caress his skin.

"You got me," Kian said when he let her come up for air. "I also don't want anyone calling security because of the ruckus we are making."

The scent of her arousal flaring, she wiggled in his lap. "We are going to have so much fun."

Looking into his wife's beautiful eyes, Kian smiled. Why the hell had he been fighting the idea of a vacation for so long? Four days of just him and Syssi, relaxing, having fun, sounded like paradise.

"I've been a fool for objecting. I can't wait to have you all to myself for four days straight."

"Are we being selfish?" Syssi wrapped her arms around his neck. "Leaving Tessa to her fate and Nathalie to deal with your mother?"

"Yes, we are. But so what? Annani is right. Us staying here will not affect the outcome either way, and tomorrow it will be another thing, then another. It never ends."

"True. We have to make us a priority."

"My woman is smart and beautiful. How the hell did I get so lucky?"

LOSHAM

"This was the last one," the doctor said.

Losham pulled out the wad of cash in the amount they had agreed on. "Thank you, Doctor. It was a pleasure doing business with you." He offered the human his hand.

The man shook it. "The pleasure was all mine." He stuffed the four thousand dollars inside his leather briefcase.

"My assistant will take you back."

"Yes, thank you."

The guy followed Rami out.

Implanting his men with trackers was one of Losham's better ideas. In fact, he should recommend that all Doomers be implanted with them. No more defections, and no more loss of men in mysterious circumstances.

In addition to the human, two out of his twelve men were missing.

The human was dead. An obituary had been posted in one of the newspapers. The cause of death hadn't been mentioned, and it didn't matter enough to merit further investigation. The only thing that bothered Losham was the money he'd lost.

His two missing men, however, could have either defected or been captured by Guardians—either imprisoned or dead.

Not knowing what had befallen them was eating at him. Losham almost hoped they had been captured. There was no shame in that. But defecting? That was shameful, more for him than his men because it implied lack of leadership.

Regardless of what had happened to the missing men, his official story would be that they'd been taken out by Guardians.

He could get away with losing two, but no more. That was why he had halted the operation. Now with the implants, he could resume the murders. If another man went missing, he would track the son-of-a-bitch, and if the man had indeed defected, Losham would make an example out of him in the most gruesome way.

Not that any of the men would be stupid enough to try to run now.

Not with the implants in their backs.

His ten remaining warriors were recuperating in the back of the warehouse. It shouldn't take more than a couple of hours for the muscles to close over the trackers and the skin to knot itself back to its pre-operation pristine condition.

While waiting, Losham sat down with his laptop and began a new search for rumors and theories about the murders. Most speculated that it was a madman who believed himself a vampire. Not bad as far as alerting the clan, but not great. He needed two murders to occur at the same time in two separate locations for the authorities and the clan to realize it wasn't the work of a single man. Perhaps he should send half of his remaining crew to San Francisco. Two simultaneous murders, one in Los Angeles, the other in San Francisco, would put an end to the lone madman theory.

The thing was, could he trust them to operate independently?

"Sir?" Gommed knocked on the door to the warehouse's dusty office.

"Come in."

"We have a problem, sir."

"Yes?"

The man turned his bare back to Losham. "Our bodies are rejecting the trackers."

The device projecting from the guy's back was almost completely out.

Losham rose to his feet, gripped the protruding tracker with his fingers, and yanked it the rest of the way out.

Blood trickled down Gommed's back, but the warrior didn't move or utter a sound.

"That's what is happening with the others as well?"

"Yes, sir."

It wasn't as if Losham hadn't considered the possibility. After all, immortal bodies pushed out bullets and blades as they healed. But the dealer who'd sold him the trackers had sworn that they were made from a special material the body didn't recognize as foreign and therefore didn't reject.

Losham should have known not to trust the human. Or maybe it was true for human bodies but not immortal.

He hated having wasted more money for nothing.

Between the cost of the trackers and what he'd paid the doctor, Losham was out another ten thousand dollars or so.

"What's going on?" Rami asked as he walked in.

"Their bodies are rejecting the trackers."

"What are we going to do, sir?"

Indeed.

"Did you thrall the doctor?" he asked Rami.

"Of course. But just to be on the safe side, tomorrow I'll go to his office and do it again."

"If he retains any of the memories, get rid of him."

"Yes, sir."

As the two left him alone in the warehouse's office,

Losham sat behind the desk and began working on a new plan.

Failure wasn't the end of the story. It was the beginning of a new one. Successful people failed as many times if not more than those who didn't achieve much. The difference was that they didn't let failure bring them down. They got up and started anew—again, and again, and again.

49

CALLIE

*B*rundar leaned against the kitchen counter. "I'm going to work today."

"Why? Aren't you on leave until Monday?" Callie cracked two eggs into the mixing bowl.

"I need to go over the schedule and get updates."

She had no doubt it could have waited for Monday, but it was obvious that being cooped up at home was making Brundar antsy. His work at the club didn't provide him with a sense of purpose like his day job did.

Brundar was a defender, and he prided himself on keeping his people safe.

Besides, ever since he'd gotten injured, he seemed to have lost interest in the club scene and was spending barely any time in the basement. Instead, he occupied himself with drawing plans for the expansion that he and Franco had planned, and crunching the numbers.

Callie wasn't sure what had caused his change of heart. Was it the injury? Or was it her?

Apparently, Brundar was a one-woman man, and once he'd committed to her, in his noncommittal way, he'd lost interest in the activities of the club's lower level.

A pity.

She was glad he didn't want to play with anyone else, but that didn't mean he had to give up the entire thing.

Callie was still curious as hell, but without Brundar to watch over her, there was no chance he and Franco would allow her to attend any of the demonstrations or classes.

But that was a worry for another day.

Her only worry for now was the state of her wardrobe. It was good to have such mundane, everyday problems. No more psychotic husband to fear, no more hiding, no more fake identity.

She felt years younger—carefree for the first time in forever.

"I need to go shopping," Callie said while folding the omelet over a spinach and mushroom sauté.

"Perfect. You can do it while I'm at the office." Brundar took the plate she handed him.

She started on the second omelet. "I'm not talking about a quick run to the supermarket. I need to go clothes and shoe shopping."

Brundar poured them both coffee and put the mugs on the counter. "How long do you think it will take?"

"At least a couple of hours."

"That's how long I need too. Do you want to meet for lunch?"

The offer was as wonderful as it was unexpected. So unlike Brundar, who still struggled with the very basics of couple interactions. Except for sex, of course; that part he'd mastered. Hell, he was so good he could teach it.

But wait, he already did.

"I would love to." She slid the other omelet onto a plate and took it to the counter. "I'll text you when I'm done with shopping. Any place in particular you have in mind?"

He shrugged. "No. You choose."

"Does it have to be someplace fancy?" Other than steak-houses, she wasn't familiar with high-end restaurants.

"Whatever you choose is fine with me. Hamburgers and fries will do."

They had only been out once to that Italian restaurant Brundar had taken her to. Their one and only date. The other time, when Brundar had brought her a gourmet meal from his cousin's place, didn't count because they'd eaten at home. Besides, it had been a reconciliation gesture, not a romantic one.

Today, they were going to have their second actual date, and she didn't want to waste it on hamburgers and fries even though she loved them.

"I'll think of something."

After spending every hour of the day for the past ten days with him, it was weird to kiss Brundar and watch him leave.

Alone in the apartment, Callie realized that the strange sensation in her gut was separation anxiety, which was ridiculous. In ten days she'd gotten addicted to Brundar's presence and dreaded being away from him.

This wasn't healthy.

Callie shook her head. It was probably the result of the trauma. She and Brundar were like survivors of a catastrophe, clinging to each other for dear life. Once things went back to normal, that feeling should pass.

Hopefully.

Because if it didn't, she would need to see a shrink about it. A grown woman shouldn't feel anxious when separated from her partner for a few hours.

Shopping should take her mind off Brundar.

Callie needed a nice new dress, a pair of high-heeled shoes, and a new strapless bra that didn't dig into her skin— if such a thing existed.

At the mall, Callie found the dress first. Another black one, but with wide shoulder straps to cover a regular bra. It was simple, with a square neckline that didn't reveal too much, and not too short, just a couple of inches above the knees.

"May I suggest the jacket that goes with it?" the salesgirl asked.

"Is it also on sale?"

"Everything in the store is thirty percent off until the end of the weekend."

"Then let's see that jacket."

Nice, Callie thought as she looked herself over in the mirror. Waist length, with three-quarter sleeves, the jacket made the outfit look like something from a sixties fashion magazine—a Jackie look. The outfit was very elegant. Perhaps she could wear it to her lunch date with Brundar.

"Do you have shoes that go with this?" she asked the girl. After all, she couldn't wear an outfit like that with socks and sneakers. That look might work in New York but not in Los Angeles.

"What's your size?"

"Seven."

"I'll be right back."

The girl brought back a pair of black, three-inch-heel pumps. Perfect. Not too extreme to finish her shopping, and not too plain for the dress. The best part was that all three items ended up costing her less than a hundred dollars, which left enough of her budget for another bra on top of the strapless, maybe a sexy number with matching panties.

It would be fun to have something beautiful to surprise Brundar with. Most of Callie's underwear was made from cotton and came in packs of six. Not that she thought Brundar cared one way or another, but she wanted it for the way it would make her feel. A femme fatale.

Unfortunately, her favorite lingerie store was closed for remodeling, which left her with two options—try to find what she needed in one of the department stores, or drive over to another mall.

Difficult decision.

The thing was, a beautiful set in black satin and lace had caught her eye in one of the advertisements the store was running, and now that she'd decided to splurge on it, Callie didn't want to compromise on something else. Heck, the next mall was only twenty minutes away, and besides, she had plenty of time before lunch, even if she made it an early one.

On the way back to the parking lot, Callie's new outfit earned her a few appreciative glances, and one guy even went as far as whistling. Rude, but at the same time flattering.

Working as a drink server in a nightclub, she couldn't consider every inappropriate glance and remark a harassment, even if she was inclined to. But she wasn't. Flirting was okay unless the guy crossed the line, becoming offensive or persisting without any encouragement on her part.

It happened sometimes, but she had no problem dealing with the offender herself. A stern look or a snide remark was usually enough.

Callie dropped the bag with her old clothes and her purse on the floor of the passenger seat, turned the engine on, and backed out from her parking spot. She turned left at the first light.

Idling at the next intersection, Callie closed her eyes for what seemed like a couple of seconds when someone behind her honked the horn.

"What's your problem, asshat?"

The light must've turned green right at that moment, and the driver was very impatient.

"People."

She continued down the boulevard, deciding to use surface streets instead of going on the freeway.

When someone honked at the next red light, Callie began to worry. Why was she closing her eyes at all? She wasn't tired.

Furthermore, the honking implied that she was closing them for longer than she thought she was.

Should she pull over?

Nah, she needed to find a Starbucks and get a double-shot cappuccino. That would wake her up.

A few blocks later it happened again.

This time, though, Callie wasn't idling at a red light, she was driving, and it wasn't a honk that woke her up, but the sound of screeching tires.

She had a split second to panic before the impact, and then everything turned black.

50

BRUNDAR

"Stop looking at your watch every goddamned minute." Anandur rolled his eyes.

They had finished the Guardian meeting with Kian an hour ago, going over everything he wanted them to do and not do in his absence. The guy was going away for a long weekend but was preparing as if he was leaving for at least a year.

"And stop looking at your phone too. Your fidgeting is making me nervous."

Brundar couldn't help it. Calypso had planned to leave the apartment shortly after he had, which was a little after ten in the morning. She'd said that shopping would take her no more than two hours, but it was already after one in the afternoon, and she hadn't texted him yet.

"I should call her." He selected her contact.

Anandur stayed his hand. "Don't. You told me that this is the first time since the incident that she is taking some time to herself. Let the girl shop in peace."

"I worry about her."

"That's exactly why you shouldn't call her. You'll make her feel guilty and cut her fun time short."

Maybe, but if Brundar didn't hear from her in the next fifteen minutes, he was going to lose his shit.

Something was wrong, he could feel it in his gut. "I'm calling her."

"What if she's driving? Does she have Bluetooth in her car?"

"No. It's an older model."

"Then she would have to reach into her purse to find the damn thing, and that's not safe."

Brundar put the phone back, pulled one of his knives from its holster, and started twirling it between his fingers.

"I hate it when you do that. I know how sharp you keep them."

"I've never nicked myself before." Brundar twirled faster, the knife turning into a blur as he tried to quiet the unease churning in his gut by keeping his focus on the sharp blade.

"You should've put a tracker on her car. Then you would have had peace of mind."

Yeah, he should have, but it hadn't crossed his mind. "I'm calling her."

Anandur shrugged. "You do what you have to do. But don't say I didn't warn you."

The phone rang and rang and rang, finally going to voicemail. Brundar dialed again with the same results.

"She is not answering."

"It's noisy in the mall. She probably can't hear the ring."

Brundar typed a quick message. *Call me as soon as you can.*

Pacing the corridor in front of Kian's office, Brundar waited for Calypso's response.

Ten minutes later he was done waiting. "Fuck it. I'm going to look for her."

"Where? It's a big city."

Brundar called Calypso's number again, but again it went to voicemail. "What else can I do?"

"Do you know her license plate number?"

"No. How the hell should I?"

Anandur scratched his beard. "Maybe Roni can get it from the security camera footage in her apartment building. Does the building have one in the parking garage?"

"It does." Brundar started walking toward the elevators.

"Stop. Roni is working in William's lab now."

Brundar reversed direction and headed for the lab, with Anandur following closely behind him.

The kid lifted his head from an array of monitors. "How can I help you, gentlemen?"

"I need you to find a license plate number." Brundar typed the address, Calypso's car model and color, then handed his phone to Roni. "This is her address. See if you can find the parking lot feed."

"Was it parked there last night?"

Brundar nodded.

It took the kid five minutes to find the feed, then enlarge it so he could copy the number. "Here you go." He handed Brundar a piece of paper.

"You're not done. I need you to check if that car was involved in an accident. Check reports from ten o'clock this morning until now."

Roni frowned. "What happened?"

Anandur waved a dismissive hand. "My brother is overreacting. His friend went shopping, and he can't get a hold of her."

Brundar gritted his teeth. "I have a bad feeling."

"You should have said so." Anandur's tone changed from mocking to worried in an instant. The big oaf had always been superstitious. He believed in omens and lucky numbers and all that shit.

Roni's fingers were a blur on his keyboard. If Brundar hadn't known better, he would have thought the kid was an immortal. Humans just didn't operate at speeds like that.

"Got it. You were right."

Brundar's gut flipped and then twisted in a tight knot. "Talk."

"She was involved in an accident, another car hit her when she didn't stop at a red light. She was taken to the nearest hospital with a broken arm, a light concussion, and some superficial cuts. Nothing life-threatening."

"Thank the merciful Fates." Anandur clutched at his heart.

Brundar wasn't going to thank the sadistic bitches. As if she hadn't suffered enough, Calypso was hurting again. But at least she was alive.

"Which hospital?" he asked.

Roni scribbled the name and address on a note and handed it to Brundar.

"I'll come with you," Anandur offered.

"No. I'm going to get Bridget. You stay here. I don't want to stir up a storm that would reach Kian."

Anandur scratched his head. "Bridget is kind of busy at the moment. Tessa is at the clinic."

"Is she transitioning?"

"Bridget doesn't know yet."

"I'm going to the hospital with Bridget or without."

Anandur nodded. "Give Callie my love."

Brundar dialed the doctor's number. "Can you drop everything and come with me? Calypso was in a car accident."

"What's the damage?"

Fucking Bridget and her cold heart. He'd been expecting a gasp, or an 'oh no', but all he got was a fucking 'what's the damage?'

"A broken arm, a concussion, and some superficial cuts."

"She doesn't need me. I'm sure the human doctors can handle that."

Cold-hearted woman.

"I'm asking a favor. I want you to examine her and then decide whether she needs your help or not."

"I'll meet you in the parking garage in fifteen minutes."

51

JACKSON

"*H*ow are you feeling?" Jackson asked the moment Tessa's eyelids fluttered open.

"It hurts all over."

He pushed out from the chair and moved to sit next to her on the bed. "I'll call Bridget to give you something for the pain." He brushed a strand of hair away from her cheek.

"It's not so bad. It's not an acute pain. Did you eat anything? You've been sitting in this chair since last night."

Sweet girl, worrying about him even when she was the one in a hospital bed and hurting.

"Bhathian brought me a sandwich from the café this morning."

"What time is it?"

"Around one o'clock."

"And you haven't eaten since breakfast? Go get yourself something to eat." She waved a hand, shooing him away.

Jackson leaned and kissed her damp forehead. "Sylvia is on her way, and she is bringing me lunch. What about you? Are you hungry?"

Tessa hadn't been able to keep anything down, not even

water, and was hooked up to an intravenous drip, but maybe after so many hours of sleep, her stomach had settled.

"No. I don't want to puke again."

Smoothing his hand over her hair, he kissed her forehead again. "Poor baby. Is there anything I can do to make you more comfortable?"

"You're here. That's enough. Who is running the shop?"

"Vlad and Gordon. I told them to close up if they can't manage. I'm not leaving your side."

Tessa's smile was a feeble attempt at one. "Thank you. I know I'm being selfish, but I don't want to be alone here."

"Nonsense. You couldn't get rid of me even if you tried."

She cupped his cheek. "I love you."

"Ditto."

"Ditto? That's it?"

She was teasing, which was a good sign. If she were in a lot of pain, humor would've been the last thing on her mind.

"I love you this much." He spread his arms wide.

"Then hug me."

It was a request Jackson was happy to oblige, provided he could figure out a way around all the tubes and sticky pads attached to her. He ended up wrapping his arms over everything and lifting her very gently to his chest.

Tessa sighed. "That feels so good."

Holding her to him with one hand, he caressed her exposed back with his other. Was it his imagination or had she gotten even thinner overnight? The girl was all bones.

A quick knock on the door was all the notice they got before Bridget strode in.

"I'm sorry to interrupt, kids, but I want to run a quick check on Tessa before I have to leave."

"You're leaving?" he asked.

"I won't be gone long, and Hildegard is here if you need anything."

Jackson laid Tessa back on the bed. "Do you need me to move?"

"Yes, please."

Leaning against the wall, Jackson crossed his arms over his chest as he watched Bridget perform her checkup.

"Tell me what you feel, Tessa," Bridget asked.

"I hurt everywhere, not like in unbearable pain, but a constant low-level pain."

"Is it a stabbing sort of pain, or does it feel like pressure?"

"I think, it's more like pressure."

"Does it feel like pins and needles or like a squeeze?"

"Not a squeeze. More like my skin is too tight and everything inside me is swelling."

He was no doctor and knew nothing about human ailments, but that didn't sound good.

Bridget nodded as if she knew exactly what Tessa was complaining about and pulled a measuring tape out of her white coat's pocket.

She'd measured Tessa last night, and now again? What was she expecting to find?

Once the doctor was done taking dozens of measurements and notating them on her tablet, she put the tape back in her pocket and smiled. "I have great news for you, Tessa. Since last night, you've gained one-eighth of an inch in height."

Tessa looked confused, and so was he.

"What does it mean?" Tessa asked.

"It means that you're transitioning."

They had suspected it, but it was just a possibility. Now Bridget sounded as if it was a done deal.

"Can you explain a little bit more?" Tessa squeaked her question.

"I had a feeling that your growth had been stunted for some reason. I could've made sure by taking X-rays of your joints, but I was waiting for your stomach to settle first. Now

I don't need to. The fact that you're growing means that you're transitioning and your body is working on reaching its full potential. Andrew gained a couple of inches during his transition, though in his case I don't think he would've reached that height as a human even under perfect conditions. It's just the size he was supposed to be as an immortal. The difference is that he was unconscious for days during his transition, most likely because of his age."

"Did Nathalie grow taller?"

"No. She didn't change at all. Every person is different."

Tessa closed her eyes. "I can't believe it is actually happening," she whispered.

"Congratulations." Bridget pushed to her feet. "Before I leave, do you want anything for the pain?"

Tessa shook her head. "No. Now that I know why it hurts, I want to savor it. My body is fixing itself."

"If you change your mind, Hildegard can help you."

"Thank you, Doctor."

Bridget patted Tessa's slim shoulder. "You're welcome."

As Jackson took Bridget's place on the bed, his smile grew into a face-splitting grin that was almost painful. "Is my kitten going to turn into a cat?" He clasped Tessa's hand and brought it to his lips for a kiss.

"Would it bother you? I know you like it that I'm small."

"I love you. Small, big, average, it doesn't matter. You'll always be my kitten."

Tessa smiled sheepishly. "I wouldn't mind being a couple of inches taller, or a couple of cup sizes bustier." She glanced down at her small breasts, their outline barely visible under the loose hospital johnny.

Jackson would've loved nothing more than to show her how much he worshiped her breasts, but it would have to wait for when she felt better.

"As I said. It doesn't matter to me. You're perfect the way

you are, and you're going to be just as perfect after your transition."

Tessa opened her arms. "Come here."

He embraced her gently, careful not to dislodge any of the tubes and wires. "Do you realize that all of our dreams will now become a reality?"

"Don't tempt the Fates, Jackson," she whispered in his ear. "Nothing is guaranteed, not even for immortals."

Unfortunately, it was true.

The Fates bestowed and the Fates took away, and no one's life was without trials and hardships. Except, Tessa had already paid her dues and then some. For the rest of her immortal life, she deserved nothing but good fortune and happiness.

Jackson, on the other hand, had been blessed with a wonderful life. At some point, the Fates might decide it was his turn to pay up.

BRUNDAR

"*How* ow is your thralling ability?" Bridget asked as they stepped through the hospital's sliding doors.

"It's above average. Why do you ask?"

As she looked up at him, Bridget's expression was condescending, but he was too anxious to care.

"We are not Callie's family. They might not let us in. I need you to make them believe you're her husband and I'm her sister. My thralling ability is decent but not excellent, and I don't get much practice."

He nodded.

"What name is she using now?" Bridget asked.

"She is back to Calypso. Calypso Meyers, that's her maiden name."

"Is that the name on the driver's license she is using?"

Damnation. He wasn't sure. She'd registered her car under Heather Wilson, and Brundar doubted she'd had time to transfer ownership to Calypso Meyers. She might've been using the fake driver's license.

"Let me check with Roni. He was the one who found out where she was."

Since he didn't have the kid's number, Brundar texted William his question.

The answer came a few moments later. *Calypso Meyers.*

"It's Calypso. Let's go."

"Does she have medical insurance?"

"Yes." Franco had all of his employees covered even before it became mandatory, including the part-timers.

They walked over to the reception, where Brundar didn't waste time with niceties, taking over the receptionist's mind right away. "I'm looking for my wife. Calypso Meyers. She was admitted about an hour ago."

Eyes glazed over, the woman nodded and typed the name into the computer.

Brundar had used brute force, too much for such a simple task, but he wasn't in the right frame of mind for delicate probing. Bridget remained silent beside him, but he sensed no disapproval from her.

The woman gave them Calypso's room number, together with two visitor passes to clip on their shirts.

"She is not in the emergency room, which is a good sign," Bridget said as they entered the elevator. "If her injuries were severe, they would have kept her there for observation."

On the fifth floor, they passed the nurses' station and went straight into Calypso's room.

They found her sleeping, her mouth slightly agape and drooling.

Brundar winced. Calypso's face hadn't had time to recover from the previous abuse she'd suffered, and now it was covered in new bruises and shallow cuts. Her left arm was in a cast and her forehead was bandaged, probably hiding a bigger gash.

Bridget walked in and opened the chart.

"She was given mild pain medication, that's all. The arm was reset without an operation." As Bridget kept reading, her eyebrows dipped in a frown. "She is scheduled for a CT scan.

Apparently, she fell asleep or blacked out while driving." The doctor cast him an accusing sidelong glance. "Did you keep her up all night long?"

"She had an adequate number of sleeping hours for a human," he said quietly. "There was no reason for her to fall asleep at the wheel. Something must be wrong."

"I agree. We should take her to the clinic."

"Why?"

"She might be transitioning," Bridget whispered.

Brundar shook his head. "She is not a Dormant. Quit thinking of her as one. Focus on finding what's wrong instead."

Lately, Bridget had been dealing almost exclusively with transitioning Dormants. No wonder that was the direction her mind went for answers. But unfortunately, in Calypso's case, there had to be some human biological malfunction that had caused her to black out.

"I can do both at the clinic. But if she is transitioning, it is imperative that we take her out of here."

"And how do you suggest we do it?"

"One of us carries her out while the other thralls the staff and has one of the doctors write her a release."

"What about Kian?" It was the middle of the day, and there was no way they could sneak Calypso into the clinic without anyone noticing. Besides, with Tessa there, people would be coming to visit the girl, and it would be impossible to hide the extra patient in the room next to her.

"I have the authority to override him when it comes to medical emergencies. This certainly qualifies as one."

"What emergency?" Calypso startled them both.

Brundar sat on the bed next to her and took her uninjured hand. "Your accident, sweetling. How are you feeling?"

"Like I was hit by a truck, which I was."

"How did it happen?"

Calypso tilted her head to look at Bridget. "Hi, it's so nice of you to come, but it looks worse than it is. They need to run some more tests, but after that, they are going to let me go home tomorrow."

Bridget came closer. "I know. I read your chart. Can you tell us what happened?" She repeated Brundar's question.

Calypso touched her hand to the bandage on her forehead. "I don't know. I remember closing my eyes while idling at a red light, twice. Both times people behind me honked, and when I opened my eyes the light was green. I thought they were impatient. But what if I had my eyes closed for longer than I thought I did? I must've done it again, this time not with the brake on, but I don't remember anything. One moment I'm driving, the next one I'm on a stretcher and paramedics are hovering over me. They later told me that I ran a red light, just kept on driving. Lucky for me, the guy that hit me wasn't going fast."

A tear slid out of the corner of her eye. "My car is totaled, and so is the guy's truck. We are both lucky to be alive."

Brundar leaned over her and took her into his arms. "You're okay, and the other guy is alive. Right?"

She sniffled and nodded.

"Then nothing else matters. Your injuries are mild, and you'll be okay in no time. The car is just a piece of metal. It's replaceable."

"I know, but I still feel like crap. Why is it happening to me? Why can't I catch a break?" Calypso started sobbing openly.

Lost, Brundar cast a pleading glance at Bridget. Maybe as a female and a doctor she had the right words to soothe the crying woman in his arms? Because he sure as hell had no idea what to do.

Taking pity on him, or maybe on Calypso, Bridget said, "Would you feel better recuperating in my clinic? I have all the equipment needed to run tests and find out why you blacked out. It might be something as benign as dehydration, or a vicious virus."

Calypso nodded. "I would love that. But I don't think they are going to let me go without first running those tests the doctor ordered."

"I can call the doctor in, and you can say that you want to be discharged. No one can keep you against your will. They'll just have you sign papers releasing them from liability."

"Should I?"

"Yes, you should."

"Okay. But I don't have anything to wear. I think they cut off my clothes."

"I'll get you something from the gift shop while Brundar deals with the doctor. Right, Brundar?"

"Right. I'll go get him. Or is it her?" Brundar asked.

Bridget looked at the chart. "Her. Doctor Belinda Hernandez."

"Got it."

It took over an hour for all the paperwork to get filled in and signed, but in the end he didn't even have to thrall anyone to get Calypso out of there. Doctor Hernandez wasn't happy about it, but apparently, she had no choice. It was Calypso's prerogative to release herself. They even provided an orderly with a wheelchair to take Calypso to Brundar's car.

"I'll drive," Bridget volunteered. "You guys sit together in the back."

"Thank you," he and Calypso said at the same time.

"I need you to hold me," Calypso whispered in his ear as he lifted her off the wheelchair and into the Escalade's back seat.

"And I need to do the holding."

Up front in the driver seat, Bridget sighed, and then mumbled quietly, "Always the bridesmaid, never the bride."

53

CALLIE

*C*allie opened her eyes to a dimly illuminated room. Was she in the hospital?

She had a hazy recollection of being taken to an ambulance, and another one of someone telling her that her arm was broken. She lifted her right arm, then the left. The left was much heavier—the one with the cast.

Had she dreamt about Brundar holding her? Taking her away?

But she was still in a hospital room, so it must've been a dream. It had been daytime when she'd last closed her eyes. Apparently, night had fallen because it was dark in her room. Maybe someone closed the blinds.

Her head felt as if it was stuffed with cotton balls. Her thoughts couldn't travel freely or connect. Bits and pieces were stuck in random places, not coalescing into something that made sense.

She must have hit her head pretty bad. Evidently, the airbag hadn't deployed. Callie remembered hitting the steering wheel, not the impact itself—she'd blacked out before it had happened—but she remembered anticipating it.

As proof, her head was throbbing with pain. She reached

with her uninjured arm and lightly touched her forehead, or rather the bandage covering it. Even that feather-light touch caused her to wince.

Callie closed her eyes and took in a shallow breath in case her ribs were broken too. It hurt a little. Her ribs were bruised but not broken.

Thank God. If the damage was limited to a broken arm and a cut on her forehead, she should count herself lucky.

It could've been worse.

In the adjacent bathroom, she heard the toilet flush, then the water run as whoever was using it washed their hands. Probably the patient in the next room with whom she was sharing the bathroom. Once that lady was done, Callie needed to use the facilities herself.

Should she call the nurse to help her?

Nah, first she would try without anyone's aid. If that didn't work, and she felt dizzy, she could then call for the nurse. Carefully, Callie pushed to a sitting position, waited for a moment to see if that was okay, then dropped her legs over the side of the bed.

So far, so good.

The question was whether she could stand.

The bathroom door opened, spilling light into the room, but the silhouette that appeared in that doorway was way too big to be a woman.

"What are you doing?" asked a familiar gruff voice.

"Brundar?"

He crossed the distance in two long strides, stopping in front of her and blocking her way. "Where do you think you are going?"

Why did he sound so agitated? Was she still dreaming? "The bathroom."

"I'll carry you."

She was in his arms before she had a chance to object. "When did you get here?"

He looked at her with a puzzled expression on his face. "I never left."

Now that her eyes had gotten used to the sudden burst of light, she could see his features more clearly, but that didn't help with her confusion. "I don't understand."

"What is the last thing you remember?"

"The doctor saying something about my arm being broken."

Brundar frowned, his puzzled expression turning worried. "Let's get you to the bathroom first, and then we will talk."

"Okay."

As he set her down on the toilet, Callie took a look around. The bathroom looked familiar and yet strange at the same time. But the mystery would have to wait for later. First, she needed to empty her bladder.

"Can you turn around, please?"

When he did as she asked, Callie lifted the flaps of her hospital johnny, expecting to be naked under it, but someone had put panties on her.

Crap. Pushing them down with one hand proved to be much harder than she'd expected, but after some wiggling, she finally managed.

Putting them back, though, was a different story. "Um, Brundar? A little help, please?"

He turned around, crouched at her feet, and gently pulled her panties up. "Good?"

Callie smiled, reminded of how he used to ask her if she was okay every step of the way on her sexual journey of exploration. "Yeah. Though I think that maybe I shouldn't be wearing panties at all. It would make going to the bathroom easier."

"Do you want me to take them off?"

"Maybe before you have to leave. When are the visiting

hours over?" She pushed to her feet and turned to the sink to wash her hands.

"Visiting hours? There are no visiting hours. I can stay as long as I want to."

"That's nice. Most hospitals have rules about that. I think ten o'clock is the latest. Unless you're the spouse, but we are not married." She dried her hands with a paper towel.

"You're not in the hospital, Calypso. You're in Bridget's clinic. Don't you remember getting yourself discharged so you could come with us?"

Callie turned around and leaned against the vanity. "I don't. Maybe, I don't know. I'm so confused." She had no reason to doubt him, which meant that her brain was playing tricks on her. "Maybe they gave me something at the hospital? Some drug that I had a reaction to?"

Brundar scooped her into his arms and carried her back to the bed. "I'm no expert. But I think that your brain couldn't handle yet another trauma so soon after the last one, and decided to take a vacation. But I might be talking nonsense. We should consult Bridget."

Actually, what he'd said made a lot of sense. During her previous short stay in Bridget's clinic, Callie remembered the doctor telling her that she hadn't fully internalized what had happened to her. Maybe it had finally caught up with her.

"What time is it?" she asked after he tucked the blanket around her.

"Early. It's a little after five in the morning."

"Crap, how long was I out? I thought it was still yesterday evening."

Brundar sat on the bed next to her. "Bridget and I got you out of the hospital at around three in the afternoon, you fell asleep in the car, and I carried you here. You've been asleep ever since."

"No wonder I'm so thirsty. Is there anything to drink here?"

"I'll get you water."

Her lips twisted in distaste. "I was thinking coffee. But I'll start with water."

"I'm not giving you anything other than that until Bridget approves it." He went outside the room and a moment later returned with a paper cup filled with water.

"When is she coming in?" Callie let the water wet her dried out, cracked lips before gulping it down.

"I don't expect her to be here before seven. She stayed late, taking your vitals several times until she was sure you're fine."

"I need to thank her." She finished the cup and handed it to Brundar. "Could you get me another one?"

"Of course."

Her eyelids felt heavy, and Callie let them drop as soon as Brundar had left the room to fill up her cup.

Just for a few seconds until he comes back.

54

BRUNDAR

*W*hen Brundar returned with the water Calypso had asked for, he found her sleeping again. Something wasn't right, but all he could do was wait and worry until Bridget got there.

It had been her idea to put Calypso in the after surgery recovery room. With the OR and lab separating it from the front of the clinic, it was secluded and as far away from Tessa as possible.

Security was well aware of the visitor, but Bridget had told them to keep it quiet. Whether they'd informed Kian or not was anyone's guess. But since the guy hadn't called to chew Brundar or Bridget's heads off, they probably hadn't. It made sense that they had instructions not to bother him on his vacation unless it was an emergency.

In either case, it was important to keep Calypso hidden from the clan members, or rather the other way around.

Yesterday, with people coming to visit Tessa throughout the afternoon, Brundar had done his best to stay out of their way. Now, there was no one there except for Jackson, who refused to leave the girl's side even for a moment.

In a way, Brundar envied the kid. Tessa wasn't a secret

stowaway like Calypso. Jackson's friends and his mother had brought him a change of clothes and food and whatever else was needed.

Brundar had only Anandur and Bridget to help him out, which wasn't much.

Anandur had stopped by last night, but he'd left early that morning for Hawaii. And Bridget had her hands full with two patients. Besides, it wasn't her job to take care of him.

If Brundar wanted to eat, he had to slink out like a thief, get something from the vending machine upstairs, and then sneak back in without any of Tessa's visitors seeing him, which wasn't an easy feat given that they were all immortals.

At seven-thirty, Bridget walked into the recovery room. "Did she wake up at all?"

"She woke up early in the morning, used the bathroom, and had a drink of water. But when I went to refill her cup she fell asleep again. That's a lot of sleeping even for a human."

Bridget put a finger to her lips, shushing him. Calypso was sleeping, not unconscious, and he should watch what he said in front of her.

The doctor adjusted the lights in the room, making it a little brighter before checking on her patient.

"Brundar, come over here." She motioned for him to get closer. "Look at the cuts on her cheeks. They are almost gone."

Brundar hadn't noticed before, but now that he was paying closer attention, he saw that not only were the cuts much less visible, but her bruises had faded too. Even the old ones. His gut flipped and twisted into a knot. Did it mean that she was transitioning? But Calypso wasn't a Dormant.

"How is it possible?" he whispered.

Bridget patted his shoulder. "The Fates have smiled upon you, Brundar. Your woman is a Dormant, and she is transitioning. Offer them your thanks."

He shook his head. "I don't get it. Unless you count superb culinary skills, she has zero special abilities."

"Affinity, my dear Brundar. You felt it, I felt it, your brother felt it. It's the immediate connection we rarely feel for anyone outside our family. It doesn't even have to be a liking. Fates know there are some clan members I can't stand, but I still feel connected to them. Do you get what I'm trying to say?"

He shook his head. "I'm afraid not." It wasn't easy for him to talk about his shortcomings, but confiding in Bridget wasn't like talking to just anyone. She was a doctor and therefore bound to keep it confidential. "My emotional intelligence is subpar. I don't feel connected to anyone aside from my brother to an extent, and now to Calypso. Even my own mother feels like a mere acquaintance to me."

Bridget threw him a pitying look, then quickly masked it with her all-knowing doctor expression. "When you open yourself up to it, you'll get it."

She leaned over Calypso and gently started unwrapping the bandage over her forehead. "Look at this. It's nothing more than a scratch. Give it a couple of hours, and it will fade completely. I bet her arm is going to be as good as new by the end of the day or tomorrow morning."

"What is going to be as good as new?" Calypso asked.

"Your arm," Bridget answered.

With her eyes still closed, Calypso smiled. "I'm dreaming, right?"

"No, you're awake." Bridget walked over to one of the cabinets and pulled out a mirror. "Take a look." She handed it to her, then lifted the back of the bed to a reclining position.

Calypso opened her eyes, but it was too dark for her to see. Apparently, her eyesight was still human. "What am I looking at?"

"Get the lights, Brundar," the doctor ordered.

He turned them up, but not all the way. There was no

reason to flood the room with a bright light that would hurt Calypso's eyes.

"Oh, wow. My bruises are gone. What did you give me, a magic potion?"

"Not a single thing."

Calypso frowned and looked closer. "I thought the cut on my forehead was deep. But look at this, it's only a scratch. I don't know why they made such a big fuss about it."

Her mind was looking for an explanation within her frame of reference. Unless someone told her what was going on, she would never think in that direction.

But damn, where to begin?

Bridget took the mirror away. "Let me show you something, Callie." She loaded a tray with a few packets of sterile gauze and a small surgical knife.

"Give me your hand."

Calypso eyed the tray suspiciously. "What are you going to do?"

"A little test."

She offered the doctor her uninjured hand. Bridget held it, palm up, then struck fast, making a tiny cut.

"What the fuck? Why did you do that?" Calypso tried to yank her hand out of Bridget's grasp.

"Just look at the cut, Callie." Bridget wiped the blood off with a gauze square.

It wasn't closing as fast as it would for an immortal, but it was much faster than humanly possible. She was still transitioning. Her body would probably get more adept at healing itself when the process was completed.

"I'm dreaming." Calypso dropped her head on the pillow and closed her eyes. "Some really fucked up dreams. Where the hell is my brain coming up with that?" she mumbled, talking to herself.

Bridget rose to her feet and threw away the soiled gauze. "I did my part, but she is still in denial. Now it's your turn."

Brundar swallowed.

"Where do I start?"

"At the beginning, of course." Bridget cast him a smile over her shoulder as she headed out the door.

Right. At the beginning.

55

CALLIE

*B*ridget had told Brundar to start at the beginning. What had she meant by that?

The beginning of what?

Brundar sat on the bed next to Callie and kissed the palm Bridget had nicked with her wicked knife. "You're not dreaming. This is all real, and after I explain, it will all make sense. But first, you need to drink some more. You were thirsty before you fell asleep again."

"I still am."

Heck, even if it was a dream, it was for sure interesting. She would play along and see what her mind was capable of inventing.

Brundar got up and walked over to the sink, filling her cup with tap water. "All the water in the keep is filtered." He handed her a cup.

Did he say the keep? Like a castle? Both times Callie had been taken to this place, she hadn't seen where it was. The first time she'd been blindfolded, the second time asleep. But from the one she'd been conscious for, Callie remembered that the drive wasn't long. As far as she knew, there were no castles within driving distance of her old house.

"Thank you." She gulped the contents in one go.

Brundar sat on the bed again and clasped her hand. "Remember how you wondered about my incredible recovery? It wasn't because of some revolutionary new procedure. I heal fast because I am immortal. And so are Anandur and Bridget and every other member of my family. That is the real reason I couldn't be with you, and it's also the reason Kian was so angry about us bringing you to the keep. Our existence must be kept secret from the human world. Can you imagine what would happen if word got out that there are people who don't age?"

If they were real, they would be hunted and collected like the most precious treasure in the world, and experimented on. But of course, they weren't. Brundar would not be talking about it so openly either.

"So if it is such a big secret, why are you telling me about it now?"

"Some humans carry our dormant genes. They are very rare and almost impossible to find. Typically they exhibit some paranormal abilities, like precognition or telepathy."

Callie frowned. "I remember you asking me if I had any." Immortals were not a new concept, there were plenty of movies and books featuring some sort of creatures that couldn't die, but she didn't remember ever reading anything about Dormants, and it was unlikely that her mind had conjured that idea out of nothing. Could it be that it wasn't a dream after all?

He nodded. "I was hoping against hope that you were one of these rare humans. Because if you were, I could activate those dormant genes and you would turn immortal, which would mean a possible future for us."

Lifting her palm, Callie glanced at the spot Bridget had nicked with her surgical knife. It was completely healed as if it had never been injured. "Are you telling me that I am one of those humans who carry immortal genes and that you accidentally turned me into an immortal?"

She had one hell of an imagination to come up with a story like that. Nice story, though, where she and Brundar could live happily ever after. Forever. Which brought her back to the dream theory. This was the sort of fantasy she was capable of inventing.

"That's exactly what I'm saying. The Fates have smiled upon me. There is no other explanation for you appearing in my life. Dormants are extremely rare, and finding a true love match is even rarer. It cannot be a coincidence."

As crazy as it sounded, Callie held similar beliefs. From the very start, she'd felt that her meeting with Brundar had been fated. Except, she'd thought it had to do with him rescuing her from Shawn.

But what if the picture was bigger than that?

"What is the catalyst for activating those dormant genes?"

Brundar smiled. "Kiss me, and I'll show you." He lowered his head and took her mouth in a gentle kiss. She wrapped her good arm around his neck and held him close, savoring his warmth, his solid chest.

There was nothing in her world that compared to the feeling Callie got every time their bodies touched like that, and it wasn't only the attraction. It was a coming together.

They were like two halves that needed to fuse in order to breathe easy.

"Open your eyes," he said as he let go of her mouth.

The lights must be playing tricks on her because it looked as if Brundar's eyes were glowing from the inside.

And then he smiled.

"Oh, my God!" She pointed. "You have fangs." Now Callie was certain she was dreaming.

"That's what happens when I am aroused, or when I get aggressive. That's why I insisted on the blindfold. Obviously, I couldn't allow you to see me like this."

Why did it make so much sense?

Maybe because she was the one making it up?

But what if all of it was real?

How would she know?

"Are you in shock?" Brundar asked when she remained quiet.

Callie shook her head. "I have to find a way to ascertain if I am dreaming or hallucinating. If this is real or not. But I can't think of anything that would prove it beyond a shadow of a doubt. I often have very realistic dreams."

"Would it help if I pinched you?"

"Not really. If pain were a convincing sign, then Bridget cutting into my palm would've been proof enough. I've dreamt about pain, and I've dreamt about pleasure, and both felt very real."

Brundar rubbed his jaw. "If I tell you my clan's history, and it will be a tale that you could've never imagined on your own, would you believe me then?"

"I have to hear it first."

Brundar took in a deep breath. "I'm not the best at telling stories, but I'll give it a try. The gods you've learned about in mythology were real. The furthest back our known history goes is ancient Sumer. The mother of our clan—"

More than an hour passed until Brundar was done with his story. And one hell of a story it was. Callie had about a thousand questions, but she'd asked none, listening to Brundar's tale from beginning to end without interruptions. Here and there she'd tried to guess where the story was going, but most of the time had gotten it wrong, proving to herself that it wasn't a product of her imagination.

"I have so many questions that I don't know where to start."

"Do you believe me, though? That this is not a dream?"

She nodded, fighting the tears stinging the back of her eyes. "It's such a sad story. Poor Annani, to lose her one true love so tragically and then everyone else she'd ever loved. To be all alone in the universe. She was so incredibly brave."

"Indeed, she is. But the most amazing thing about her is her heart and her joy in life. After all that she's been through, she should be bitter and jaded, but she is not."

Callie hoped to meet the goddess one day, even if only to see her from afar. After all, it wasn't likely that a powerful being like Annani would deign to talk to a simple ex-human like Callie. "Annani could be such a fantastic role model. Especially for girls. It's a shame her story can't be taught in schools."

With a smile, Brundar pulled her into his arms for a gentle hug. "You're amazing, Calypso. Always thinking of others. I'm so proud to call you my mate."

She cleared her throat. "About that mate thing. Can we call it something else?"

Brundar pulled back, amusement dancing in his glowing eyes. "Would you prefer wife?"

"Is that a proposal?"

"Only if you want it to be."

56

BRUNDAR

*I*t wasn't the most romantic proposal, even Brundar knew that. Calypso would probably say no, or not yet. She hadn't grown up with the myth of a true love match, and she might not realize the gift they had been given.

In time, she would.

Except, with her history of being pushed into a marriage that had resulted in a catastrophe, she might never be ready.

It didn't matter. Brundar didn't need a ceremony to bind him to Calypso, or her to him. They were bound by much stronger forces than that.

Love and fate.

But she was so damn young.

What if she decided to follow the advice he'd given her about not rushing into another commitment before partying for a while?

Over his dead body, or rather that of any male she partied with, which now included his immortal clansmen.

He should dissuade her from that idea. "You don't need to answer me yet. But just so you know, the venom is addictive. You'll be repulsed by other males. Human and immortal alike."

Calypso cupped his cheek. "Since you and I are never going to have other partners, that's not a problem. You are it for me, and I am it for you."

"So, is it a yes?"

"If you can find someone to marry us now, I'll do it here in this hospital room with Bridget and the nurse as witnesses."

He shook his head. "First, you need to get well, which fortunately is not going to take much longer now that you're immortal, or rather on your way to becoming one. According to Bridget, it takes up to six months for the body to complete the transition."

Calypso lay back on the pillows and closed her eyes. "Yeah, you're right. I don't want to black out in the middle of the ceremony. I keep falling asleep."

"That's because of the transition. The first stages wreak havoc on the body, and it tries to preserve energy by becoming inactive. You're lucky to only fall asleep. Syssi was unconscious for over a day, and Andrew for several days."

Calypso's eyes widened. "Syssi was a human? No wonder she seemed so normal."

"She was the first Dormant Amanda found. And what do you mean, Syssi seemed normal? Amanda and Bridget didn't?"

"Not really. I felt a different vibe from them, same with you and Anandur."

Brundar frowned. As far as he was aware, humans couldn't detect immortals unless they were showing glowing eyes and fangs. If something was giving them away, he needed to know about it. "Different in what way?"

"It's hard to explain. I thought it was because you guys were all originally from Europe, and Europeans have a different vibe than Americans. But maybe that's not it. I really can't put my finger on it."

"If you come up with something later, please let me know. Staying hidden and undetectable is crucial to our survival."

"I'll try. Maybe this is my special talent? Sensing immortals?"

"Could be. But, apparently, there is another Dormant here who exhibits no unique abilities. So maybe it's not a prerequisite."

When Calypso didn't respond, Brundar realized she'd fallen asleep again. Except, now that he knew why this was happening, he was no longer worried. She needed the sleep.

Careful not to disturb the bed, he got up and walked out. Leaning against the wall of the reception room outside the recovery area, he pulled out his phone and called his brother.

Anandur answered before the first ring ended. "What happened?"

"Everything is all right," Brundar calmed his brother. No wonder Anandur assumed he was calling with news of some disaster. He never called unless it was an emergency. "I have good news. Calypso is transitioning."

Aside from Anandur's heavy breathing, the line was silent for a long moment. "How?"

"Apparently, she is a Dormant."

"Are you sure she is transitioning?"

"Positive. Bridget performed the cut test. Calypso blacked out while driving because she was transitioning. I thank the merciful Fates for her getting away with only minor injuries. She could've been killed." His gut clenched uncomfortably at the thought.

"Right. But you were together for weeks, and I assume it wasn't a platonic relationship."

"Where are you going with that?"

"She should've transitioned a long time ago. Why only now?"

Brundar rubbed his jaw, trying to figure out what had been different about last week. Well, since he'd been staying with Calypso, they had been having sex more frequently. That could've been the difference. "Before my injury, we hadn't had sex as often."

"Nothing else?"

"Calypso started using birth control. Could that have anything to do with it?"

"What did you do before that? Did you thrall her every time to make her think you had protection?"

What kind of a man did his brother think he was?

"Of course not. I tried to keep the thralling to a minimum. I used condoms. And thanks to the blindfold, I didn't need to thrall her after every bite either."

"You need to tell Bridget. It might be important."

"True. I also wanted to tell you that I asked Calypso to marry me and she said yes."

"Yes!" Anandur shouted.

"Keep it down. Is Kian with you?"

"He and Syssi are taking a nap. But, bro, we no longer need to keep it a secret. Do you want me to tell him? Or do you want to do the honors yourself?"

"I'd rather wait until he is back."

"Do you have a date? Or is it just in the agreement stage?"

"You know who is here. It's an opportunity." Even though their sat phones were using a secured and heavily encrypted connection, Brundar preferred not to mention the goddess's name.

"Right. Are you going to wait for me to come back?"

"Of course I will, you moron. I'm not getting married without you. Besides, Calypso needs to heal completely first, and then she would probably want to get a nice dress and maybe plan a party or something."

"Aha, so it's not that you are waiting for me to come back because you want your brother to be your best man. It's all about a dress."

Brundar chuckled. "Of course, it's about the dress. You can't come to my wedding wearing jeans."

Anandur gasped dramatically. "Brundar, you told a joke! You are cured!"

57

JACKSON

It was the middle of the night when a small cloaked figure practically floated into the room and closed the door behind her. Even with the cloak's hood hiding her face and her inner glow subdued, Jackson knew who it was.

He pushed to his feet and bowed. "Greetings, Clan Mother."

"Shush." Annani pulled the hood back and put a finger to her lips. "No one knows I am here." She smirked. "I was supposed to stay in Kian's penthouse, but I wanted to give my blessing to the new member of my clan. How is the girl doing?"

Jackson bowed again, moved by Annani's concern for Tessa, a girl she'd never met. "Thank you. Tessa is doing well. She is sleeping."

The goddess glided closer and put her hand on Tessa's forehead. "She is not unconscious. This is good. I was worried, but I see that she is very young. The young fare better through the transition."

"Could you bless her anyway?"

Annani smiled. "Of course, child." She glided toward him and lifted a small palm to his cheek. "Such a handsome boy."

"Thank you." Jackson dropped to his knees so the goddess wouldn't have to look up.

She sighed, but it wasn't a sad sigh. "I sense so much love in you. Your heart has a boundless capacity for feelings. I hope the Fates bless your union with many children. They will be loved and cherished."

Jackson looked into the goddess's warm, smiling eyes. "Is this a blessing, or a prediction?"

"Both." She leaned and kissed his forehead. "Do not tell anyone I was here. My presence in the keep is known only to the Guardians and council members, and it needs to stay that way."

Tessa would've loved to see the goddess. But now he couldn't even tell her. Jackson hesitated for a split second before asking, "Can I tell Tessa? Knowing that you came to see her will mean so much to her."

Annani turned her head to look at the sleeping girl. "I will do better than that. I will wake her."

Jackson was speechless. He hadn't expected Annani to be so accommodating. The rumors painted her as unyielding, a prima donna that had to have her way in all things—as was her due. After all, she was the last remaining goddess and the mother of their clan. They were lucky she wasn't a tyrant, and that her demands weren't too outrageous.

As Annani walked over to the bed in that floating way she moved, Jackson looked down at her feet, checking if they were even touching the floor, but her cloak was too long, dragging on the floor behind her.

She leaned and kissed Tessa's forehead. "Wake up, sleeping beauty."

Annani laughed at her own joke, the sound of her laughter so sweet it sent shivers up and down Jackson's spine. There was an unearthly quality to her voice, especially when she sang or laughed.

From the other side of the bed, Jackson saw Tessa crack

her eyes open, and then open them wider. "Am I dead? Are you an angel?"

Annani laughed again. "If I am, then I am a very naughty one."

"Your voice is so beautiful. It sounds like little crystal bells." Tessa reached out a hand to touch a lock of Annani's hair. "So soft." She lifted her eyes back to Annani's face. "Are you here to escort me to the other side?"

The Goddess smiled and patted Tessa's cheek. "You are not dead, child, and I am not an angel. But I am a goddess. I am sure you have heard about me. I am Annani, otherwise known as Clan Mother."

Tessa gasped and pushed back on the bed. "Oh, my, God. I mean Goddess." She turned frantic eyes to Jackson. "What am I supposed to do?"

Annani patted her cheek again. "Nothing at all except get better. I came to give you my blessing, but you are doing splendidly without it." She leaned closer. "You and Jackson are already blessed beyond measure. Your love for each other shines like a thousand suns."

BRUNDAR

a text arrived at three in the morning, or rather night, waking Brundar from the short nap he'd allowed himself. Calypso was still sleeping for long stretches at a time, and he was afraid that during one of them she would slip into unconsciousness. Which meant that he kept checking on her throughout the night.

He pulled his phone out of his pocket and looked at the screen.

The text was from Kian. *Congratulations. Best news I've got in a long time,* Kian wrote at midnight Hawaiian time. An apology for the way he'd kicked Calypso out was apparently too much to expect from the guy.

Fucking Anandur. He was supposed to keep his mouth shut.

Brundar dozed off for what seemed like a few minutes when another text came in, jarring him awake. This time from Syssi. *I'm so happy for both of you. This is a miracle, and it deserves a grand celebration. Tell Callie we are going to have one as soon as I'm back from Hawaii.*

Apparently, Anandur hadn't told them about the wedding plans. Maybe he'd misunderstood, thinking that he wasn't supposed to talk about the wedding but that telling Kian and Syssi about Calypso's transition was okay.

He would give him the benefit of the doubt. After all, he owed his brother not only his life but Calypso's as well. For as long as he lived, Brundar was never going to forget Anandur's arrival at the scene at Shawn's house.

He fired a couple of quick *thanks* to both and closed his eyes again. When he opened them again, it was seven in the morning.

Frantically, Brundar pushed to his feet and clasped Calypso's hand, relaxing when she squeezed back.

"What time it is?" she mumbled.

"Seven."

"Morning or evening? I lost track of time."

"Morning."

Calypso swung her legs over the side of the bed and got up.

He was at her side in the blink of an eye. "What do you think you're doing?"

"I'm going to the bathroom."

"Let me help you."

"No, I can do it. I feel strong."

"Can I come with you anyway? I know you need help with your panties."

She smiled. "If I can't manage, I'll call for you to come in. Okay?"

He didn't have much choice. The woman was trying to prove something. "I'll stand outside the door."

Calypso rolled her eyes. "Fine."

He listened as she used the toilet, then washed her uninjured hand and brushed her teeth, all while having only one arm to work with. Stubborn woman. He could've made it so much easier for her.

"Brundar," she finally called out.

He opened the door.

"Can you find me a hairbrush? My hair looks like a bird's nest."

"I'll ask Bridget. But first I want to see you get in bed without falling down and breaking more bones."

She smiled sheepishly. "If everything heals as fast as those cuts and bruises, then I have nothing to worry about. Look at my face." She pointed with her good hand. "Perfect."

"I agree." He guided her back to the bed and helped her up.

"Can you find me a cup of coffee too?"

"I'll ask Bridget if it's okay."

"Ask Bridget what?" The doctor walked in.

"I want coffee," Calypso said. "And food. I'm starving."

"All taken care of." The doctor turned her head towards the door. "You can come in, Amanda. Callie is awake."

Amanda sauntered in pushing a loaded cart in front of her. "Good morning, darlings. My butler prepared breakfast for you."

Calypso eyed it hungrily. "Thank you and your butler. I would kill for a cup of coffee."

Amanda lifted the carafe. "No need to kill anyone." She poured dark liquid into the cup. "Cream and sugar?"

"Yes, please."

She fixed Calypso's coffee and handed it to her. "You take yours black, right?" she asked Brundar.

He nodded.

"Here you go." She handed him a steaming mug.

Calypso took a few grateful sips, then looked at Bridget. "Do you have a hairbrush I can borrow?"

"I got you covered, girl." Amanda pulled out a large paper bag from the cart's lower shelf and put it on the bed. "A brush and a change of clothes. No bra, I'm afraid. Mine wouldn't fit you."

"Thank you. You're awesome." Calypso got off the bed

with surprising ease. "I'm going to change and brush my hair. I need to feel human again." She giggled. "But I'm not, am I?"

Bridget lifted a hand. "Not yet. I want to remove your cast, and it will get messy. You'll need a shower after that."

"Are you sure the bone is already mended?"

"If you still need a little support, I'll give you a sling. Eat something first, though. You said you were starving."

A few minutes later, when Calypso was done with a sandwich and another cup of coffee, Bridget shooed Brundar and Amanda out. "And take the cart with you. I need room to move."

"How did you know we were here?" Brundar asked as they stepped out into the waiting room.

"Anandur told Syssi, and Syssi told Nathalie and me, and we told everyone else. You know how the rumor machine works."

Damnation. Now he wouldn't have a moment's peace.

As if to prove him right, there was a knock on the waiting room's door.

"Come in," Amanda said.

The Guardians piled into the small room, sucking up all the air, or at least it felt like it to Brundar. The anxious knot in his gut refused to ease even though Calypso was doing exceptionally well. Everything was happening so fast and so unexpectedly, Brundar was having a hard time adjusting to his new reality.

Yesterday morning Calypso was a human, and they had zero prospects as a couple, and now they were talking forever.

Several embraces and backslaps later, the questions began.

"How did you find her?"

"Did you know she was Dormant?"

"Did you suspect?"

He tried to answer them patiently. After all, these men and Kri were almost like brothers and sister to him.

"When can we see your mystery woman?" Bhathian asked.

Amanda crossed her arms over her chest. "Not today, gentlemen and lady. Give the girl a breather. Once she is ready, Brundar will invite you over to his apartment. Right, Brundar?"

"Right." As long as it got them to leave as soon as possible, he was willing to promise a lot of things.

Amanda uncrossed her arms and headed for the door as well. "I need to get going, or I'll be late to my morning class. I'll call you when I'm back. Oh, and Annani told me that she wants to talk to you. Not right now, but at your earliest convenience."

Brundar frowned. "Do you know what she wants?"

"Probably to give you some words of wisdom and ask about a wedding date." She winked.

He was going to strangle Anandur. "Why? What did you hear?"

"Nothing. But Calypso is your true-love match, and I assume you would like to make it official at some point."

"What about you and Dalhu? You guys don't seem in a hurry."

"We are very comfortable the way we are." She pushed the door handle down. "Do whatever feels right for you and Calypso. You can get married tomorrow, or next week, or in a year, or never. It doesn't matter. The bond between you is indestructible."

For some reason, Amanda's words managed to ease the knot in his gut. He didn't know whether it was the reassurance that he and Calypso would never have to part, or the realization that they didn't need to rush into a wedding only because Annani was there. They had all the time in the world.

He was about to head back into the recovery room when there was another knock on the door. Who the hell was it this time?

He yanked it open. "Carol. You heard too?"

She flung herself into his arms, and he had no choice but to catch her. What had gotten into her? She knew he didn't like to be touched.

Surprisingly, though, he felt no revulsion, not even the slightest discomfort.

Carol was family, and she was excited for him. He hugged her back.

He hadn't expected her to burst into tears. "What's the matter? Aren't you happy for me?"

"I'm ecstatic." She pulled away and plopped down on one of the chairs. "Those are tears of joy, Brundar. Sometimes females get overemotional, and the only way to let the pressure out is to cry."

He sat next to her. "Are you still trying to teach me how to interpret emotions?"

She shrugged. "You need it now more than ever. This is just the beginning for you. Relationships need constant work."

"Calypso knows who and what I am."

Carol threw him a sidelong glance. "Does she, now?"

He frowned. "What are you trying to say?"

She sighed. "I get you, Brundar. More than you realize. We are both survivors. I haven't told anyone the complete story of what was done to me. I can't. Not because I'm ashamed, or anything like that, but because to talk about it would mean to relive it. But if one day I'm lucky enough to find my true love match, I'll have to tell him."

"Why?"

"True love means true acceptance. The good, the bad, and the ugly."

59

CALLIE

*C*allie's arm was healed.

In fact, she hadn't felt so good in a long time. After what she'd suffered at Shawn's hands, the visible bruising had been only part of the story. She'd been aching all over and putting a brave face on it because it was nothing compared to Brundar's injuries.

"I think I'll head into the shower now," she told Bridget.

"By all means. As far as I'm concerned, you're free to go. But just in case those blackouts return, I want you to stay in the keep for a few days, and absolutely no driving."

"I know. I wouldn't dare."

"Good, and please stop by my office on your way out. I'll print out a list of instructions for you."

"Thank you."

"You're welcome." Bridget patted her shoulder.

In the bathroom, Callie dropped the johnny on the floor and examined what she could see in the vanity mirror. The bruising was all gone, but she had somehow lost a lot of weight over the last twenty-four hours. Her skin was stretched over her protruding ribs. Not a sexy look. She needed to go on a calorie-dense diet.

Other than that she was still the same Callie. Same color eyes, same messy hair, same everything. Apparently, the change didn't make people look better.

Don't be greedy, Callie. You're an immortal, and so is the man you love.

Immortal.

Wow.

Life was sure stranger than fiction.

Except, standing in front of the mirror and staring at her reflection wasn't going to help her wrap her head around this new reality she'd found herself in. In the meantime, life went on, and she needed to get busy to keep from freaking out.

Step one, shower.

When she was done, Callie put on the clothes Amanda had so thoughtfully lent her. They were nothing fancy, a pair of black leggings and a black T-shirt, but the labels were enough to make Callie suck in a breath. She'd never even tried on anything like that. A pair of new panties with the price tag still attached, another sticker shocker, but no bra. No big deal. The T-shirt was loose and the fabric substantial. Unless someone looked closely, it was hard to tell Callie wasn't wearing one.

She pulled her wet hair back, tucking it behind her ears, and opened the door to the recovery room.

Brundar was leaning against the wall, his arms crossed over his chest and his legs at the ankles. "You look good."

"Thank you." She looked down at her outfit. "I've never worn anything so expensive in my life."

"I'm not talking about your clothes." He pushed off the wall and sauntered toward her, the predatory gleam in his eyes giving her pause. He'd told her a lot yesterday, but that was only the tip of the iceberg. She knew so little about the man she'd fallen in love with.

God, he'd proposed last night, but he hadn't told her he

loved her yet. Not that she doubted he did, but she needed to hear him say it.

As he pulled her into his arms and kissed her, hungrily, savagely, crushing her to him, Callie realized that he'd been holding back until now, mindful of her human fragility. How strong was she anyway?

Suddenly, she was reminded of Donnie's story about Brundar lifting an SUV with one hand. How strong was he?

"Ready to go home?"

"Bridget said I need to stay here for a few days."

"I know. I was talking about my and Anandur's apartment."

"Oh. Let me just pick up my things." Using the same bag Amanda had brought her change of clothes in, Callie put in the sweats and underwear Bridget had gotten for her in the hospital's gift shop and her purse that the paramedic had pulled out of her wrecked car, then went to the bathroom for the toothbrush Bridget had given her.

"Now I'm ready." Sort of.

Callie still felt as if she'd been transported into a parallel universe.

On their way out, they stopped at Bridget's office for the set of instructions.

Bridget handed them to Brundar. "Make sure she follows this. Especially the part about the food." She pointed a finger at Callie. "Your body needs a lot of calories for what it is doing. This is not the time to think about your figure."

Callie waved a dismissive hand. "Don't worry. I don't like seeing my own ribs. I'm going to indulge in every sinful dish I skipped over because it was too fattening."

That had proven to be a bit of a problem, as she'd discovered looking into Brundar's empty fridge. "I see that Anandur went back to his old ways after I left. All you have is beer and peanut butter. Nothing else."

"I'll get us something from the café downstairs."

She shook her head. "I don't want more sandwiches. I want real food. Can you stop at a grocery store and get me some supplies?"

"I want you to rest, not cook. I'll bring takeout from wherever you want."

Given the stubborn expression on his face, it was pointless to argue. She would let him win today, but tomorrow she was going to cook no matter what. She would find someone to bring her groceries. Perhaps Amanda could lend Callie her butler.

"Can you also stop by our apartment and bring me more clothes? And my lotions and my hairbrush."

"Anything else?"

"Shoes. And socks. My nightshirt. And don't forget panties and bras."

A smile tugged at the corner of his lips. "Is that all?"

"I can't think of anything else right now. I'll text you if I remember. But please, stop by a supermarket and at least get some eggs and butter and bread and a few vegetables. Maybe some cookies. If I'm to stay here for a few days, I don't want to depend on takeout alone."

He nodded. "I can do that."

"Thank you." She wrapped her arms around his neck and stretched to give him a kiss. "It's strange to adjust to the reversal of roles. Again. First, you took care of me, then I took care of you, and now you're taking care of me again."

"That's what people who love each other do."

Did Brundar just say the L word?

"Say it again."

He lifted a brow. "What? That people who love each other take care of each other?"

"Yes, that. You said love."

"I know what I said."

"That's the first time you told me that you love me."

Brundar frowned. "I might have not used that specific word, but I think it was pretty obvious."

"Yes, but I still needed to hear it."

He smiled. "I love you, Calypso."

"And I love you, Brundar. Forever."

He nodded. "Forever."

60

BRUNDAR

*B*y the time Brundar finished unloading his car, the elevator was full of grocery bags, clothes bags, and Chinese takeout. He'd emptied Calypso's closet and brought everything that was there, which wasn't much. It was time the girl started thinking about herself, and stuffed her closet full of clothes like any other female.

Perhaps he could ask Amanda to help Calypso out. Even better, he could give the princess his credit card and ask her to order things online. That way Calypso couldn't argue or fuss over the prices.

He would get rid of the price tags before she saw them. Brundar wanted her to have the same kind of luxuries Amanda took for granted and take them for granted as well. He hadn't liked the way she'd referred to the borrowed clothes as if they were things she could never have.

The thought of taking care of his mate filled Brundar with a profound sense of satisfaction. Living as long as he had and spending very little, he'd amassed a small fortune. He could spoil Calypso with fancy stuff until she forgot ever living without it. There was nothing he wouldn't get for her.

He was Calypso's mate, and therefore she could no longer refuse his support or his gifts.

Mate.

Fates, the word felt good on his lips. He had a mate. His true love match.

Brundar had never thought he would get that lucky. Even when Amanda had discovered Syssi, and the entire clan had been buzzing with hope, he'd never believed one would be found for him. And later, when it had become clear that Amanda had been overly optimistic and finding Syssi and Michael had been a lucky fluke, he hadn't been disappointed because he'd never expected to have one.

Calypso was a gift.

Which reminded him that he still owed Annani a visit, and making the goddess wait was never a good strategy.

Both hands holding multiple bags, he kicked the door to his apartment. "Calypso, open up," he said without raising his voice, hoping her hearing had improved with her transition.

It had. A moment later he heard her footsteps and then the door opened. "Need help?" she asked.

"I've got it." As if he would let her lift anything.

He dropped everything on the floor and went back to bring the rest of the stuff from the elevator.

Calypso was already pulling things out from the bags. "Did you bring every last piece of clothing from the apartment?"

"Just about. There wasn't much."

"Yeah. And the new beautiful outfit I bought at the mall got ruined in the accident." She looked sad.

He pulled her into his arms. "We will get you a new one. A lot of new ones. One ruined outfit is no reason for sorrow."

She hugged him back, holding him tight to her. "I know. But it was a nice one. You would've liked it."

He caressed her back, noting how thin she'd gotten in the

span of one day. "I brought Chinese takeout. You need to eat." He let go of her.

Her stomach rumbled in agreement. "It smells amazing. Let me set up the table."

He caught her hand. "We can eat straight from the boxes. I have a meeting I have to get to. I don't have time."

For a change, Calypso didn't argue. She was either too hungry or too tired to bother with plates.

Sitting at the counter, they demolished the six different dishes he'd brought, including all the rice and the fortune cookies.

"Look." Calypso handed him the thin strip of paper with her fortune.

He read it out loud. "Out of misfortune, a blessing will arise."

"Creepy," she said.

"Very apt." He put the piece of paper inside his pocket for safekeeping.

"What are you going to do with that?"

"I don't know yet, but I want to keep it. Maybe frame it. Or perhaps put it inside one of those little decorative boxes."

Calypso lifted a brow. "I didn't peg you as sentimental."

He leaned and kissed her lightly. "I didn't either. But I find myself feeling and doing a lot of things I never did before."

"Because of me?"

"Thanks to you."

61

CALLIE

*H*er belly full to bursting, Callie felt like taking a nap, but the bags on the floor bothered her. Until she put everything away and made sure the place was nice and tidy, she wouldn't be able to sleep.

Besides, Brundar's meeting was a perfect opportunity to clean up and organize without him fussing and demanding that she rest and not touch a thing.

Callie poured herself another cup of coffee and got to work.

After putting the groceries away, she took her things to Brundar's closet, which had enough unused space to accommodate all of them with plenty of room to spare. The guy didn't have much, but what he had was neatly organized. Obviously, he used some laundry service because everything was professionally pressed.

She picked up a sweater and brought it to her nose for a sniff. It had been laundered, but some of Brundar's unique scent remained. Closing her eyes, she buried her nose in it and breathed his scent in, a sense of calm suffusing her.

Was it part of the addiction he'd told her about? Or was it normal for a woman in love?

She was still sniffing and pondering that question when someone knocked on the door. Brundar would have just walked in, and Anandur was in Hawaii. So who could it be?

Maybe Amanda. Or Bridget.

It turned out to be Amanda and another woman Callie had never met before, who was holding an adorable baby girl.

"Callie, meet Nathalie and her daughter Phoenix. Nathalie, meet Callie." Amanda made the introductions as the two women stepped in.

Nathalie offered her hand. "Hi. I'm a new immortal too. I thought you would like to talk with a kindred spirit."

Callie shook what she was offered, but her eyes remained glued to Phoenix's toothless smile. "She is adorable."

Nathalie adjusted the baby to a more comfortable position. "Thank you."

"Please come in and take a seat. Can I offer you a cup of coffee? I have some freshly brewed."

"I'll get it." Amanda waved a hand. "You sit with Nathalie and have a chat."

For some reason, Callie had a feeling that it would be just as pointless to argue with Amanda as it was with Brundar.

"There are cookies next to the coffeemaker."

"I'll get them."

"How are you feeling?" Nathalie asked. "Amanda said you had no idea you were a Dormant and that the transition took you and Brundar by surprise."

"It happened while I was driving. I'm lucky to be alive."

"By the way," Amanda said as she came in with three cups of coffee. "Bridget is on her way as well. I wish Syssi were here, then the welcoming party would be complete. She is also an ex-human turned immortal. Our first one." She handed Callie her coffee mug and put Nathalie's on the coffee table.

"Brundar told me. We had a very long talk yesterday. Or rather he talked, and I listened."

Amanda shook her head. "I wish I could've seen that. I don't think I ever heard Brundar string more than two words together."

There was a knock on the door and Amanda, who was still standing, opened the way. "Bridget. You're just in time for coffee."

"I need one. With two Dormants transitioning at the same time, I've hardly had any sleep."

"How is Tessa doing?" Callie asked.

"She is still down in the clinic. Your transition went pretty smoothly, aside from the accident that is, but her body is going through more changes so it will take longer."

"Why is that?"

"I have a theory. I think that during the transition the body reaches its full potential. Tessa should have been a bit taller, but growing up she didn't get proper nutrition. She is compensating for it now."

Callie frowned. "I looked myself over in the mirror, and I look exactly the same as I did before."

"So do I," Nathalie said. "My butt is still too big and my boobs too small. I guess I was destined to be disproportioned."

Callie chuckled. "I have the opposite problem. My butt is too small, and my boobs are too big."

Amanda looked at the two of them as if they were nuts. "You girls are being silly. You are each beautiful in your own way. The world would have been a boring place if we all looked the same."

"Says the most gorgeous woman in the universe," Nathalie mumbled.

"I am not. That title belongs to my mother."

The goddess. Kian and Amanda's mother. No wonder the brother and sister were so inhumanly beautiful.

"I have a question," Callie said. "My father and step-mother just had a baby boy. Is he a Dormant like me?"

"Not likely," Bridget said. "If you had the same mother then the answer would have been yes. The immortal genes come from the mother. Are your parents divorced?"

"No. My mother was killed in a car accident when I was a toddler."

Nathalie patted her knee. "I'm so sorry."

Callie shrugged. "I don't even remember her. All I have are a few pictures and home movies. My dad never really got over her death, and it was very difficult for him to talk about her, so I don't even know much about what kind of a person she was. She seemed nice in the home movies, and happy. My father did too."

"That's so sad," Nathalie said.

"He is better now. Iris, his new wife, brought the smile back to his face, and now with the new baby, he sounds really happy. I can't wait to see my baby brother." She glanced at the little girl in Nathalie's arms. "I absolutely adore babies."

Bridget cleared her throat. "Did you think about what you are going to tell him?"

"I'm not going to tell him anything." Callie snorted. "If I come up with a story like that, he will have me committed to a mental institution."

"Eventually he will notice that you're not aging," Bridget said.

Right. But there was plenty of time to think about that. Callie was only twenty-one. Her father would not expect to see wrinkles on her face for many years to come.

BRUNDAR

"Good evening, Clan Mother." Brundar bowed.

"Come sit with me." She patted the spot next to her.

He did as she asked, but sat as far away from her as the couch allowed. It wasn't that he feared her, but sitting so close to the goddess seemed disrespectful.

She smiled. "I heard the wonderful news. Congratulations."

He bowed his head again. "Thank you, Clan Mother."

"Please." She waved a hand. "Call me Annani. We are not meeting in any official capacity. This is family business."

"As you wish." He would swallow his own tongue before using her given name.

"It is very fortunate that I happen to be here. If you so wish, I can perform a joining ceremony for you and your beloved."

The goddess's eyes sparkled with enthusiasm. There were two things that made the Clan Mother especially happy. One was babies, and the other was weddings. He would have to disappoint her.

"I thank you for your offer, but it's too early for us to be talking about a wedding." Hopefully, Anandur had kept his yap shut and hadn't told Kian or Syssi about Brundar's proposal.

The last thing he needed was to antagonize the goddess. If she'd heard from Kian or Syssi about his proposal, she would think he was lying to her on purpose.

Annani frowned, and his gut twisted in a knot. Did she know?

"Why is that? Are you not sure that she is the one and only for you?"

He shook his head. "It's not that. I know Calypso is my true love match. But we haven't been together long. I need her to get to know me better first."

"I see." The spark in the goddess's eyes dimmed a little. "You are not sure of her love for you."

"It's not that either. I know Calypso loves me."

Frustrated, the goddess lifted both hands in the air. "So what is the problem, young man?"

He wasn't going to tell Annani his deepest secret, but maybe he could ask her advice. "Do you believe that mates need to know everything about each other?

A naughty smile brought back the sparkle in her eyes. "Well, not everything. Some mystery makes the relationship more interesting."

It was obvious that she was not talking about his type of secret. "What about traumatic events that happened a long time ago? Things that might affect the way she sees me?"

Annani's expression turned somber. "You are a warrior, Brundar. Whatever you have done in the line of duty is nothing to feel ashamed of. Your beloved should know who you are, including your past deeds, and accept you, warts and all. If she does not, then she is not worthy of you."

Again, Annani had mistaken his question to mean something else. Brundar was not ashamed of his past deeds as a soldier. He hadn't told Calypso any details, but she knew he had killed in defense of his clan and had no problem with that.

Still, the goddess had it right. If he never told Calypso about what had happened to him, he would always wonder if it might change the way she saw him. It was better to get it over with, and not let it fester indefinitely.

"Thank you for the advice, Clan Mother. I will tell Calypso everything there is to know about me. But I need to find the right time to do it."

The goddess put her tiny hand on his thigh. "Do not delay. The more you think about it, the harder it will become. Things of this nature always seem worse than they actually are."

"Words of wisdom."

She smiled. "I have not always been so wise. It comes with age. Talk with your Calypso. If you change your mind about the wedding, do so soon. I am leaving the day after Kian and Syssi are back."

"I will. Thank you." He pushed to his feet.

"I want to meet your mate when she feels better. Perhaps tomorrow?"

That was unexpected. He hadn't told Calypso about Annani staying at the keep because it was supposed to be classified information. "I'm under orders to keep your presence here a secret. Only the Guardians, the council members, and Phoenix's parents are allowed to know."

Annani waved a dismissive hand. "I am amending your orders to include Calypso in that shortlist. As long as I am here, I want to meet the new additions to my clan. I already met Tessa, and now I want to meet Calypso."

He bowed again. "Of course, Clan Mother."

She sighed. "I see that it is no use with you. Hopefully, your mate will soften you some. You are too rigid."

"Yes, Clan Mother."

CALLIE

"*I*'m scared," Callie said.

Her, plain Callie Meyers, meeting a real freaking goddess face to face?

Someone please wake me from this insane dream. What was she saying? *No, please don't. If this is a dream I never want to wake up.*

"Don't be. Annani is powerful, but she is kind. She just wants to get to know you."

"What if she doesn't like me?"

"Why wouldn't she? You're smart and kind and brave and beautiful. What else is there?"

"I'm a waitress, for God's sake." She chuckled. "I guess I need to change that to a for Goddess's sake."

"So what? What's wrong with being a waitress?"

She shrugged. "A lot of people look down on waitressing because it doesn't require education."

"Not Annani. She is smarter than that."

Callie nodded. "I guess I have no choice either way. It's not like I can refuse a summons from a goddess."

"No, you can't. Can I knock on the door now?"

"Yeah." She sucked in a deep breath and forced her hands to stop fidgeting with the bottom of her shirt.

Crap, if only she had something nicer to wear. But the strapless black dress was not appropriate for a formal meeting, and everything else she had was limited to jeans, leggings and T-shirts. The outfit she'd bought before the accident would have been perfect, but unfortunately, it hadn't made it.

A short, kind of square-looking man wearing a suit opened the door and bowed. "Greetings, master and mistress. Please enter, the Clan Mother is awaiting you."

A strange little man, but then everything in Callie's new reality was.

Brundar's hand on the small of her back propelled her forward as her eyes darted around for her first glimpse of the goddess.

She found her sitting on the couch. A small woman with a massive head of hair, soft red curls cascading down her back and front and pooling around her. Callie had never seen hair like that.

But then the woman turned toward them, and Callie's knees buckled. She barely stifled the "Oh, my God," she felt compelled to exclaim.

Amanda had been right. As stunning as the daughter was, her mother, who at first glance looked much younger than her daughter, was incomparable. It was hard to put her finger on what exactly made the goddess so inhumanly beautiful. Callie had a feeling that a mere picture could have never translated all this otherworldly creature was. Her beauty emanated from the inside, striking Callie like a force field.

An immense power was contained in that small package.

"Calypso, come sit with me." She patted the couch next to her.

Callie glanced at Brundar.

He encouraged her with a nod, and when she didn't move, led her to the couch. She lowered herself down to sit on the very edge, looking down at her feet instead of facing the nuclear power plant sitting next to her.

What if the radiation made her face melt off? Callie felt like giggling hysterically at the absurd notion. Or was it? The goddess was glowing. Didn't it imply some form of radiation?

Brundar nudged her, reminding her of her manners.

"It's an honor to meet you, Clan Mother." She whispered the words Brundar had instructed her to say.

The goddess reached for her clammy hand and clasped it. "Call me Annani. Clan Mother is a title I tolerate at ceremonies. I am not too fond of it in private."

"Oh," was the only response Callie could come up with. Brilliant.

The goddess turned to look at Brundar. "You may leave us. I want a few moments alone with your mate. I will summon you when we are done."

He bowed, ignoring Callie's panicked expression. "As you wish, Clan Mother." He turned on his heel and left.

The traitor.

When the door closed behind him, the goddess sighed. "You have your work cut out for you, child. That boy needs to loosen up, and you seem like the right girl to pull that stick out of his backside."

Shocked, Callie looked up at the goddess's smiling face.

The goddess waved a hand. "Do not look so shocked. You know I am right."

Callie swallowed. "I guess," she whispered.

"Use your outside voice, Calypso," the esteemed Clan Mother singsonged the tune from a *Saturday Night Live* skit.

Callie giggled, the frog in her throat shrinking. "I would've never expected a goddess to watch television."

Annani rolled her eyes. "How else am I going to learn all

about popular culture? Besides, I enjoy a good laugh. That skit is so funny."

"It is." It was also vulgar, but apparently, the goddess was no prude.

"You are probably wondering why I wanted to see you."

Callie nodded. "Brundar said you wanted to get to know me."

"Yes. It is a rare opportunity for me to welcome a new member to my clan who is not of my line. A new blood, if you will. I do not know if Brundar explained how important it is to us to find people like you. Especially females who could become the mothers of new genetic lines."

"He told me a lot, but I don't remember everything. It was so much to absorb. But I understand that those who are your descendants can't intermarry, and that up until recently there weren't any other known immortals other than your clan and your enemies the Doomers, who are all male and are obviously not considered good marriage material."

"That is it in a nutshell. You understand perfectly. Now tell me about yourself, including how you and Brundar found each other." The goddess smirked. "If I ask him, I will get a three-word answer at best. I would rather hear the story from you."

Callie took a deep breath and decided to tell the goddess everything. After all, she had nothing to hide or be ashamed of, and even if she had, it would be foolish to tell half-truths to a goddess who might be able to read her mind.

"You are a very brave young woman," Annani said after Callie was done.

She felt herself blush at the undeserved compliment. "It's very kind of you, but I'm not. I just did what I had to do to survive." She looked into the goddess's warm eyes. "You are the brave one. I know you are a goddess and that you are very powerful, but from what Brundar told me I understand that you were still a young girl when you lost the love of your life and then your entire family. If I were you, I would've crawled into a hole and waited to die."

As sadness replaced the mirth in Annani's eyes, Callie regretted letting herself blabber like that.

"That is exactly what I did, child. But at some point, I realized it was selfish. I was the only survivor of an advanced civilization, and without me and the knowledge I carried humanity would be lost for thousands of years. I had to do all I could to preserve my people's legacy and help humanity evolve."

"As I said, you were incredibly courageous to take on such a monumental task, and at such a young age, despite the despair that must've weighed you down."

"My despair was illuminated by a tiny glimmer of hope, and it was enough to keep me going. It still does."

"The hope for humanity?"

Annani tilted her head as if deliberating whether she should answer or not. "Not only that. It was more personal than that."

What could it be? Brundar had said that the goddess had vowed to never love again. So that could not have been it. "Do you hope some of your people survived? Or maybe got away?"

"No, child. At the beginning I did. But after I'd learned all the facts I knew they were all gone."

The goddess sighed and smiled a sad smile. "It happened before I escaped, while I was still in mourning and inconsolable in my grief. An old human fortuneteller came to see me. She was quite famous for her abilities, so I agreed to hear her out even though I did not want to talk to anyone other than my parents and my best friend, Gulan."

Annani let go of Callie's hand and wiped a lone tear from the corner of her eye. "The fortuneteller told me not to despair because all was not lost. I cannot say more because she made me swear to never repeat this to anyone, and I am not foolish enough to disregard the words of a seer, even a human one."

Callie could understand that. If the foretelling was so important that it had kept Annani going for thousands of years, she was right to follow the seer's instructions to the letter and not jinx it in any way.

"I hope it was okay for you to tell me even this little."

Annani nodded. "I do not know why I did. I never told anyone." She smiled. "There must be something special about you."

Callie put a hand over her heart. "I will never repeat this to anyone. Your secret is safe with me."

The goddess leaned over and kissed her cheek. "I know, child."

6 4

BRUNDAR

*C*alypso didn't say much as Brundar picked her up from Kian's penthouse. She seemed dazed, which was understandable following her first encounter with Annani.

The goddess's presence was unnerving even to her own descendants, let alone to a girl who'd known nothing of their world up until the day before yesterday.

"Are you okay?" he asked as they entered the elevator.

"Yes. I don't know how my head didn't explode yet, but somehow I'm holding it together."

He pulled her into his arms. "You are stronger than you realize."

She leaned her forehead on his chest. "I'm not all that strong. I have you to lean on."

Her words filled him with immense satisfaction. "Always." He kissed the top of her head.

Calypso lifted her eyes to him. "And you have me to lean on too. I hope you realize that. It's no longer just your brother and you. I'm your family too."

Brundar tightened his arms around her, then let her go as the elevator doors opened.

Hand in hand, they walked down the corridor to what would be, from now on, their home. At least until he applied for a house in the village.

Would Anandur stay with them? Did he want to keep his brother as a roommate?

Brundar didn't mind, but those kinds of decisions were no longer his own. It would be up to Calypso. His future was with her.

However, there was one more thing Brundar needed to do before he could think of a future with his mate without a dark cloud hanging over his head.

Back in the apartment, he had Calypso sit on the couch and then poured himself a hefty serving of whiskey.

She lifted a brow. "Isn't it a bit early for that?"

"Anytime after five in the afternoon is not too early."

She laughed. "I guess for Scots it never is."

"Aye." He saluted. "I would offer you a drink, but all we have are beers and whiskey."

"I'll settle for a glass of water."

He went back to the kitchen, filled a tall glass for her, then came back to sit next to her on the couch.

"I need to tell you something, and it's not going to be easy for me."

She put a hand on his thigh. "You don't need to tell me anything that makes you uncomfortable."

He shook his head. "There should be no secrets between mates. Not big ones, anyway. If I don't tell you, it will keep bothering me until I do."

She nodded, but her eyes betrayed her trepidation. He wondered what Calypso was imagining his big secret was to make her so fearful.

"Remember when I told you about what happened to me when I was a kid?"

"Of course." She let out a breath, which he took to mean that this wasn't what she'd thought he was about to tell her.

"I didn't tell you everything. No one other than Anandur knows what happened. Not even our mother."

She frowned. "Are you sure you want to tell me?"

The more outs she was giving him, the more determined he was to tell her. "Yes, I am. It was more than a severe beating. I was violated by someone I thought of as my best friend."

She nodded as if his confession didn't come as a surprise to her. "I guessed as much."

It was a tremendous relief. The worst part about telling Calypso was fear of her reaction. If she'd responded with horror or pity, it would have crushed him.

"How did you know?"

"Your aversion to touch. A beating, no matter how severe, wouldn't have caused it." She took his hand and lifted it to her lips for a kiss. "Thank you for telling me. Your trust means a lot to me."

He closed his eyes for a split second, thanking the Fates for the gift that was Calypso. Somehow she'd managed to turn this difficult moment and the memory of a vile act into something positive—a gift of trust.

"That's not the end of the story. Anandur saved me from further violation by the rest of the gang that had attacked me. He killed them all."

"How old was he?"

"He was already a grown man, a warrior. If not for him, I would've died. It was before my transition, I was still human, and a weak human at that."

Calypso's lip quivered, and tears pooled at the corners of her eyes before spilling down her cheeks. "I'm sorry. I wanted to be strong for you, but imagining a young boy tortured and murdered, I just can't handle it. I'm so sorry."

He pulled her into his arms. "Thanks to Anandur it didn't happen. But my family had to flee in the middle of the night, leaving everything behind. The villagers were coming to avenge their sons, and there were too few of us to defend our homes. After that, Annani decreed that we all needed to move to one location, far away from any human settlements. It took us decades of hardship to build our home in Scotland. And it was all my fault."

She pushed on his chest. "It wasn't your fault. You were a boy, a victim."

He shook his head. "If I had listened to my mother and stayed away from the humans, none of that would have happened."

"First of all, you were a young boy. Show me one preteen who listens to his mother. Secondly, it might have saved your clan from worse things. What happened to you was tragic and awful, but it forced your family to build a strong, defensible home. So maybe you should think of it as thanks to you and not because of you."

She was so adorable when berating him for putting himself down.

At that moment, he loved her more than ever. "I love you, Calypso. You are like an explosion of light that obliterates my darkness. I couldn't hold on to it even if I tried."

The indignation in her eyes gave way to the sweetest expression. She cupped his cheek. "This is the power of love. It is the antidote to darkness."

"I agree."

As long as he was on a roll, he should get it all out. "There is more."

Calypso flinched.

He squeezed her hand. "No more tragedies, I promise. But you might get angry after you hear my last confession."

"What is it?"

"When I first met you at the club, I couldn't just let you go. You were married, off limits to me, but I peeked into Shawn's mind and knew you weren't safe with him. I've watched over you ever since." He smoothed his hand over his jaw. "It was straight out stalker behavior, but I couldn't help myself. I guess I knew on a subconscious level that you were my fated one."

Again, Calypso didn't look shocked or surprised. "Did you park across the street from my house?"

He nodded.

"I felt it. I would look out the window and get this peaceful feeling as if someone was watching over me. I thought it was just my imagination."

"So you're not mad?"

"Mad? No way, I'm grateful. Knowing that I was never really alone during those hard times is such a relief."

"You are never going to be alone again. Not as long as I breathe. We are one."

She cuddled up to him. "Always and forever."

TURNER

*D*eath.

The bastard finally came to collect, much earlier than Turner had been expecting him.

Forty-six was too young to die.

For a civilian.

As a soldier in an elite commando unit, he hadn't expected to live long, but then he was no longer one—hadn't been for a long time. Turner had been retired for a good number of years, and even before that, his field days had been a distant memory. His tactical abilities had become apparent early on in his military career, making him a much more valuable asset with a pen and paper behind the desk than with a rifle behind enemy lines.

The irony wasn't lost on him.

With a rifle, he would have had much less blood on his hands than what he'd accomplished from behind the fucking desk. As a brilliant tactician, Turner had no doubt that his missions had resulted in lower casualties compared to missions planned by others, but that didn't mean he hadn't sent many to their deaths.

Knowingly.

He had an uncanny ability to predict the precise outcome of every mission. Unfortunately, he could count those with no lives lost on the fingers of one hand.

Over the course of his military career, and later as a civilian operator, Turner had fed the Grim Reaper countless lives. But the monster wasn't satisfied with that offering. He came back for Turner with one of his most deadly hatchets.

Lung cancer.

Turner had never smoked, had never shared an office with a smoker, and as far as he knew, he hadn't been exposed to any toxic substances either. He watched what he put in his mouth, kept a gruelingly intense workout routine, and was a black belt in several martial arts disciplines.

One of the advantages of being a single man who didn't date much was plenty of free time. His lifestyle had been Spartan. He'd kept to his strict regimen, believing it would keep him in good shape and healthy into old age.

But fate was a vindictive bitch.

The disease had come out of the blue. A persistent cough that had finally prompted him to see a doctor, leading to the diagnosis less than a week later.

Not that death was imminent. With treatments he could forestall the fucker for years, maybe even for good, but Turner refused to live under his dark shadow.

He wasn't ready to go.

What had he done with his life?

A lot for others, but very little for himself.

And yet, if Turner cared to be honest with himself, he had to admit that this wasn't entirely true. Even though his job had been about the most complicated rescue and extraction operations, seemingly a noble task, he'd done it because he'd loved the game.

Outsmarting the enemy had given him the kind of satisfaction he couldn't derive from anything else; he lived for the thrill, and the collateral damage hadn't bothered him too much.

He was an analytical man, not an emotional one.

Even now, facing the possibility of his own premature death, Turner didn't feel despair or anger. He wasn't even overly surprised. But that didn't mean he was going to throw in the towel and accept defeat. That wasn't his style.

He was Turner, the guy who always found another angle, another solution.

There was no cure for what he had. The doctor had talked about treatment and remission, not a cure. But that didn't mean there was no other way to cheat death.

Permanently.

It was a long shot.

Turner had always suspected that there were hidden forces at work behind the seemingly unpredictable machinations of global affairs, and that what was considered occult often had a scientific explanation, albeit one yet to be discovered.

Apparently, the mythological gods hadn't been the construct of human imagination, but an advanced species that had become extinct.

Kian and Andrew hadn't shared many details with him, but after further investigation, Turner had deduced the rest by putting the puzzle pieces together.

A very small portion of the human population carried their immortal genes. Those lucky humans tended to exhibit a wide array of paranormal talents with varying strengths.

The only thing that had made Andrew special was his ability to tell truth from lie. A useful trick that Turner had exploited on more than one occasion during the years Andrew had served under him. But that little trick was nothing in comparison to what Turner could do.

Of course, that didn't mean he was a Dormant carrier of immortal genes, but there was a small chance that he was.

A chance was all he was going to ask for, and Kian was going to give it to him.

Willingly or not.

Turner wasn't above blackmail. On the contrary, it was one of the better tools in his arsenal. Kian needed to keep his people's existence secret, and Turner was more than happy to comply.

For a price.

A chance at immortality.

Victor Turner still had a lot of living to do.

The end... for now.

TURNER'S STORY IS COMING UP NEXT!
BOOK 17
DARK OPERATIVE: A SHADOW OF DEATH

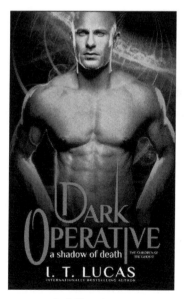

Available on Amazon

Dear reader,

Thank you for joining me on the continuing adventures of the *Children of the Gods*.

As an independent author, I rely on your support to spread the word. So if you enjoyed the story, please share your experience, and if it isn't too much trouble, I would greatly appreciate a brief review on Amazon.

Click here to leave a review

Love & happy reading,

Isabell

THE CHILDREN OF THE GODS SERIES

THE CHILDREN OF THE GODS ORIGINS

1: GODDESS'S CHOICE

When gods and immortals still ruled the ancient world, one young
goddess risked everything for love.

2: GODDESS'S HOPE

Hungry for power and infatuated with the beautiful Areana, Navuh
plots his father's demise. After all, by getting rid of the insane god he
would be doing the world a favor. Except, when gods and immortals
conspire against each other, humanity pays the price.

But things are not what they seem, and prophecies should not to be
trusted...

THE CHILDREN OF THE GODS

1: DARK STRANGER THE DREAM

Syssi's paranormal foresight lands her a job at Dr. Amanda Dokani's
neuroscience lab, but it fails to predict the thrilling yet terrifying
turn her life will take. Syssi has no clue that her boss is an immortal
who'll drag her into a secret, millennia-old battle over humanity's
future. Nor does she realize that the professor's imposing brother is
the mysterious stranger who's been starring in her dreams.

Since the dawn of human civilization, two warring factions of
immortals—the descendants of the gods of old—have been secretly
shaping its destiny. Leading the clandestine battle from his
luxurious Los Angeles high-rise, Kian is surrounded by his clan, yet
alone. Descending from a single goddess, clan members are
forbidden to each other. And as the only other immortals are their
hated enemies, Kian and his kin have been long resigned to a lonely
existence of fleeting trysts with human partners. That is, until his
sister makes a game-changing discovery—a mortal seeress who she
believes is a dormant carrier of their genes. Ever the realist, Kian is
skeptical and refuses Amanda's plea to attempt Syssi's activation.

But when his enemies learn of the Dormant's existence, he's forced to rush her to the safety of his keep. Inexorably drawn to Syssi, Kian wrestles with his conscience as he is tempted to explore her budding interest in the darker shades of sensuality.

2: DARK STRANGER REVEALED

While sheltered in the clan's stronghold, Syssi is unaware that Kian and Amanda are not human, and neither are the supposedly religious fanatics that are after her. She feels a powerful connection to Kian, and as he introduces her to a world of pleasure she never dared imagine, his dominant sexuality is a revelation. Considering that she's completely out of her element, Syssi feels comfortable and safe letting go with him. That is, until she begins to suspect that all is not as it seems. Piecing the puzzle together, she draws a scary, yet wrong conclusion...

3: DARK STRANGER IMMORTAL

When Kian confesses his true nature, Syssi is not as much shocked by the revelation as she is wounded by what she perceives as his callous plans for her.

If she doesn't turn, he'll be forced to erase her memories and let her go. His family's safety demands secrecy – no one in the mortal world is allowed to know that immortals exist.

Resigned to the cruel reality that even if she stays on to never again leave the keep, she'll get old while Kian won't, Syssi is determined to enjoy what little time she has with him, one day at a time.

Can Kian let go of the mortal woman he loves? Will Syssi turn? And if she does, will she survive the dangerous transition?

4: DARK ENEMY TAKEN

Dalhu can't believe his luck when he stumbles upon the beautiful immortal professor. Presented with a once in a lifetime opportunity to grab an immortal female for himself, he kidnaps her and runs. If he ever gets caught, either by her people or his, his life is forfeit. But for a chance of a loving mate and a family of his own, Dalhu is prepared to do everything in his power to win Amanda's heart, and that includes leaving the Doom brotherhood and his old life behind.

Amanda soon discovers that there is more to the handsome Doomer than his dark past and a hulking, sexy body. But succumbing to her enemy's seduction, or worse, developing feelings for a ruthless killer is out of the question. No man is worth life on the run, not even the one and only immortal male she could claim as her own…

Her clan and her research must come first…

5: DARK ENEMY CAPTIVE

When the rescue team returns with Amanda and the chained Dalhu to the keep, Amanda is not as thrilled to be back as she thought she'd be. Between Kian's contempt for her and Dalhu's imprisonment, Amanda's budding relationship with Dalhu seems doomed. Things start to look up when Annani offers her help, and together with Syssi they resolve to find a way for Amanda to be with Dalhu. But will she still want him when she realizes that he is responsible for her nephew's murder? Could she? Will she take the easy way out and choose Andrew instead?

6: DARK ENEMY REDEEMED

Amanda suspects that something fishy is going on onboard the Anna. But when her investigation of the peculiar all-female Russian crew fails to uncover anything other than more speculation, she decides it's time to stop playing detective and face her real problem —a man she shouldn't want but can't live without.

6.5: MY DARK AMAZON

When Michael and Kri fight off a gang of humans, Michael gets stabbed. The injury to his immortal body recovers fast, but the one to his ego takes longer, putting a strain on his relationship with Kri.

7: DARK WARRIOR MINE

When Andrew is forced to retire from active duty, he believes that all he has to look forward to is a boring desk job. His glory days in special ops are over. But as it turns out, his thrill ride has just begun. Andrew discovers not only that immortals exist and have been manipulating global affairs since antiquity, but that he and his sister are rare possessors of the immortal genes.

Problem is, Andrew might be too old to attempt the activation process. His sister, who is fourteen years his junior, barely made it through the transition, so the odds of him coming out of it alive, let alone immortal, are slim.

But fate may force his hand.

Helping a friend find his long-lost daughter, Andrew finds a woman who's worth taking the risk for. Nathalie might be a Dormant, but the only way to find out for sure requires fangs and venom.

8: DARK WARRIOR'S PROMISE

Andrew and Nathalie's love flourishes, but the secrets they keep from each other taint their relationship with doubts and suspicions. In the meantime, Sebastian and his men are getting bolder, and the storm that's brewing will shift the balance of power in the millennia-old conflict between Annani's clan and its enemies.

9: DARK WARRIOR'S DESTINY

The new ghost in Nathalie's head remembers who he was in life, providing Andrew and her with indisputable proof that he is real and not a figment of her imagination.

Convinced that she is a Dormant, Andrew decides to go forward with his transition immediately after the rescue mission at the Doomers' HQ.

Fearing for his life, Nathalie pleads with him to reconsider. She'd rather spend the rest of her mortal days with Andrew than risk what they have for the fickle promise of immortality.

While the clan gets ready for battle, Carol gets help from an unlikely ally. Sebastian's second-in-command can no longer ignore the torment she suffers at the hands of his commander and offers to help her, but only if she agrees to his terms.

10: DARK WARRIOR'S LEGACY

Andrew's acclimation to his post-transition body isn't easy. His senses are sharper, he's bigger, stronger, and hungrier. Nathalie fears that the changes in the man she loves are more than physical. Measuring up to this new version of him is going to be a challenge.

Carol and Robert are disillusioned with each other. They are not destined mates, and love is not on the horizon. When Robert's three months are up, he might be left with nothing to show for his sacrifice.

Lana contacts Anandur with disturbing news; the yacht and its human cargo are in Mexico. Kian must find a way to apprehend

Alex and rescue the women on board without causing an international incident.

11: Dark Guardian Found

What would you do if you stopped aging?

Eva runs. The ex-DEA agent doesn't know what caused her strange mutation, only that if discovered, she'll be dissected like a lab rat. What Eva doesn't know, though, is that she's a descendant of the gods, and that she is not alone. The man who rocked her world in one life-changing encounter over thirty years ago is an immortal as well.

To keep his people's existence secret, Bhathian was forced to turn his back on the only woman who ever captured his heart, but he's never forgotten and never stopped looking for her.

12: Dark Guardian Craved

Cautious after a lifetime of disappointments, Eva is mistrustful of Bhathian's professed feelings of love. She accepts him as a lover and a confidant but not as a life partner.

Jackson suspects that Tessa is his true love mate, but unless she overcomes her fears, he might never find out.

Carol gets an offer she can't refuse—a chance to prove that there is more to her than meets the eye. Robert believes she's about to commit a deadly mistake, but when he tries to dissuade her, she tells him to leave.

13: Dark Guardian's Mate

Prepare for the heart-warming culmination of Eva and Bhathian's story!

14: Dark Angel's Obsession

The cold and stoic warrior is an enigma even to those closest to him. His secrets are about to unravel...

15: Dark Angel's Seduction

Brundar is fighting a losing battle. Calypso is slowly chipping away his icy armor from the outside, while his need for her is melting it from the inside.

He can't allow it to happen. Calypso is a human with none of the

Dormant indicators. There is no way he can keep her for more than a few weeks.

16: Dark Angel's Surrender

Get ready for the heart pounding conclusion to Brundar and Calypso's story.

Callie still couldn't wrap her head around it, nor could she summon even a smidgen of sorrow or regret. After all, she had some memories with him that weren't horrible. She should've felt something. But there was nothing, not even shock. Not even horror at what had transpired over the last couple of hours.

Maybe it was a typical response for survivors--feeling euphoric for the simple reason that they were alive. Especially when that survival was nothing short of miraculous.

Brundar's cold hand closed around hers, reminding her that they weren't out of the woods yet. Her injuries were superficial, and the most she had to worry about was some scarring. But, despite his and Anandur's reassurances, Brundar might never walk again.

If he ended up crippled because of her, she would never forgive herself for getting him involved in her crap.

"Are you okay, sweetling? Are you in pain?" Brundar asked.

Her injuries were nothing compared to his, and yet he was concerned about her. God, she loved this man. The thing was, if she told him that, he would run off, or crawl away as was the case.

Hey, maybe this was the perfect opportunity to spring it on him.

17: Dark Operative: A Shadow of Death

As a brilliant strategist and the only human entrusted with the secret of immortals' existence, Turner is both an asset and a liability to the clan. His request to attempt transition into immortality as an alternative to cancer treatments cannot be denied without risking the clan's exposure. On the other hand, approving it means risking his premature death. In both scenarios, the clan will lose a valuable ally.

When the decision is left to the clan's physician, Turner makes plans to manipulate her by taking advantage of her interest in him.

Will Bridget fall for the cold, calculated operative? Or will Turner fall into his own trap?

18: Dark Operative: A Glimmer of Hope

As Turner and Bridget's relationship deepens, living together seems like the right move, but to make it work both need to make concessions.

Bridget is realistic and keeps her expectations low. Turner could never be the truelove mate she yearns for, but he is as good as she's going to get. Other than his emotional limitations, he's perfect in every way.

Turner's hard shell is starting to show cracks. He wants immortality, he wants to be part of the clan, and he wants Bridget, but he doesn't want to cause her pain.

His options are either abandon his quest for immortality and give Bridget his few remaining decades, or abandon Bridget by going for the transition and most likely dying. His rational mind dictates that he chooses the former, but his gut pulls him toward the latter. Which one is he going to trust?

19: Dark Operative: The Dawn of Love

Get ready for the exciting finale of Bridget and Turner's story!

20: Dark Survivor Awakened

This was a strange new world she had awakened to.

Her memory loss must have been catastrophic because almost nothing was familiar. The language was foreign to her, with only a few words bearing some similarity to the language she thought in. Still, a full moon cycle had passed since her awakening, and little by little she was gaining basic understanding of it--only a few words and phrases, but she was learning more each day.

A week or so ago, a little girl on the street had tugged on her mother's sleeve and pointed at her. "Look, Mama, Wonder Woman!"

The mother smiled apologetically, saying something in the language these people spoke, then scurried away with the child looking behind her shoulder and grinning.

When it happened again with another child on the same day, it was settled.

Wonder Woman must have been the name of someone important in this strange world she had awoken to, and since both times it had been said with a smile it must have been a good one.

Wonder had a nice ring to it.

She just wished she knew what it meant.

21: DARK SURVIVOR ECHOES OF LOVE

Wonder's journey continues in *Dark Survivor Echoes of Love*.

22: DARK SURVIVOR REUNITED

The exciting finale of Wonder and Anandur's story.

23: DARK WIDOW'S SECRET

Vivian and her daughter share a powerful telepathic connection, so when Ella can't be reached by conventional or psychic means, her mother fears the worst.

Help arrives from an unexpected source when Vivian gets a call from the young doctor she met at a psychic convention. Turns out Julian belongs to a private organization specializing in retrieving missing girls.

As Julian's clan mobilizes its considerable resources to rescue the daughter, Magnus is charged with keeping the gorgeous young mother safe.

Worry for Ella and the secrets Vivian and Magnus keep from each other should be enough to prevent the sparks of attraction from kindling a blaze of desire. Except, these pesky sparks have a mind of their own.

24: DARK WIDOW'S CURSE

A simple rescue operation turns into mission impossible when the Russian mafia gets involved. Bad things are supposed to come in threes, but in Vivian's case, it seems like there is no limit to bad luck. Her family and everyone who gets close to her is affected by her curse.

Will Magnus and his people prove her wrong?

25: DARK WIDOW'S BLESSING

The thrilling finale of the Dark Widow trilogy!

26: DARK DREAM'S TEMPTATION

Julian has known Ella is the one for him from the moment he saw her picture, but when he finally frees her from captivity, she seems indifferent to him. Could he have been mistaken?

Ella's rescue should've ended that chapter in her life, but it seems like the road back to normalcy has just begun and it's full of obstacles. Between the pitying looks she gets and her mother's attempts to get her into therapy, Ella feels like she's typecast as a victim, when nothing could be further from the truth. She's a tough survivor, and she's going to prove it.

Strangely, the only one who seems to understand is Logan, who keeps popping up in her dreams. But then, he's a figment of her imagination—or is he?

27: DARK DREAM'S UNRAVELING

While trying to figure out a way around Logan's silencing compulsion, Ella concocts an ambitious plan. What if instead of trying to keep him out of her dreams, she could pretend to like him and lure him into a trap?

Catching Navuh's son would be a major boon for the clan, as well as for Ella. She will have her revenge, turning the tables on another scumbag out to get her.

28: DARK DREAM'S TRAP

The trap is set, but who is the hunter and who is the prey? Find out in this heart-pounding conclusion to the *Dark Dream* trilogy.

29: DARK PRINCE'S ENIGMA

As the son of the most dangerous male on the planet, Lokan lives by three rules:

Don't trust a soul.

Don't show emotions.

And don't get attached.

Will one extraordinary woman make him break all three?

30: DARK PRINCE'S DILEMMA

Will Kian decide that the benefits of trusting Lokan outweigh the risks?

Will Lokan betray his father and brothers for the greater good of his people?

Are Carol and Lokan true-love mates, or is one of them playing the other?

So many questions, the path ahead is anything but clear.

31: DARK PRINCE'S AGENDA

While Turner and Kian work out the details of Areana's rescue plan, Carol and Lokan's tumultuous relationship hits another snag. Is it a sign of things to come?

32 : DARK QUEEN'S QUEST

A former beauty queen, a retired undercover agent, and a successful model, Mey is not the typical damsel in distress. But when her sister drops off the radar and then someone starts following her around, she panics.

Following a vague clue that Kalugal might be in New York, Kian sends a team headed by Yamanu to search for him.

As Mey and Yamanu's paths cross, he offers her his help and protection, but will that be all?

33: DARK QUEEN'S KNIGHT

As the only member of his clan with a godlike power over human minds, Yamanu has been shielding his people for centuries, but that power comes at a steep price. When Mey enters his life, he's faced with the most difficult choice.

The safety of his clan or a future with his fated mate.

34: DARK QUEEN'S ARMY

As Mey anxiously waits for her transition to begin and for Yamanu to test whether his godlike powers are gone, the clan sets out to solve two mysteries:

Where is Jin, and is she there voluntarily?

Where is Kalugal, and what is he up to?

35: DARK SPY CONSCRIPTED

Jin possesses a unique paranormal ability. Just by touching someone, she can insert a mental hook into their psyche and tie a string of her consciousness to it, creating a tether. That doesn't make her a spy, though, not unless her talent is discovered by those seeking to exploit it.

36: Dark Spy's Mission

Jin's first spying mission is supposed to be easy. Walk into the club, touch Kalugal to tether her consciousness to him, and walk out.

Except, they should have known better.

37: Dark Spy's Resolution

The best-laid plans often go awry...

38: Dark Overlord New Horizon

Jacki has two talents that set her apart from the rest of the human race.

She has unpredictable glimpses of other people's futures, and she is immune to mind manipulation.

Unfortunately, both talents are pretty useless for finding a job other than the one she had in the government's paranormal division.

It seemed like a sweet deal, until she found out that the director planned on producing super babies by compelling the recruits into pairing up. When an opportunity to escape the program presented itself, she took it, only to find out that humans are not at the top of the food chain.

Immortals are real, and at the very top of the hierarchy is Kalugal, the most powerful, arrogant, and sexiest male she has ever met.

With one look, he sets her blood on fire, but Jacki is not a fool. A man like him will never think of her as anything more than a tasty snack, while she will never settle for anything less than his heart.

39: Dark Overlord's Wife

Jacki is still clinging to her all-or-nothing policy, but Kalugal is chipping away at her resistance. Perhaps it's time to ease up on her convictions. A little less than all is still much better than nothing, and a couple of decades with a demigod is probably worth more than a lifetime with a mere mortal.

40: Dark Overlord's Clan

As Jacki and Kalugal prepare to celebrate their union, Kian takes every precaution to safeguard his people. Except, Kalugal and his men are not his only potential adversaries, and compulsion is not the only power he should fear.

41: Dark Choices The Quandary

When Rufsur and Edna meet, the attraction is as unexpected as it is undeniable. Except, she's the clan's judge and councilwoman, and he's Kalugal's second-in-command. Will loyalty and duty to their people keep them apart?

42: Dark Choices Paradigm Shift

Edna and Rufsur are miserable without each other, and their two-week separation seems like an eternity. Long-distance relationships are difficult, but for immortal couples they are impossible. Unless one of them is willing to leave everything behind for the other, things are just going to get worse. Except, the cost of compromise is far greater than giving up their comfortable lives and hard-earned positions. The future of their people is on the line.

43: Dark Choices The Accord

The winds of change blowing over the village demand hard choices. For better or worse, Kian's decisions will alter the trajectory of the clan's future, and he is not ready to take the plunge. But as Edna and Rufsur's plight gains widespread support, his resistance slowly begins to erode.

44: Dark Secrets Resurgence

On a sabbatical from his Stanford teaching position, Professor David Levinson finally has time to write the sci-fi novel he's been thinking about for years.

The phenomena of past life memories and near-death experiences are too controversial to include in his formal psychiatric research, while fiction is the perfect outlet for his esoteric ideas.

Hoping that a change of pace will provide the inspiration he needs, David accepts a friend's invitation to an old Scottish castle.

45: Dark Secrets Unveiled

When Professor David Levinson accepts a friend's invitation to an old Scottish castle, what he finds there is more fantastical than his most outlandish theories. The castle is home to a clan of immortals, their leader is a stunning demigoddess, and even more shockingly, it might be precisely where he belongs.

Except, the clan founder is hiding a secret that might cast a dark shadow on David's relationship with her daughter.

Nevertheless, when offered a chance at immortality, he agrees to undergo the dangerous induction process.

Will David survive his transition into immortality? And if he does, will his relationship with Sari survive the unveiling of her mother's secret?

46: Dark Secrets Absolved

Absolution.

David had given and received it.

The few short hours since he'd emerged from the coma had felt incredible. He'd finally been free of the guilt and pain, and for the first time since Jonah's death, he had felt truly happy and optimistic about the future.

He'd survived the transition into immortality, had been accepted into the clan, and was about to marry the best woman on the face of the planet, his true love mate, his salvation, his everything.

What could have possibly gone wrong?

Just about everything.

47: Dark haven Illusion

Welcome to Safe Haven, where not everything is what it seems.

On a quest to process personal pain, Anastasia joins the Safe Haven Spiritual Retreat.

Through meditation, self-reflection, and hard work, she hopes to make peace with the voices in her head.

This is where she belongs.

Except, membership comes with a hefty price, doubts are sacrilege, and leaving is not as easy as walking out the front gate.

Is living in utopia worth the sacrifice?

Anastasia believes so until the arrival of a new acolyte changes everything.

Apparently, the gods of old were not a myth, their immortal descendants share the planet with humans, and she might be a carrier of their genes.

48: Dark Haven Unmasked

As Anastasia leaves Safe Haven for a week-long romantic vacation with Leon, she hopes to explore her newly discovered passionate side, their budding relationship, and perhaps also solve the mystery of the voices in her head. What she discovers exceeds her wildest expectations.

In the meantime, Eleanor and Peter hope to solve another mystery. Who is Emmett Haderech, and what is he up to?

THE PERFECT MATCH SERIES

Perfect Match 1: Vampire's Consort

When Gabriel's company is ready to start beta testing, he invites his old crush to inspect its medical safety protocol.

Curious about the revolutionary technology of the *Perfect Match Virtual Fantasy-Fulfillment studios*, Brenna agrees.

Neither expects to end up partnering for its first fully immersive test run.

Perfect Match 2: King's Chosen

When Lisa's nutty friends get her a gift certificate to *Perfect Match Virtual Fantasy Studios*, she has no intentions of using it. But since the only way to get a refund is if no partner can be found for her, she makes sure to request a fantasy so girly and over the top that no sane guy will pick it up.

Except, someone does.

Warning: This fantasy contains a hot, domineering crown prince, sweet insta-love, steamy love scenes painted with light shades of gray, a wedding, and a HEA in both the virtual and real worlds.

Intended for mature audience.

Perfect Match 3: Captain's Conquest

Working as a Starbucks barista, Alicia fends off flirting all day long, but none of the guys are as charming and sexy as Gregg. His frequent visits are the highlight of her day, but since he's never asked her out, she assumes he's taken. Besides, between a day job and a budding music career, she has no time to start a new relationship.

That is until Gregg makes her an offer she can't refuse—a gift certificate to the virtual fantasy fulfillment service everyone is talking about. As a huge Star Trek fan, Alicia has a perfect match in mind—the captain of the Starship Enterprise.

FOR EXCLUSIVE PEEKS AT UPCOMING RELEASES & A FREE COMPANION BOOK

Join my *VIP Club* and gain access to the VIP portal at ITLUCAS.COM
CLICK HERE TO JOIN

Included in your free membership:

- **FREE** Children of the Gods companion book 1
- **FREE** narration of Goddess's Choice—Book 1 in The Children of the Gods Origins series.
- Preview chapters of upcoming releases.
- And other exclusive content offered only to my VIPs.

Also by I. T. Lucas

THE CHILDREN OF THE GODS ORIGINS

THE CHILDREN OF THE GODS

ALSO BY I. T. LUCAS

DARK HAVEN
47: DARK HAVEN ILLUSION
48: DARK HAVEN UNMASKED

PERFECT MATCH
PERFECT MATCH 1: VAMPIRE'S CONSORT
PERFECT MATCH 2: KING'S CHOSEN
PERFECT MATCH 3: CAPTAIN'S CONQUEST

THE CHILDREN OF THE GODS SERIES SETS

BOOKS 1-3: DARK STRANGER TRILOGY—INCLUDES A BONUS SHORT STORY: **THE FATES TAKE A VACATION**
BOOKS 4-6: DARK ENEMY TRILOGY —INCLUDES A BONUS SHORT STORY—**THE FATES' POST-WEDDING CELEBRATION**
BOOKS 7-10: DARK WARRIOR TETRALOGY
BOOKS 11-13: DARK GUARDIAN TRILOGY
BOOKS 14-16: DARK ANGEL TRILOGY
BOOKS 17-19: DARK OPERATIVE TRILOGY
BOOKS 20-22: DARK SURVIVOR TRILOGY
BOOKS 23-25: DARK WIDOW TRILOGY
BOOKS 26-28: DARK DREAM TRILOGY
BOOKS 29-31: DARK PRINCE TRILOGY
BOOKS 32-34: DARK QUEEN TRILOGY
BOOKS 35-37: DARK SPY TRILOGY
BOOKS 38-40: DARK OVERLORD TRILOGY
BOOKS 41-43: DARK CHOICES TRILOGY
BOOKS 44-46: DARK SECRETS TRILOGY

MEGA SETS

THE CHILDREN OF THE GODS: BOOKS 1-6—INCLUDES CHARACTER LISTS

THE CHILDREN OF THE GODS: BOOKS 6.5-10 —INCLUDES CHARACTER LISTS

TRY THE CHILDREN OF THE GODS SERIES ON AUDIBLE
2 FREE audiobooks with your new Audible subscription!